In the
Company
of Others

Also by Claude Whitmyer
Mindfulness and Meaningful Work:
Explorations in Right Livelihood
(editor)
Running A One-Person Business
(with Salli Rasberry)

This New Consciousness Reader is part of a new series of original and
classic writing by renowned experts on leading-edge concepts in
personal development, psychology, spiritual growth, and healing.

Other books in this series include:

Dreamtime and Dreamwork
EDITED BY STANLEY KRIPPNER, PH.D.

The Erotic Impulse
EDITED BY DAVID STEINBERG

Fathers, Sons, and Daughters
EDITED BY CHARLES SCULL, PH.D.

Healers on Healing
EDITED BY RICHARD CARLSON, PH.D., AND BENJAMIN SHIELD

Meeting the Shadow
EDITED BY CONNIE ZWEIG
AND JEREMIAH ABRAMS

Mirrors of the Self
EDITED BY CHRISTINE DOWNING

The New Paradigm in Business
EDITED BY MICHAEL RAY AND ALAN RINZLER

Reclaiming the Inner Child
EDITED BY JEREMIAH ABRAMS

Spiritual Emergency
EDITED BY STANISLAV GROF, M.D., AND CHRISTINA GROF

To Be a Man
EDITED BY KEITH THOMPSON

To Be a Woman
EDITED BY CONNIE ZWEIG

What Survives?
EDITED BY GARY DOORE, PH.D.

SERIES EDITOR: CONNIE ZWEIG

IN THE COMPANY OF OTHERS

Making Community in the Modern World

EDITED BY

CLAUDE WHITMYER

JEREMY P. TARCHER/PERIGEE

To my mother, Donna Fay Estill, who taught me to read, write, and ask questions, and who introduced me to the experience of community by making the effort to be part of one herself.

To Lu Phillips, who embodied the ideal of the servant leader, who encouraged diversity by leaving no one out, and whose way of life simply *was* "community."

To my wife, Gail Terry Grimes, with whom I share the pleasures of the company of others. Our partnership enhances our ability to be in community because of the strength of the community between us.

•

Jeremy P. Tarcher/Perigee Books
are published by
The Putnam Publishing Group
200 Madison Avenue
New York, NY 10016

Jeremy P. Tarcher, Inc.
5858 Wilshire Blvd., Suite 200
Los Angeles, CA 90036

Library of Congress Cataloging-in-Publication Data

In the company of others : making community in the modern world / edited by Claude Whitmyer.
p.   cm.—(New consciousness reader)
Includes bibliographical references.
ISBN 0-87477-735-6 (pbk : alk. paper)
1. Community life. 2. Community organization. I. Whitmyer, Claude. II. Series.
HT65.I5 1993   92-37836 CIP
307—dc20

Design by Rhea Braunstein

Printed in the United States of America
1   2   3   4   5   6   7   8   9   10
This book is printed on acid-free paper.
∞

Contents

CONTENTS

CONTENTS

Foreword

I am because we are

For the past two or three years, every *Utne Reader* editorial
salon—those bimonthly gatherings where we ask a group of 8 to 12
invited guests "What have you been thinking and obsessing about
lately?"—has turned at some point to the issue of community. Why
do so many of us feel the lack of it? What are the forces that
undermine it in our culture? Why are there so many tribal wars and
ethnic conflicts raging across the nation and the globe? How can
traditional tribal communities deal with the forces that would destroy them? And is it possible to create real multicultural community for ourselves in the modern world?

I've been interested in community since living and working in
communal arrangements in the 60s and 70s. But living with 20
other macrobiotic devotees was often too much for a group of
people raised on the Lone Ranger, *Catcher in the Rye*, and *The
Stranger*. We simply weren't very good at it. And trying to run a
magazine *(New Age Journal)* by group consciousness and consensus decision-making often turned into group tyranny. Still, something felt natural and right about being in groups. Then, in 1977,
Margaret Mead confirmed my feelings when she told me that "99
percent of the time humans have lived on this planet we've lived
in groups of 12 to 36 people. Only during times of war, or what we
have now, which is the psychological equivalent of war, does the

nuclear family prevail, because it's the most mobile unit that can ensure the survival of the species. But for the full flowering of the human spirit we need groups, tribes, community."

I suspect that most readers of this book would not consider themselves "tribal." Your community, if you feel you have one at all, is probably defined by friends and family scattered across town and around the country. You may say that you are part of several communities, but these are probably more accurately described as *networks* of people with whom you work or share a particular hobby or interest.

Most of the people I know, indeed, most Americans, haven't a clue as to the social skills necessary to live in a real community. We tend to live, work, and hang out with people of similar education, income, age, race, physical attributes, and worldview. We rarely, if ever, have to deal with the Other. We put our older people in nursing homes and our young ones in day-care centers. Lawbreakers are kept behind bars and the physically disabled and mentally ill are kept out of sight. Through our tax dollars we ask trained service personnel to handle these others for us so that we can get on with our careers and our personal growth.

We modern Westerners have much to learn about community. How did the ancients weave their intricate and time-tested webs of inclusion? What do the salons of pre-Revolutionary France have to teach us about the community's need for conversation, and especially for listening and speaking from the heart? What do tribal people know about ritual, place and the invisible world that can help us in our efforts to rebuild community for ourselves and our children?

Claude Whitmyer has assembled a veritable pantheon of some of the best thinkers and visionaries of our time. Their writings on where we've come from, who we are, and where we might (or ought to) be going, are the best collection I've seen on the subject of community, a subject that will soon be widely recognized as among the most crucial issues humans have to face in this decade and indeed well into the next millennium.

Perhaps these writings will help begin the conversations that will lead to the re-creation of real community. Perhaps some day our children will know the experience of community conveyed by this common phrase of the Xhosa people of southern Africa: "I am because we are."

Eric Utne, Founder, Editor-in-chief
Utne Reader
Minneapolis, Minnesota
September 1992

Acknowledgments

As I write, the phone and the doorbell ring simultaneously. I am near the end of the creative part of this book, and I look forward to a long-awaited vacation. Over the years I have observed that the closer I get to vacation time, the more the phone and door need answering. While working on this anthology I have had an enlightening insight as to why this happens.

I belong to a community. My family, friends, and fellow community members look to me, as I do to them, for comfort, aid, and just plain company. When I am about to become inaccessible, even for just a few weeks, they rush to interact, asking for my attention or offering me theirs. These interruptions are an integral part of belonging, and I am just now learning to welcome them as the positive signs they are.

I am grateful to the entire membership of the Briarpatch community for the unique opportunity of being their servant leader. I acknowledge Michael Phillips for his role in recruiting me to that position, and I am especially grateful to my core supporters and advisors: Sara Alexander, Anisa Allan, Andy Alpine, Charmian Anderson, Kristen Anundsen, Cathy Beaham, Clarke Berry, Barbra Blake, Joni Blank, Bart Brodsky, Ernest Callenbach, Saundra Durgin, Jack Fitzwater, Andora Freeman, Anthony Giovanniello, Gordon Grabe, Lynn Gravestock, Tom Hargadon, Judith Jenna, Willa Kacy, Irene Kane, Fenton Kay, Dyanne Ladine, Vicki

Lee, Moses Ma, Jack McCurdie, Joan McIntosh, Karen Moawad, Peggi Oakley, Sophie Otis, Shali Parsons, Fran Peavey, Norman Prince, Roger Pritchard, Carole Rae-Watanabe, Salli Rasberry, Maureen Redl, Deborah Reinerio, Tom Rose, David Rowley, Morgan Rowley, Patricia Ryan-Madsen, David Sibbet, Valerie Skonie, Lee Spiegel, Michael Stein, Randall Sugawara, Paul Terry, Judy Vasos, Nancy Vernon-Burke, Jake Warner, Arek Whitmyer, and Lyla Wilson. They lift me up when my spirit droops, pull me to the ground when my ego soars, and help me find the way when I'm lost. I also wish to thank the coordinators of the satellite Briarpatches, Jim Bucheister, Trician Comings, Yoshio Miwa, Harry Pasternak, Portia Sinnott, Joan Leslie Taylor, and Goran Wiklund, for helping those in other parts of the world to build their own communities. Most especially, and with great affection, I thank my apprentices, Mart Pearson, Victoria Maki, Kathleen Gorman, Sarah Parton, June Cheng, and Chris Mays, for service above and beyond the call of duty and for helping me make my community a better one.

I am also indebted to the Briarpatch and to the other communities I have known for allowing me to create an anthology informed by personal experience. I am equally indebted to the authors in this volume for their contributions to the study of community and the issues that affect it.

I want to give particular thanks to my editor, Connie Zweig, who has the uncommon ability to remain in the background until she is needed and who ventured forward at just the right moments to help me clarify my thinking, remember my focus, and meet my deadlines. Credit also goes to the staff members at Jeremy P. Tarcher, Inc., who were invisible most of the time but whose presence was definitely felt and appreciated at key moments.

I also want to acknowledge Peter Beren, who encouraged me to offer this idea to Tarcher, and Brad Bunnin, who introduced me to Peter and helped me with the contract.

Finally, I wish to register a special appreciation for my partner in life and love, Gail Terry Grimes, who encouraged me, listened to my ideas, and shared in the editing of the entire manuscript. My skill as a writer has improved greatly under her tutelage.

A Note on Language

Given the efforts we have made in the last twenty years toward equality of the sexes, we should have devised a better way of handling the neutral gender in the written word. Unfortunately we have not. For this reason, I apologize in advance for the archaic use of the masculine forms *he, his, him,* and *a man,* which designate hypothetical individuals throughout these copyrighted excerpts, especially in the older pieces.

Prologue

Waking Up to the Company of Others

> *At certain points along their journey, people begin to crave a larger context . . . They long to be in the supportive and joyful company of others who are seekers like themselves.*
>
> JACQUELYN SMALL

> *Everyone forges his inner self year after year. One must try to temper, to cut, to polish one's soul so as to become a human being. And thereby become a tiny particle of one's own people.*
>
> ALEXANDER SOLZHENITSYN

I awoke to the voice of my mother telling us it was time to go. In the cold autumn air of those last few hours before dawn my four sisters, two brothers, and I arose reluctantly from the warmth of sleep.

We dressed quickly and loaded the cars. Then the nine of us and two or three boys from the nearby air force base, who had spent the night on our living-room floor, piled into three cars. We were headed for the Murdocks', another church family, to celebrate the breaking of the annual nineteen-day fast.

The Murdocks' house was across town, and the car heater was just beginning to thaw out my frozen, ten-year-old toes when we pulled into their driveway. A few church members were already there, and others were arriving. We exchanged hearty greetings in the glow of the Murdocks' porch light, which was already beginning to pale as the eastern horizon turned from cherry red to orange.

Everyone carried something inside: groceries, cooking utensils, and Thermoses of hot chocolate to push away the morning chill. We had no church building, no hall, only one another and our homes. In the Murdocks' kitchen, Effie was cracking eggs into a bowl, fresh from her farm on the edge of town. George had a kitchen whip in hand ready to fluff them up. Sharon was laying out thick slices of bacon on the broiler tray and Willa added milk to the pancake ingredients while a square griddle preheated on the stove. All over the house, kids were horsing around with their friends, while grown-ups talked about the weather, work, births, deaths, and the price of new cars. We were in the company of others, and it felt good.

Belonging to a Community

In my teen years, driven by a curiosity to discover how life worked, and encouraged by the teachings of the founder of my family church regarding "independent investigation of the truth," I visited the churches of many denominations. To my surprise, many of the people I met only saw each other at Sunday services. They didn't have the strong bonds that our community had built from countless shared experiences at homes like the Murdocks'.

Our church believed in "equality of the races" and "equality of the sexes," so women and people of color were among our leaders. Compassion and community involvement were implicit in our daily lives. Members of the church came to visit our group every year from Africa, Europe, Asia, and the Pacific.

Growing up in this way, I felt as if I were part of a community of global proportions, populated by many different kinds of very interesting, warm, compassionate people. Thus, in the most critical years of my early development, I experienced the strongest sense of community I have ever known. These early experiences were, I'm certain, greatly responsible for my ongoing efforts to rediscover a sense of community long after I had gone away to college and then to the big city to work.

Although college and graduate school provided a semblance of community, from the time I entered college in 1965 until I moved to San Francisco in the early 1970s, I was without the feeling of belonging that had given such richness to my childhood and adolescent years. And I think I was quietly afraid I might never know that feeling again.

Then, in 1974, I became involved with what, at the time, was called the Briarpatch Society, a group of people who had been social activists in the 60s and who had become entrepreneurs. What drew us together was a shared belief that business did not have to be synonymous with greed, corruption, and profit at all cost. We were among the early pioneers in a movement that has come to be known by the watchwords "environmental preservation" and "social responsibility."

To this day, Briar businesses are either directly involved in the environment or are operated in a way that greatly reduces their impact on the planet. Briars believe in providing the highest quality product or service and in giving something back to our local community. We share resources—from information and financial statements to shovels and pickup trucks. From the beginning, we have shared a belief that it was important to do all we can to ensure the long-term survival of our businesses and our community. To this end, we donate money to hire a coordinator who arranges technical advice and emotional support for members, as it is needed.

In 1983, I was invited to join the team of volunteers that provides the technical advice to Briarpatch businesses, and, in 1984, I was asked to serve as the coordinator. My experience with Briarpatch has given me back that sense of community I had as a child. By sharing resources and interests in the course of the day-to-day operations of our businesses, members of Briarpatch have access to a rich community experience that has no geographical boundaries. While most Briars live in the San Francisco Bay Area,

I have corresponded with and talked by phone with at least 200 other members scattered around the U.S. and in other countries. Over the years I have worked with Briars from Canada, the U.K., Japan, New Zealand, and Sweden, entertaining them when they visited San Francisco and traveling to work with them in their own communities. Through parties, workshops, networking, and other social activities, we interact and provide mutual support as if we were all in the same village, much like Marshall McCluhan's "global village."

Briars have basic values very much like the ones I grew up with, including diversity in the membership, and a tolerance (bordering on encouragement) of a wide range of behavior. Through my involvement with Briarpatch, I have developed an active curiosity about how communities come about, why they succeed or fail, and whether anything can be done to increase their likelihood of success. And I have come to know once again the comfort and joy of belonging to a community.

What Is Community?

We hear a lot these days about a "sense of community." More and more of us, we're told, are seeking it. We talk about the African American, Hispanic, and Asian communities; the gay and lesbian community; the New Age community; the political community; the university community; a community of peers; a community of interest; the local community. But what is this thing called community? Why do we seek it? How do we know when we find it?

There is something about being human that makes us yearn for the company of others, to be with and be touched by our family, friends, and clan. Moving about in the world, stuck inside our own skin, we often feel alone and isolated from the rest of creation. Fear and anger at the outrages perpetrated by the irresponsible drive us further into isolation. Introspective solitude can help us learn to live with this deep loneliness, but the only way to truly diminish the feeling is by making deep connections with others. This is what we mean by community.

Many people discount community as a utopian ideal, something unrealistic or destined to fail. Anticipating disappointment, they shy away from trying to find or build one. The truth is a bit more complicated than that, though. Many utopian communities have been quite successful, as the examples in this book will illustrate. But even these are not necessarily perfect. In every group that comes together in community, whether it is utopian or simply a small town, there arises a unique set of problems, challenges, and opportunities.

We don't have to give up our dreams about community just because there are difficulties. Nor do we have to sell everything, pack up, and move to a communal farm to experience community. We can begin by inviting friends into our home, or by using the increasingly ubiquitous personal computer to join an electronic community. We can organize a ritual men's group, a women's group, or a business support group. More and more people are finding a real sense of community at the workplace or within a collaborative housing project. Churches are seeing a renewal of interest in activities that bring people together for mutual support and the betterment of the church community.

A sense of community can also be found within small groups created to meet special needs. There are support groups for battered women, cancer survivors, people living with AIDS, and spouses of soldiers sent overseas. There are groups organized to accomplish a community goal, such as planting neighborhood trees, building a community garden, or starting a day-care center. Hiking clubs, intellectual salons, and softball teams are sprouting up everywhere, just for fun. And there is no shortage of groups—such as Debtors Anonymous, Overeaters Anonymous, Gamblers Anonymous, or Adult Children of Alcoholics, to name a few—that are part of the "recovery community" created around the twelve-step program of Alcoholics Anonymous. This is only a partial list, but it is proof that alternative ways of connecting with others are as numerous as the number of groups attempting to connect.

The key to turning your contact with people into a sense of connectedness is the effort you are willing to make for it to happen. The rewards can be just as great as the feeling of warmth and love I felt that morning in the Murdocks' kitchen so long ago.

What This Book Is About

There is a swelling wave of interest in the concept of "community." By the time this book reaches your local bookseller this wave will have produced numerous magazine articles and talk show interviews with the authors of the books you find standing on the shelf next to this one. But this book is not just a rehash of the usual words of wisdom on the subject. I have attempted to include a balanced sampling of the best writing on community of the past fifty years, and I have organized it in a way that I hope you will find easily accessible and highly informative. This is a foundational collection that addresses the full range of the human need to belong.

This book offers practical suggestions and examples to help you understand what community is and how to go about creating it for yourself. The underlying themes throughout the collection are these: 1) We need not be isolated one from another. 2) With focus and perseverance, we *can* build a sense of community for ourselves even in the pervasive urban settings of today's world. A lot of us today, and I mean people of all ages and all cultures, are anxious to escape today's lifestyle of consumption, greed, and isolation. Television sets, CD players, and microwave ovens disappoint us as comrades. We yearn for a chance to belong, to find comfort in the company of others, to feel a sense of connectedness and mutual support. We hunger for some clear guidance in how to rediscover this sense of community. The concept of "community building" is fundamental, and it will become even more important in the coming decades, especially if our cities, states, and nations increasingly fail to meet our basic needs for health, work, and physical security.

There is a conspicuous absence of media reports on successful alternatives to the "lifestyles of the rich and famous." This leads many to believe that there are few models for a new and better way of life. We fear that the greed and corruption that fed on the failing savings and loan industry in the late 1980s, and the blind rage and sense of hopelessness that fueled the urban riots of 1992, predict a future in which nobody cares about anybody but themselves. It is the premise of this book, however, that there is no real shortage of positive role models for community building. To illustrate this, I have included, in every section, samples of what real people are doing to shape a meaningful sense of community in their lives.

How to Use This Book

These essays are organized into six major sections based on the common steps that all of us take in our exploration of community. In Part 1, "Seeking Community: The Need," we focus on why we need community at all. What is it about us as human beings that makes community such an integral part of our behavior? What do we mean by "a sense of community," "common ground," or "the common good?" What do we long for and what do we fear? What do we know about the dynamic tension between our longing to be together and our need for privacy; the push and the pull between our quest for community and the ideal of "rugged individualism"? Part 1 concludes, as does every section, with descriptions of actual communities.

In Part 2, "Making Community: The Task," we switch our focus to the actual tools we will need and the steps we will take to create our own sense of community. We explore that special sense of belonging and the psychological processes and patterns of group interaction required to make it happen. We also examine the pragmatic aspects of community economics and local self-reliance. In the sample community described in this section, we hear a personal story about the blending of group process and community economics necessary for a community to survive.

In Part 3, "Finding Community: The Satisfaction," we look at the special circumstances that bring a feeling of satisfaction to our community experience. We explore kinship and friendship, mutual service, the use of ritual, and mindfulness of the daily tasks and intimate relationships which act as the keystones to community building. Description of a community that exemplifies the integration of these keystones appears in this section.

In Part 4, "Living Community: A Wide Range of Choices," we explore some of the many options available in today's world. We begin with a look at so-called "intentional communities" made up of people who live and work together with a common focus. Then we move on to explore the experience of community in such varied settings as the ritual men's group, the corporate work place, collaborative housing projects, living room salons, and computer bulletin boards. And we conclude this section with a fascinating account of the gay community as it learns to cope with the AIDS epidemic.

In Part 5, "The Dark Side of Community: Facing and Overcoming the Pitfalls," we turn our attention to the forces that stand in the way of successful community. There is an all-too-common human tendency to create a destructive tension between the "I, me, mine" of our personal ego (which can be extended to include our family, clan, race, or nation) and the "them, they, theirs" of the Other so easily identified by how "they" are different from us and me. Because this tendency is a strong destructive force working against the establishment of community, we explore it in some depth. Our dual desires for a meaningful work life and a meaningful community are investigated as the two primary driving forces behind the experience of being drawn into the destructive influence of a cult. A checklist for telling if you're involved with a cult (no doubt our biggest fear in joining a community) is also included. Finally, we have a chilling, true story of the worst cult nightmare in modern times, the Jonestown massacre. My intention here is not to frighten or thrill, but to provide an opportunity to look the monster squarely in the face and thereby diminish his power.

Part 6, "Tomorrow's Communities," opens with an essay describing what it will take to create the kind of democratic, self-sustaining communities that could be our legacy to future generations. Any description of future communities is by definition fiction. It comes as no surprise then that this section moves from conjecture about a future society built on the religious principles of Buddhism to a community example drawn from a work of speculative fiction describing an ecological utopia. This section also includes an argument for why we need to reintroduce the Anglo-European concept of "the commons" into our future communities.

———•———

I have come to think of community as a kind of vitamin. The experience of connectedness with others is as necessary to a fully healthy life as the minimum daily amount of each of the essential vitamins is to a balanced diet. This book will have served its purpose if it helps give you:

- knowledge of what works and what can go wrong
- insight into the many different ways you can experience a sense of community
- exposure to the practical skills necessary to build and maintain a community
- examples of communities that work
- ideas about helping to make community a part of our future and the future of our children

It is likely that what you know about community will be informed and expanded by this book, making you less susceptible to the traps of cults and political movements that use "community" as a justification for imposing destructive beliefs on hungry followers.

One of the fathers of the community movement in America, Arthur E. Morgan, who has done much to articulate what community means, puts it this way: "The problem of community, as of all society, is to save and to enlarge the priceless values of freedom, while yet developing the qualities of mutual regard, mutual help, mutual responsibility, and common effort for common ends. . . . For the preservation and transmission of the fundamentals of civilization, vigorous, wholesome community life is imperative. Unless many people live and work in the intimate relationships of community life, there can never emerge a truly unified nation, or a community of mankind. If I do not love my neighbor whom I know, how can I love the human race . . . If I have not learned to work with a few people, how can I be effective with many?"

1

SEEKING COMMUNITY: THE NEED

*Behold, how good and how pleasant it is for breth-
ren to dwell together in unity!*

PSALM 133

*Man is the only being who feels himself to be
alone and the only one who is searching for the
Other.*

OCTAVIO PAZ

*There is something in the human condition that
eternally yearns for a greater sense of connectedness, yearns to reach out and deeply touch others,
throwing off the pain and loneliness of separation
to experience unity with others. In all times and
all places people have consciously reached out to
feel their connectedness with a larger whole. This
is the experience of community.*

CORINNE MCLAUGHLIN AND GORDON DAVIDSON

Years ago—hundreds of years, in fact, before the Age of Industry—we took community for granted. We had our family, our village, our clan. We belonged, that's all, we just did. It was our natural way. Today, we may banter around the word "community"; we may talk about our church or temple as a "community"; we may live in the political and geographical "communities" of township, city, and neighborhood; we may see ourselves as part of this or that "community of interest." But we have lost the unspoken, felt sense of belonging that our ancestors enjoyed. We no longer huddle around the fire in the cave. We no longer run to the town square when the crier calls. We mill about in the suburban mall on Saturday afternoon and pretend that this is the new town center. But we are wandering, for the most part, among strangers who share little in common except the sale at Macy's. The urgency and passion of real community just isn't there. It is this void which prompts the yearning we feel.

"The human spirit cannot abide the enforced loneliness of isolation," says Dr. Howard Thurman, in his book *The Search for Common Ground.* To Thurman, perhaps the single most important American theologian of the twentieth century, the question "Why do we seek community?" has a self-evident answer—one that arises from the potential for the future when we take the actual steps to be with other people in a mutually supportive way. As he explains it, "In human society, the experience of community, or realized potential, is rooted in life itself because the intuitive human urge for community reflects a characteristic of all life."

While the modern age has definitely raised our standard of living far above that of our forebears, and brought us the many miracles of technology, it also has had a diminishing effect on the natural communities we once had. Despite the reassurances of social scientists who claim that we have replaced our natural communities with neighborhoods or centers of ideological focus, our personal experience tells us that this instinctive sense of community has been weakened for all of us, and completely lost to many.

In this opening section, the contributors give us a clear understanding of our need to belong. They draw on experiences from both history and contemporary times to describe this universally human yearning for community.

In chapter 1, *The Wins of Our Fathers: Utopian Communities in Nineteenth Century America,* British scholar Mark Holloway introduces us to the widespread experiments of our recent forebears. Holloway helps us to understand what drove them to set themselves apart from the mainstream of their time. Were they successful? In many ways the answer is yes, and perhaps their greatest success was in setting an example for us to follow. The quiet, almost surreptitious pursuit of heaven on earth by American citizens of the last century led to the establishment of more than a hundred residential communities, with a total membership of more than one hundred thousand men, women, and children. There can be no better place to start our study of the possibilities of community than with a review of the successes and challenges faced by those who came before us.

In chapter 2, *The Fallacy of Rugged Individualism,* psychiatrist M. Scott Peck presents a discussion of how we become fully human through participation in community. Peck focuses on the significant difference between the process of "individuation" and the widespread fallacy of "rugged individualism." What is the relationship between individualism and community? How can we become who we are—creatures called to individual growth, personal power, and distinct wholeness—and still belong to and meet the needs of our community? This is the question Peck addresses.

Does human biology inevitably make us social creatures? In chapter 3, Homo sapiens: *The Community Animal,* community

4

advocate Arthur E. Morgan describes the role of our biological nature in our yearning for community. Though many contemporary biologists and psychologists might disagree with Morgan's thesis, he makes a strong case for the existence of a human "instinct" for community.

In the last two chapters we turn to examples of real communities. What would it be like to live in a community governed more by the seasons and the land than by the political expectations of our Western civilization? In chapter 4, *An Historical Native American Village,* author Malcolm Margolin answers this question with an introduction to the Ohlone Indians, who lived in the San Francisco Bay Area 200 years before the coming of the Spanish explorers.

The physically simple but emotionally rich community life of the Ohlone compares strikingly with today's simple life of the Northern Californians who live in Ananda, the community described in chapter 5, *A Modern Village of Spiritual Seekers.* While the community experiences in each of these villages have both benefits and drawbacks, they illustrate the fact that when we gather together for the purpose of mutual aid and comfort, then a feeling of "community" *can* and usually *will* grow among us.

CHAPTER 1

Mark Holloway

The Wins of Our Fathers: Utopian Communities in Nineteenth Century America

For nearly two thousand years men and women of the Christian heretical sects have attempted to live according to the precepts of the Sermon on the Mount. Many of them, especially during the last three centuries, have set up small societies of a [communal] nature, based upon the supposed practice of the Apostolic Church, as described in Acts iv. Seventeenth-century Europe was full of such sects. Persecution, however severe, did nothing to diminish their fervour. And when America had been colonised, vast numbers of them emigrated in search of religious liberty.

By the nineteenth century they were firmly established. Heaven had come down to earth—very much down to earth—in the Shaker Societies and other communities; and where heaven led, Utopia followed. Fleeing from the industrial problems of Europe, utopian socialists tried to solve them by setting up model societies in America. Thus it came about that the nineteenth century in that country was the golden age of community experiments.

Over a hundred communities, with a total membership of more than one hundred thousand men, women, and children, were tried out in the course of the century. Some features of these experiments, whether they were sectarian or not, were more revolutionary than those of the much larger democratic and working-class movements in Europe, from which they differed fundamentally in that they attempted to dissociate themselves completely from established society. Instead of trying to change society from within, by parliamentary reform or by violent revolution, they tried to set up models of ideal commonwealths, thus providing examples which (in some cases) they hoped the world would follow. The ideals they sought, and often succeeded in achieving, included equality of sex, nationality, and colour; the abolition of private property; the abolition of property in people, either by slavery or through the institutions of monogamy and the family; the practice of non-resistance; and the establishment of a reputation for fair-dealing, scrupulous craftsmanship, and respect for their neighbours.

The history of these experiments is one of few successes, many failures, and constantly renewed endeavour. Only three or four communities have lasted longer than a hundred years. Many vanished within a few months of their foundation. But all have contributed something of value, not only to the fund of experience upon which succeeding experiments of the same kind have relied, but also to the history of American society. When they failed, going down before the advance of large-scale industry and 'scientific' socialism, one of the most valuable qualities of revolutionary man suffered an eclipse from which it has not yet emerged. Socialists would be unwise to spurn the idealism with which these utopians were endowed, for although it led them up strange backwaters and provided them with fantastic hallucinations, the heart of socialism lies in it. It is better, perhaps, to be slightly mad with a sound heart, than to be sane without one.

Slightly mad, indeed, some of them were. From the emaciated Kelpius, who searched the heavens night after night for a portent of the Millennium, to Fourier, who thought that the sea would turn into lemonade; from the two Shaker girls who were ordered to whip one another for watching 'the amour of two flies in the window', to Bronson Alcott, who refused to 'enslave' animals by using them on his farm—from first to last, as was inevitable in a movement that tested the validity of almost every belief and almost every convention, there was a large number of cranks and a high proportion of fanatics. Emerson was certainly thinking of some of them when he wrote to Carlyle in 1840: 'We are all a little wild here with numberless projects of social reform. Not a reading man but has a draft of a new community in his waistcoat pocket. . . . One man renounces the use of animal food; and another of coin; and another of domestic hired service; and another of the State. . . .'

Surrounded by such men, it is not surprising that Emerson wrote as he did, for 1840 was to initiate the busiest decade in community history. The well-established Shakers, Rappites, and Zoarites were still flourishing and were to be joined by half a dozen new religious communities—Hopedale, Bethel-Aurora, Bishop Hill, Amana, and Oneida. Brook Farm, almost on Emerson's doorstep; the ephemeral Fruitlands; and the numerous Fourierist Phalanxes that were to spring up like mushrooms from New York to Iowa, were all established in the 'forties. And, finally, at the end of the decade, the Icarians were to begin their long and persevering struggle against bitter odds.

But however many religious, vegetarian, socialist, or anarchist fanatics may have been included in these schemes, they were merely the by-products of some of the most searching social experiments in modern times—experiments which although they will provide a certain amount of incidental amusement, nevertheless deserve serious consideration.

The utilitarian outlook that brought efficiency and material success to these communities was also responsible for certain disadvantages. 'You will look in vain,' says Nordhoff, 'for highly educated, refined, cultivated, or elegant men or women. They profess no exalted views of humanity or destiny; . . . they do not speak much of the Beautiful with a big B. They are utilitarians. Some do not even like flowers; some reject instrumental music. . . . Art is not known among them; mere beauty and grace are undervalued, even despised.' Solitude, either physical or mental, was also unobtainable. The safeguards of celibacy, which obliged Shakers to go about in pairs of the same sex, the system of keeping a check on the whereabouts of each person, the constant communal activities of every kind, and the practices of criticism and confession ensured, even if they were not specifically designed to encourage, lack of individual thought and action. Such disadvantages, however, did not trouble the stolid peasants and unintellectual working men who, partly on account of this very capacity for simplicity and austerity, were the most successful communists. If they had no Art with a capital A, they were excellent craftsmen;

if they rejected Beauty with a big B, they were nevertheless surrounded by the beauty of the countryside, and no doubt found a spiritual beauty in their peculiar forms of worship. Intellectuals, on the other hand, found the austerity that was forced upon them by economic conditions a trial hard to bear; and if they attempted to place culture and amusement before hard work and financial security, they were almost invariably faced with disaster. This was the experience of New Harmony and of many Fourierist Phalanxes. Only Brook Farm and Oneida managed to combine work, culture, and pleasure in an harmonious manner; but life at the Farm, as Hawthorne discovered, was no picnic, and there is no telling how the experiment would have ended if it had not been cut short.

———•———

Allowing for such limitations, the success of [these] societies cannot be denied. What were the reasons for their success? That [most] of them were religious communities is an important but not a necessary condition of successful communal living. Owing final allegiance to God, implicitly obeying His representatives—who were often credited with supernatural powers—and using [communalism] as a means to an end, it was natural that the sectarians should submit easily to order and discipline. The non-religious did not submit so easily. Many of them, such as the younger Icarians, had been rebels against civil authority before joining communities, and they were only too inclined to remain rebels against all discipline. For them communalism was an end in itself, and they would not tolerate the strict moral government exercised by the religious groups. They were impatient for change; but the abolition of evil by a mere change of environment, as predicted by Owen and Fourier, never came; instead, dissension usually proved that human waywardness dies hard. The Icarians were exceptional. They alone succeeded in substituting [communalism] for religion—but at tremendous cost in hardship and misadventure. However, they prove the truth of Nordhoff's assertion that 'a commune, to exist harmoniously, must be composed of persons who are of one mind upon some question which to them shall appear so important as to take the place of a religion, if it is not essentially religious; though it need not be fanatically held.'

If religion was not an essential condition of success, nor was the abolition of the family. The Inspirationists, the Zoarites, and the Bethel-Aurorans permitted, even if they did not encourage marriage; and the Icarians almost enforced it. In these communities separate households were also the general rule.

One of the most important ingredients of success was frequent meetings in which the morale was kept at as high a pitch as possible, aided by such devices as confession and mutual criticism. Among the Shakers, the Inspirationists, and the Perfectionists such meetings were held daily, and no communities were more successful than these three. Yet the Zoarites and Bethel-Aurorans had no such system of moral discipline. . . .

In short, there is no complete recipe for success. What applies in one case, does not apply in another. Safeguards that protect one community fail to prevent disaster elsewhere, while a society with hardly any safeguards at all survives unscathed. It is a matter party of [genetic] temperament, partly of prudence, partly of trust, partly of strong faith; but in communities, no less than in other societies, success or failure depends ultimately upon chance or a complex concatenation of events.

It is certain, however, that there must be some fundamental belief to which all members subscribe—a belief capable of sustaining them in all crises and uniting them in spite of minor dissensions; and that this belief, if it is not already so embedded in the personalities of each individual as to need no evocation or encouragement, must be ritualised until it provides a sanction for all conduct. To ensure that this solidarity shall be maintained, a very careful system of admission must be devised; and to ensure that there shall be solidarity to maintain, previous acquaintance of the founder-members is essential. Nothing could provoke disruption more speedily than the foolhardy calling together of a heterogeneous collection of individuals with little in common but a vague desire for community life—as Owen proved at New Harmony and many of the Phalanxes substantiated.

The community experiment was certainly worth while. The lowest possible estimate must admit that it was harmless, alike to the nation, the State, and the individual. This cannot be said of violent revolutions, or even of the militant working class organisations. If they achieved better conditions for the working-class, they did so at the cost of bloodshed—which brought violent reaction—

or of the independence of the worker. Whatever benefits it may have brought with it, the trade union movement has taught the worker to expect a master. It has not taught him to take control into his own hands, or to co-operate independently of the central government. By perpetuating a traditional slave-mentality, it is in danger of producing a body of negative and irresponsible men, in whom true self-reliance is supplanted by allegiance to a machine for inflating those very desires and appetites which the working man finds obnoxious in the rich. This acquisition of a whole set of false values and material follies is very natural and very understandable after the centuries of deprivation and oppression; but it is not admirable. It perpetuates the existing lack of interest in work, and accentuates the exclusive interest in hours and money.

Communities, on the other hand, produced a high standard of living and workmanship, were pioneers in Negro and feminine emancipation, in democratic government, in eugenics, in the primitive psycho-analysis of mutual criticism, and in education and social reform. They were a benefit to their neighbours and also to the nation; and they showed by example that associative effort of this type can be highly satisfactory. It is well for us that these examples exist, with all their faults and follies; for whether we like the idea or not, it is always possible that necessity may force such a life upon us. If so, we should be grateful for this fund of experience. It may prove to be invaluable.

Certainly, if centralisation were to break down or become intolerable, or if a devastating war were to destroy national organisation, some such movement might well be expected.

Meanwhile communities still exist, and are still in process of formation.

CHAPTER 2

M. Scott Peck

The Fallacy of
Rugged Individualism

I am lonely.

To a degree my loneliness—and yours—is inevitable. Like you, I am an individual. And that means I am unique. There is no one else like me in this whole wide world. This "I-entity" that is me is different from each and every other "I-entity" that ever lived. Our separate *identities*, like fingerprints, make all of us unique individuals, identifiable one from another.

This is the way it must be. The very genetic code is such that (except for the rare aberration of identical twins) each of us is not only subtly different biologically from any other human being who ever existed but is substantially dissimilar. From the moment of conception. And if that were not enough, all of us are born into different environments and develop differently according to a unique pattern throughout our own individual lives.

Indeed, many believe this is not only the way it must be but is also the way it *should* be. Most Christians believe God designed it that way; He designed each soul differently. Christian theologians have reached a well-nigh universal conclusion: God loves variety. In variety He delights. And nowhere is that variety more apparent and inevitable than among the human species.

Psychologists may or may not agree with notions of divine creation, but almost all agree with the theologians that the uniqueness of our individuality is called for. They envision it as the goal of human development that we should become fully ourselves.

Theologians sometimes speak of this as the call to "freedom"—the freedom to be our true individual selves as God created us to be. The psychiatrist Carl Jung named this goal of human development "individuation." The process of human development is one of becoming fully individual.

Most of us never totally complete the process and may never get very far at all. Most, to a greater or lesser degree, fail to individuate—to separate—ourselves from family, tribe, or caste. Even into old age we remain figuratively tied to the apron strings of our parents and culture. We are still dictated to by the values and expectations of our mothers and fathers. We still follow the direction of the prevailing wind and bow before the shibboleths of our society. We go with the crowd. From laziness and fear—fear of loneliness, fear of responsibility, and other nameless dreads— we never truly learn to think for ourselves or dare to be out of step with the stereotypes. But in light of all we understand, this failure to individuate is a failure to grow up and become fully human. For we are called to be individuals. We are called to be unique and different.

We are also called to power. In this individuation process we must learn how to take responsibility for ourselves. We need to develop a sense of autonomy and self-determination. We must attempt, as best we can, to be captains of our own ships if not exactly masters of our destiny.

Furthermore, we are called to wholeness. We should use what gifts or talents we are given to develop ourselves as fully as possible. As women, we need to strengthen our masculine sides; as men, our feminine sides. If we are to grow, we must work on the weak spots that prevent growth. We are beckoned toward that self-sufficiency, that wholeness required for independence of thought and action.

But all this is only one side of the story.

It is true that we are called to wholeness. But the reality is that we can never be completely whole in and of ourselves. We cannot be all things to ourselves and to others. We cannot be perfect. We cannot be doctors, lawyers, stockbrokers, farmers, politicians, stonemasons, and theologians, all rolled into one. It is true that we are called to power. Yet the reality is that there is a point beyond which our sense of self-determination not only becomes inaccurate

13

and prideful but increasingly self-defeating. It is true that we are created to be individually unique. Yet the reality is that we are inevitably social creatures who desperately need each other not merely for sustenance, not merely for company, but for any meaning to our lives whatsoever. These, then, are the paradoxical seeds from which community can grow.

So we are called to wholeness and simultaneously to recognition of our incompleteness; called to power *and* to acknowledge our weakness; called to both individuation *and* interdependence. Thus the problem—indeed, the total failure—of the "ethic" of rugged individualism is that it runs with only one side of this paradox, incorporates only one half of our humanity. It recognizes that we are called to individuation, power, and wholeness. But it denies entirely the other part of the human story: that we can never fully get there and that we are, of necessity in our uniqueness, weak and imperfect creatures who need each other.

This denial can be sustained only by pretense. Because we cannot ever be totally adequate, self-sufficient, independent beings, the ideal of rugged individualism encourages us to fake it. It encourages us to hide our weaknesses and failures. It teaches us to be utterly ashamed of our limitations. It drives us to attempt to be superwomen and supermen not only in the eyes of others but also in our own. It pushes us day in and day out to look as if we "had it all together," as if we were without needs and in total control of our lives. It relentlessly demands that we keep up appearances. It also relentlessly isolates us from each other. And it makes genuine community impossible.

On my lecture tours across the country the one constant I have found wherever I go—the Northeast, Southeast, Midwest, Southwest, or West Coast—is the lack of—and the thirst for—community. This lack and thirst is particularly heartbreaking in those places where one might expect to find real community: in churches. Speaking to my audiences, I often say, "Please don't ask me questions during the break times. I need those times to get my thoughts together. Besides, it has invariably been my experience that the questions you have represent concerns that others have as well and that they are best addressed in the group as a whole." But more often than not someone will come to me during the break with a question. When I say, "I thought I requested you not to," the usual response is "Yes, but, Dr. Peck, this is terribly important to me, and I can't ask it in the group because some of the members of my church are here." I wish I could say this was an exception. There are, of course, exceptions and exceptional churches. But such a remark speaks of the normal level of trust and intimacy and vulnerability in our churches and other so-called "communities."

Yes, I am lonely. Since I am an utterly unique individual, there is no one who can totally understand me, who can know exactly what it is like to walk in my shoes. And there are parts of my journey—as there are in everyone's journey—that must be walked alone. Some tasks can be accomplished only in solitude. But I am infinitely less lonely than I used to be before I learned that it was human to have feelings of anxiety and depression and helplessness, before I learned that there were places where I could share such feelings without guilt or fear and people would love me all the more for it, before I knew I could be weak in my strength and strong in my weakness, before I had experienced real community and learned how to find it or create it again.

Trapped in our tradition of rugged individualism, we are an extraordinarily lonely people. So lonely, in fact, that many cannot even acknowledge their loneliness to themselves, much less to others. Look at the sad, frozen faces all around you and search in vain for the souls hidden behind masks of makeup, masks of pretense, masks of composure. It does not have to be that way. Yet many—most—know no other way. We are desperately in need of a new ethic of "soft individualism," an understanding of individualism which teaches that we cannot be truly ourselves until we are able to share freely the things we most have in common: our weakness, our incompleteness, our imperfection, our inadequacy, our sins, our lack of wholeness and self-sufficiency. It is the understanding expressed by those in the Fellowship of Alcoholics Anonymous when they say: "I'm not OK and you're not OK, but that's OK." It is a kind of softness that allows those necessary barriers, or outlines, of our individual selves to be like permeable membranes, permitting ourselves to seep out and the selves of others to seep in. It is the kind of individualism that acknowledges our interdependence not merely in the intellectual catchwords of the day but in the very depths of our hearts. It is the kind of individualism that makes real community possible.

CHAPTER 3

Arthur E. Morgan

Homo sapiens: The Community Animal

Biologically man is a social creature. His throat and mouth are formed for delicately modulated speech, and that speech is a trait of social and not of solitary animals. A man is not a normal organism by himself, but only in relations with others.

In mental constitution men are more than social creatures, they are community animals. Cattle and horses, when living wild on the plains, may thrive in vast undifferentiated herds of thousands of individuals. They are social animals, but apparently not to any marked degree community animals. Men live best in integrated groups of limited size. They crave community life, not simply social life.

Men can become adjusted to almost any kind of life and may be so habituated to it that any change to a different mode is extremely unpleasant. New York slum dwellers on being transferred to rural communities often find the new life unendurable, and drift back to the city. On the other hand, the most isolated men in the Southern mountains come to prefer their relative loneliness to any more intimate community life. Even such men generally have community relationships. They may hunt and fish together, they take care of each other's sick, they maintain churches in common. There seem to be normal degrees of association from which extremes of solitude or intimacy are variants. Men who are not parts of some small community tend to be psychopathic or

16

variants from a wholesome type. Men forced into too intimate and constant association become irritable or lose individuality.

Put a man among large masses of men and he will begin to gather a few of them together to build a small community. Such efforts take the forms of college fraternities, clubs, secret orders, church congregations, luncheon clubs, study clubs, and numberless other associations of limited numbers. We have here evidence of one of the most fundamental and universal of human traits—a craving of human nature which cannot safely be ignored.

In modern America, the village, the neighborhood, the hamlet, or the city, often has become but an economic aggregation or only an incidental grouping, without the acquaintance, the personal relationships, and the common interests and activities, which are the essential characteristics of a community. Such aggregations do not fully satisfy the emotional cravings for fellowship, common interests, and unified planning and action.

The idea that man is a small-community animal is supported by the science of anthropology. For the most part early man was a small-village dweller, and the villages in which he lived were not just accumulations of dwellings, but had well-developed social organization. In fact, the community may be older than mankind, for some of man's nearer relatives among the apes and monkeys also live in organized communities which have definite range of size, characteristic of the species.

Where men live on isolated farms, generally it is because some arbitrary circumstance has prevented action according to the tendencies of human nature. In Mexico the Aztec conquests, and after them the Spaniards, drove tribes from their villages into the hills for safety, where for centuries they have continued to live on isolated farms or in very small groups. In England the ancient villages with their common lands were broken up by the Norman conquerors, and by later enclosures of common lands by the nobility, so that through forcible means the character of English community life was largely destroyed. Brittany in France, where the people live on separate farms, was settled by a mass movement from Britain about ten centuries ago, with apparently arbitrary division of lands. In the rough mountains of Switzerland and Scandinavia many small valleys were settled which were too small to support villages. Isolation occurred because the only way for a young man to get a foothold was to go beyond the confines of village ownership and make a new clearing. In Russia the agrarian reform of 1906, which undertook to break up villages and make separate farms, so disturbed community ways that it constituted revolution. Recently Manchuria has been settled largely by individual immigrants, many of whom have not yet matured a village organization.

In the United States the somewhat crudely drafted homestead laws, written with little thought of human nature, put families far apart by giving each homesteader a tract of land half a mile square. The resulting isolation left the craving for community unsatisfied. In the rich farming states of the Middle West the more prosperous farmers sell or rent their farms and move to town, leaving the less competent and less independent people on the land. One finds fewest farms abandoned by their owners among such people as the Mennonites, the Amish, the Dunkards, and the Mormons, where there is strong community feeling and where community life is most deeply rooted and best provided for.

In several other parts of the United States the tendency to community life found expression. Most of New England was settled by communities. At one time in Massachusetts it was unlawful for a colonist to live more than a mile distant from the community center. The Acadians of Louisiana live in ribbon villages, farming the land back of their houses. In New Mexico and Arizona the Mexicans live usually in fairly compact villages, not on isolated farms.

Thus it seems that where men live in isolated situations it usually is because circumstances beyond their control caused them to deny or to repress deep-seated community impulse. Whenever those compulsions to separation are removed, men tend again to congregate in communities. A large proportion of American farmers who lived on relatively isolated farms overcame that isolation to some degree and developed real community life among themselves.

The modern town-planner, in trying to secure an impression of integration and unity in the physical planning of a village, tries to find an axis or a focus for his plan. Sometimes without fully realizing the significance of what he does, he tries to secure outward and visible evidence of an inward and spiritual condition which would characterize a true community.

CHAPTER 4

Malcolm Margolin

An Historical Native American Village

Before the coming of the Spaniards, Central California had the densest Indian population anywhere north of Mexico. Over 10,000 people lived in the coastal area between Point Sur and the San Francisco Bay. These people belonged to about forty different groups, each with its own territory and its own chief. Among them they spoke eight to twelve different languages—languages that were closely related but still so distinct that oftentimes people living twenty miles apart could hardly understand each other. The average size of a group (or *tribelet*, as it is often called) was only about 250 people. Each language had an average of no more than 1,000 speakers.

As many as thirty or forty permanent villages rimmed the shores of the San Francisco Bay—plus several dozen temporary "camps," visited for a few weeks each year by inland groups who journeyed to the Bayshore to gather shellfish and other foods. At the turn of this century more than 400 shellmounds, the remains of these villages and camps, could still be found along the shores of the Bay—dramatic indication of a thriving population.

What would life have been like here? What would be happening at one of the larger villages on a typical afternoon, say in mid-April, 1768—one year before the first significant European intrusion into the Bay Area? Let us reconstruct the scene. . . .

———•———

20

The village is located along the eastern shores of the San Francisco Bay at the mouth of a freshwater creek. An immense, sprawling pile of shells, earth, and ashes elevates the site above the surrounding marshland. On top of this mound stand some fifteen dome-shaped tule houses arranged around a plaza-like clearing. Scattered among them are smaller structures that look like huge baskets on stilts—granaries in which the year's supply of acorns are stored. Beyond the houses and granaries lies another cleared area that serves as a ball field, although it is not now in use.

It is mid-afternoon of a clear, warm day. In several places throughout the village steam is rising from underground pit ovens where mussels, clams, rabbit meat, fish, and various roots are being roasted for the evening meal. People are clustered near the doors of the houses. Three men sit together, repairing a fishing net. A group of children are playing an Ohlone version of hide-and-seek: one child hides and all the rest are seekers. Here and there an older person is lying face down on a woven tule mat, napping in the warmth of the afternoon sun.

At the edge of the village a group of women sit together grinding acorns. Holding the mortars between their outstretched legs, they sway back and forth, raising the pestles and letting them fall again. The women are singing together, and the pestles rise and fall in unison. As heavy as the pestles are, they are lifted easily—not so much by muscular effort, but (it seems to the women) by the powerful rhythm of the acorn-grinding songs. The singing of the women and the synchronized thumping of a dozen stone pestles create a familiar background noise—a noise that has been heard by the people of this village every day for hundreds, maybe thousands, of years.

The women are dressed in skirts of tule reeds and deer skin. They are muscular, with rounded healthy features. They wear no shoes or sandals—neither do the men—and their feet are hardened by a lifetime of walking barefoot. Tattoos, mostly lines and dots, decorate their chins, and they are wearing necklaces made of abalone shells, clam-shell beads, olivella shells, and feathers. The necklaces jangle pleasantly as the women pound the acorns. Not far away some toddlers are playing in the dirt with tops and buzzers made out of acorns. Several of the women have babies by their sides, bound tightly into basketry cradles. The cradles are decorated lovingly with beads and shells.

As the women pause in their work, they talk, complain, and laugh among themselves. It is the beginning of spring now, and everyone is yearning to leave the shores of the Bay and head into the hills. The tule houses are soggy after the long winter rains, and everyone is eager to desert them. The spring greens, spring roots, and the long-awaited clover have already appeared in the meadows. The hills have turned a deep green. Flowers are everywhere, and it is getting near that time of year when the young men and women will chase each other over the meadows, throwing flowers at each other in a celebration so joyful that even the older people will join in.

On a warm day like this almost all village activity takes place outdoors, for the tule houses are rather small. Of relatively simple design (they are made by fastening bundles of tule rush onto a framework of bent willow poles), they range in size from six to about twenty feet in diameter. The larger dwellings hold one or sometimes two families—as many as twelve or more people—and each house is crowded with possessions. Blankets of deer skin, bear skin, and woven rabbit skin lie strewn about a central fire pit. Winnowing, serving, sifting, and cooking baskets (to name only a few), along with several unfinished baskets in various stages of completion are stacked near the entrance way. Many of the houses also contain ducks stuffed with tule (to be used as hunting decoys), piles of fishing nets, fish traps, snares, clay balls ready to be ground into paint, and heaps of abalone shells that have been worked into rough blanks. The abalone shells were received in trade last fall from the people across the Bay, and after being shaped, polished, and pierced they will eventually be traded eastward—for pine nuts, everyone hopes.

While all the houses are similar in construction, they are not identical. One of them, off to the side of the village near the creek, is twice as large as the others and is dug into the earth. It has a tiny door—one would have to crawl on all fours to enter—and it is decorated with a pole from which hang feathers and a long strip of rabbit skin. Its walls are plastered thickly with mud, and smoke is pouring out of a hole in the roof. This is the sweat-house, or *temescal* as it was called by the early Spaniards. A number of adolescent boys are lingering around the door, listening to the rhythmic clapping of a split-stick clapper that comes from within. The men are inside, singing and sweating, preparing themselves and their weapons for the next day's deer hunt. It is here, away from the women, that the bows, arrows, and other major hunting implements are kept.

Another house is noticeably different from the rest, mainly because it is smaller and has fewer baskets and blankets. Whereas the other dwellings contain large families, this one contains only two people. They are both men. One of them leads a man's life, but the other has chosen the women's way. He wears women's ornaments, grinds acorns with the women, gathers roots, and makes baskets. The two men are living together, fully accepted by the other villagers.

There is one more house that is different from the rest. It is larger than the others, and it holds many more storage baskets filled with food. This is the chief's dwelling. A few of the wealthier men of the village have two wives, but only the chief has three. He needs both the extra food and the extra wives, for he must fulfill his responsibilities of disbursing food to the needy and entertaining guests from other areas.

Guests do arrive this afternoon, three traders from another village, and they are led at once to the chief's house. Their village is only about twenty-five miles away; and while the traders are related by marriage to some of the village families, they are very infrequent visitors, and indeed they speak a different language. But the language of trade—salt, beads, pine nuts, obsidian, abalone shells, and other desired goods—is universally understood. The language of hospitality is also universal. A great feast must be prepared in their honor.

As the afternoon wears on, a group of boys return to the village. They are carrying snares, bows and arrows, and pieces of firewood. They run to the women grinding the acorns and show what they have caught: rabbits, a ground squirrel, a few small birds. The smallest boy among them, no more than about four years old, is particularly delighted. He has caught his first animal: a mouse! There is great laughter among the women. Also, great praise.

"How fat it looks," says the mother matter-of-factly, hiding her pride lest the other women think her boastful. She will roast the mouse whole in the pit oven; it will provide about two good bites. But the food value is not nearly as important as the fact that her child is becoming a hunter. Indeed, she feels that she has done well by him. When she was pregnant she followed all the right taboos. She ate neither meat nor fish. She bathed him in cold water when he was born, and she herself burned the umbilical cord and disposed of the ashes in the proper way so that no harm would come to him. When he was still a baby she fed him quail eggs to make him fast on his feet. She nursed him for two full years during which she made love to no one, lest the love-making sour her milk.

Now he is growing up and becoming a hunter. Perhaps it is Quail who is helping him. Quail is a good helper for a little boy, she thinks. Later on, when he reaches manhood, he will seek others. Who will they be, she wonders? She is partial to Badger, and she hopes her son will someday have Badger dreams. Badger was one of her father's best helpers, a major family totem, and. . . .

But no sooner does that thought enter her mind than she shuts it out. Her father is dead. Along with her mother she had singed her hair, blackened her face with tar, and mourned him for a full year. Now she must never mention his name again. No one will ever mention his name. She must try not to think about him. He is dead.

A ripple of laughter among the other women brings her back. They are laughing and their eyes are dancing. "It feels lucky tonight. Let's gamble."

Tonight they will gamble. They will sing their gambling songs and court fortune. The woman is glad that this is not the time of her period, for then she would have to stay away from other people lest she ruin their luck.

"I'll get that necklace tonight," one woman yells, pointing at another's necklace of shells and eagle down. "I'll win it yet. Won't it look fine on me?"

Everyone laughs. The acorn grinding song resumes, and the mother continues pounding.

Toward the end of the afternoon more and more people drift back into the village. A group of women, children, and older men return from the mud flats. Everyone is carrying a digging stick, and the women have on their backs heavy baskets full of mussels, clams, and oysters. The baskets are supported by tumplines around the forehead, and they are dripping with sea water. Also from the direction of the Bay, a group of men haul onto shore a pair of small boats made of tule reeds. They hang their nets out to dry and happily approach the village with a big load of fish. Others who return—men, women, and children—carry bundles of firewood heaped high on their backs.

Suddenly all eyes turn toward the land where an old woman is making her way back to the village. Where has she been all day? Perhaps she has been collecting power plants, singing her songs in sacred places, communicating with spirit-world helpers, or visiting a secret hiding place in the woods where she keeps her medicine bundle. No one asks. The other women watch her carefully and greet her politely. She is a shaman.

So far everyone acknowledges that the shaman has been above reproach. She has accumulated much power and cured many people. Indeed, she has often danced and sung for hours at a time, and with her hollow tube she has sucked out of their bodies many malignant objects: lizards, inchworms, bits of deer bone, and pieces of quartz—hideous things, all sent to them by their enemies. But one always has to watch shamans, for sometimes they turn evil. They learn to communicate with Owls. They take on the character of Bears. The people they touch begin to die. When that happens, it is sometimes necessary for the people of the village to kill the shaman. But this is a difficult and serious business—especially if the shaman (whether man or woman) has many supernatural helpers.

So far there has been no cause for alarm. She seems above reproach. Also, she does not get along very well with the chief, and that is encouraging; for if a shaman turns evil the people often go to the chief for permission to kill him or her. But if the shaman and the chief are close friends or relatives, then the suffering a village might have to endure at their hands could be enormous. True, there is no immediate cause for suspicion, but such fears are never far from anyone's mind.

The women have finished grinding their acorns. They pile fresh wood onto their outdoor cooking fires, leach the acorn meal with hot water, and begin to make the mush that will form the basis for the night's dinner. The ovens are dug open and their savory contents added to the feast.

The men have finished sweating and dancing, and now they come forward from the direction of the sweat-house. They have scraped their bodies clean with curved deer ribs, and they have bathed in the cool creek. Many of the men have beards and moustaches, some wear hairnets made of milkweed fibers, and several have stone and shell amulets hanging around their necks. Their ears and noses are pierced, and long plugs of wood or bone have been inserted into them. Otherwise they are naked.

As they come forward to get their food, several of the men pointedly refuse any meat. Everyone knows at once that these are the ones who will go hunting the next day. Tonight they will eat only acorn food and they will spend the entire night in the sweat-house. The next day, if their dreams are favorable, they will don their deer-head masks to seek deer. The women, however, say nothing. A woman must never talk to a man about deer hunting: to say anything at all would bring bad luck to the hunter, and perhaps illness or even death to the woman.

The villagers eat in groups around the various houses. The meals are noisy, full of jokes and good humor. The people dip two fingers into their bowls of acorn gruel and slurp up more of the rich, bland food. Clam shells, mussel shells, and animal bones are tossed into a pile beyond the circle of houses.

———•———

As it gets dark the infants and toddlers crawl in among the blankets to go to sleep. Others put on rabbit-skin capes or wrap themselves in deer-skin blankets. The older children gather around their grandfathers and grandmothers, hoping for a story.

Suddenly they hear a scream. Everyone looks up. Out of one of the houses races a coyote with a piece of dried fish in its mouth. A woman runs after it, waving her digging stick. One of the old men laughs. Coyote is like that, yes indeed, Coyote is like that. And the old man tells once again the hilarious exploits of Coyote during the creation of the world.

As he tells the story, the sound of chanting rises from the far end of the village. The women have begun to gamble. The men have returned to the sweat-house. They are singing their deer chants. Some have put on their feathers and are dancing. Tonight they will tell hunting stories, smoke tobacco, and perhaps dream the right dreams. If the dreams are favorable, tomorrow they will light fires in the sweat-house again, sweat some more, paint their bodies, put on their deer-head masks, and go out to hunt.

The other people in the village smile. Perhaps tomorrow there will be fresh deer meat. That is good, very good. Everyone will get some. But more than that, if the men head out into the hills they will bring back news about the flower seeds. Perhaps the chief will give the word to move outward into the hills where the people can throw themselves face down onto the slopes and eat the delicious clover, and where they can taste again the nutty, roasted kernels of buttercup, clarkia, and redmaid seeds. The people feel glad inside just thinking about it. It is the end of winter, and soon it will be time to move out into the hills.

CHAPTER 5

*Corinne McLaughlin and
Gordon Davidson*

A Modern Village of Spiritual Seekers

Ananda is a community of two hundred members living on seven hundred acres in Nevada City, California. Founded by Swami Kriyananda in 1967, Ananda is based on the teachings of Paramahansa Yogananda, and practices daily meditation, chanting, and yoga. Calling themselves a "village," rather than a "community," Ananda members share the land and have common spiritual beliefs and practices, but they generally own individual homes and some of the businesses.

The community exists primarily to support the members in their pursuit to make God an integral part of their lives. Ananda is not a commune, but is rather more like an old New England village. The community members are supportive of one another but each person is expected to take responsibility for making their own life work. Members of the community work and live together but each individual takes personal responsibility for manifesting his or her own housing and work. There are single people who live alone, couples with and without children, and group houses where everyone shares a common kitchen. The vision of Ananda as a haven for those seeking God has been a consistent theme since the founding of the community in 1967.

There are no minimum work requirements at Ananda, but members are encouraged to volunteer in the community at various jobs that need doing in the garden, dairy, publications, office, and guest programs. For regular jobs in these areas, members receive a small salary, which is sufficient to cover rent and basic living expenses. Community salaries are not large enough for saving money to build or buy a house at Ananda, so members often get outside jobs or start businesses on their own.

Ananda Village, the land where most of the members live (as distinct from the retreat center and monastery land up the road), is organized as a non-profit corporation. The Village takes care of membership, planning, land use, and marketing. Some of Ananda's businesses, like its dairy, community store, health food store, and handicrafts store in town, are part of Ananda's non-profit corporation; others are privately owned. Sometimes members in these privately-owned businesses take lower wages in order to donate more money from the business to the community.

"The real focus of the community is our spiritual life and the deep friendships and sharing between people, as well as creativity in the arts and children's education," says Purushottama, who is co-manager of Ananda Village and oversees Ananda's businesses.

Originally the community only had a few "new age" businesses—like incense and oils and health foods—but now they've expanded and run a construction company, a clothing and jewelry store, a health clinic, a bookstore, children's schools (with over sixty students), and a hot air balloon business.

Ananda's businesses have been very successful financially. Swami Kriyananda explains why.

> Some people talk as if a practical, hard-headed approach is the secret of success in business. But the secret of our success is that people like us. And if they like the people in the store, they're going to come back there.

The consciousness with which Ananda members work is as important to them as getting the job done. A guest at Ananda who was working in their publications business on a "rush job" was told by a member that he should feel free to stop and do something else for awhile if the folding and collating work was getting to him. The guest asked, "Shouldn't the job have priority over how I feel about it?" He was told, "No, your *head* has priority!" Ananda members feel our heads are instruments for receiving intuition/guidance from God in each moment as to what is best to complete, so we have to take good care of ourselves. They also feel that their businesses are the place where they apply their spiritual lessons and see whether they've really learned them.

2

MAKING COMMUNITY: THE TASK

When the stranger says: "What is the meaning of this city? Do you huddle together because you love one another?" What will you answer? "We all dwell together to make money from each other," or, "This is a community"?

T. S. ELIOT

Community doesn't just happen. People *make* community. Every community experience that has ever been or ever will be begins when one or more individuals decide to focus their time and energy on calling others together with a clear intention.

We are born with the desire to be together, but the skills that really *make* community must be learned. Unfortunately, we don't learn these skills in school or in our families. We are given some rough guidelines for how to get along with others, and, in generations past, we were even taught the value of following the rules that promote social harmony. But more and more of us are escaping from our childhood education without a sufficient sense of social responsibility and the social skills that make it possible for us to come together for mutual support and the good of the community.

As a result, many of us feel isolated and alienated from those around us. Not belonging is often one of the most discomfiting feelings we experience in life. This pain of separateness and isolation may never be completely overcome, because we are each unique individuals with more going on inside than we can ever fully communicate to those around us. So how will we ever feel completely understood?

But, we can learn to improve our communication, disclose more about our private selves, assert our identities and ask for equal consideration, offer unconditional love and support to those in need, give everybody a chance to participate, overcome conflicts without the use of force, and so on. All these ways of being with one another offer some balance between our need to be a unique individual and our need to belong. There are few experiences more rewarding than the feelings of togetherness and camaraderie that arise from a smoothly functioning group process.

By keeping in mind the growth stages of community development as we build a community of our own, we can prepare ourselves to hang in there when the going gets rough. Learning to communicate well; to practice cooperation; to choose inspired, responsible leadership or serve as leaders ourselves; and to value and pay for the things we want to accomplish—as a group—this is how we make community a purposeful activity.

Of course, many community experiences do arise spontaneously and successfully when people come together for intellectual or commercial exchange, to create something, to celebrate, or to simply hang out. Still, for the most part, a strong community takes skill. In this section we will focus on the tools you need and the steps you can take to create your own sense of community, regardless of the size or type of group you choose.

Making community is a process that requires dedication. It is simply not enough to be inspired by or feel passion for the idea of community. Except for the very small, ad hoc groups you might join from time to time, almost every other community experience will involve long hours and hard work. Even in a small, short-term community experience (a political campaign, a support group, or even the line at the grocery store), the basic tools for getting along, communicating, reaching compromise, and seeing to it that everyone's needs are met, are the same.

Most groups begin when someone holds up a flag to see who salutes. Somebody feels a need to get something done but realizes they need help. So they begin talking to others, usually friends and associates. At first everyone makes an effort to get along and be mutually supportive. Soon, ideals clash. Group members begin trying to convert each other to their personal opinions and beliefs. This is the first critical moment in forging the identity of the group. Members attack each other, and usually the leader is blamed for the resulting chaos.

Secondary leaders emerge trying to take over. The group faces a fork in the road: organization or growth. If the group organizes itself into committees, or sub-groups, the result is "pseudocommunity," a way to be together without the deep connection of real community. But if the members of the group have the courage to go through the process of removing the barriers they have created—barriers of feelings, assumptions, ideals, and motives—they can grow to the point that they are free of the need to control or force their opinions upon the others. Then the group has a chance of moving beyond chaos into an experience of true community. This is the evolution of community outlined by psychiatrist M. Scott Peck in chapter 6, *Stages of Community Building*.

In chapter 7, *Skills for Living Together*, organizational consultant Duane H. Fickeisen presents self-understanding as the first step in our efforts to make community. Fickeisen's background in "whole systems" design and his study of group processes make him the ideal candidate to explain the general systems approach to community making. He takes a variety of viewpoints: from ecology, he draws an explanation of the importance of diversity; from psychology, the "hero's journey"; from education, a model of learning that takes into account our different learning styles; from sociology, the concepts of participation and influence; from engineering, the difference between task and maintenance functions; from decision theory, an exploration of decision-making methods; and from business, the concepts of leadership and management. Heady as it sounds, Fickeisen's presentation is easy to understand, and he encourages you to try out these ideas in a real community experience. As Fickeisen says in his closing, "You must *do* it— *experience* community. That takes courage, creativity, and commitment as well as skills. It all starts with a simple decision to *be* in community—a decision of the heart that, once taken, creates its own fulfillment."

Next we focus on the issue of what makes a good leader. As an executive at AT&T, Robert K. Greenleaf developed his ideas about "servant leadership." In chapter 8, *The Leader as Servant*, Greenleaf describes the essence of this concept, the idea that the best type of leader is one whose primary purpose is not self-advancement or domination, but a deep-seated need to serve.

"Community exists to the extent that the pattern and quality of that which really happens is in some way serving its members.

The reality is that people give each other things, do things for each other. The mechanic fixes your car, the teacher gives your child an education, the salesman gives us the goods, you give your best at work. And in exchange for these real gifts—we confer symbols on each other. You give the mechanic $325, the teacher gets $2,184 per month, the price tag is $19.99. Perhaps you get what you are worth at work." So says economist Michael Linton, and so we make the transition from the social and psychological to the economic realities of community. In chapter 9, *Money and Community Economics,* Linton offers an alternative to unemployment and poverty for any community willing to make the transition from the old way of thinking about money to the creation of "local money." "Poverty is a lack of money. Give conventional money to the poor, and they are poor again tomorrow. Show them how to use their own money, and they can manage their own affairs," says Linton. The secret, he says, is to balance the flow of capital into and out of our communities by becoming less dependent on imported goods and by increasing the circulation of cash, labor, and assets within the local community.

Finally, in chapter 10, *The Economics of a Kibbutz,* we bring this section to a close with an interview by Amia Lieblich of 70-year-old Menachem, treasurer of Makom, a large rural commune in Israel. Even though many of the issues and opportunities faced in making community arise from the economic needs of the group, they must still be worked out through social and psychological processes, as is clearly illustrated in this chapter. This is the real-life story of how one group has managed to create both a sense of community *and* a sustainable economy.

CHAPTER 6

M. Scott Peck

Stages of Community Building

Groups assembled deliberately to form themselves into community routinely go through certain stages in the process. These stages, in order, are: Pseudocommunity, Chaos, Emptiness, [and] Community. Not every group that becomes a community follows this paradigm exactly. Communities that temporarily form in response to crisis, for instance, may skip over one or more stages for the time being. I do not insist that community development occur by formula. But in the process of community-making by design, this is the natural, usual order of things.

Pseudocommunity

The first response of a group in seeking to form a community is most often to try to fake it. The members attempt to be an instant community by being extremely pleasant with one another and avoiding all disagreement. This attempt—this pretense of community—is what I term "pseudocommunity." It never works.

In pseudocommunity it is as if every individual member is operating according to the same book of etiquette. The rules of this book are: Don't do or say anything that might offend someone else; if someone does or says something that offends, annoys, or irritates you, act as if nothing has happened and pretend you are not bothered in the least; and if some form of disagreement should show signs of appearing, change the subject as quickly and smoothly as possible—rules that any good hostess knows. It is easy to see how these rules make for a smoothly functioning group. But they also crush individuality, intimacy, and honesty, and the longer it lasts the duller it gets.

In my experience most groups that refer to themselves as "communities" are, in fact, pseudocommunities. Think about whether the expression of individual differences is encouraged or discouraged, for instance, in the average church congregation. I've found it not only easy to recognize pseudocommunity but also to nip it in the bud. Often all that is required is to challenge the platitudes or generalizations. When Mary says, "Divorce is a terrible thing," I am likely to comment: "Mary, you're making a generalization. I hope you don't mind my using you as an example for the group, but one of the things people need to learn to communicate well is how to speak personally—how to use 'I' and 'my' statements. I wonder if you couldn't rephrase your statement to 'My divorce was a terrible thing for me.' "

"All right," Mary agrees. "My divorce was a terrible thing for me."

"I'm glad you put it that way, Mary," Theresa is likely to say, "because my divorce was the best thing that ever happened to me in the last twenty years."

Once individual differences are not only allowed but encouraged to surface in some such way, the group almost immediately moves to the second stage of community development: chaos.

Chaos

The chaos always centers around well-intentioned but misguided attempts to heal and convert. Let me cite a prototypical example. After a period of uneasy silence a member will say, "Well, the reason I came to this workshop is that I have such-and-such a problem, and I thought I might find a solution to it here."

"I had that problem once," a second member will respond. "I did such-and-such, and it took care of the difficulty."

"Well, I tried that," the first member answers, "but it didn't solve anything."

"When I acknowledged Jesus to be my Lord and Savior," a third member announces, "it took care of that problem and every other problem I had."

"I'm sorry," says the first member, "but that Jesus Lord-and-Savior stuff just doesn't grab me. It's not where I'm at."

"No," says a fourth member. "As a matter of fact, it makes me want to puke."

"But it's *true*," proclaims a fifth member.

And so they're off.

By and large, people resist change. So the healers and converters try harder to heal or convert, until finally their victims get their backs up and start trying to heal the healers and convert the converters. It is indeed chaos.

In the stage of chaos individual differences are, unlike those in pseudocommunity, right out in the open. Only now, instead of trying to hide or ignore them, the group is attempting to obliterate them. Underlying the attempts to heal and convert is not so much the motive of love as the motive to make everyone *normal*—and the motive to win, as the members fight over whose norm might prevail.

The disagreement that arises from time to time in a genuine community is loving and respectful and usually remarkably quiet— even peaceful—as the members work hard to listen to each other. Still, upon occasion in a fully mature community the discussion might become heated. Yet even then it is vivacious, and one has a feeling of excitement over the consensus that will be hammered out. Not so in chaos. If anything, chaos, like pseudocommunity, is boring, as the members continually swat at each other to little or no effect. It has no grace or rhythm. Indeed, the predominant feeling an observer is likely to have in response to a group in the chaotic stage of development is despair. The struggle is going nowhere, accomplishing nothing. It is no fun.

The chaos could easily be circumvented by an authoritarian leader—a dictator—who assigned them specific tasks and goals. The only problem is that a group led by a dictator is not, and never can be, a community. Community and totalitarianism are incompatible.

In response to [a] perceived vacuum of leadership during the chaotic stage of community development, it is common for one or more members of the group to attempt to replace the designated leader. He or she (usually it is a he) will say, "Look, this is getting us nowhere. Why don't we go around the circle counterclockwise and each person say something about himself or herself?" Or "Why don't we break into small groups of six or eight, and then we can get somewhere?"

The problem of the emergence of such "secondary leaders" is not their emergence but their proposed solutions. What they are proposing, one way or another, is virtually always an "escape into organization." It is true that organizing is a solution to chaos. Indeed, that is the primary reason for organization: to minimize chaos. But an organization is able to nurture a measure of community within itself only to the extent that it is willing to risk or tolerate a certain lack of structure.

The proper resolution of chaos is not easy. Because it is both unproductive and unpleasant, it may seem that the group has *degenerated* from pseudocommunity into chaos. But chaos is not necessarily the worst place for a group to be.

Emptiness

"There are only two ways out of chaos," I will explain to a group after it has spent a sufficient period of time squabbling and getting nowhere. "One is into organization—but organization is never community. The only other way is into and through emptiness."

More often than not the group will simply ignore me and go on squabbling. Then after another while I will say, "I suggested to you that the only way from chaos to community is into and through emptiness. But apparently you were not terribly interested in my suggestions." More squabbling, but finally a member will ask with a note of annoyance, "Well, what is this emptiness stuff anyway?"

Emptiness is the hard part. It is also the most crucial stage of community development. It is the bridge between chaos and community.

When the members of a group finally ask me to explain what I mean by emptiness, I tell them simply that they need to empty themselves of barriers to communication. And I am able to use their behavior during chaos to point out to them specific things—feelings, assumptions, ideas, and motives—that have so filled their minds as to make them impervious as billiard balls. The process of emptying themselves of these barriers is the key to the transition from "rugged" to "soft" individualism. The most common (and interrelated) barriers to communication that people need to empty themselves of before they can enter genuine community are:

Expectations and Preconceptions.
Prejudices.
Ideology, Theology, and Solutions.
The Need to Heal, Convert, Fix, or Solve.
The Need to Control.

I have hardly exhausted the list of things that individuals may need to give up in order to form themselves into a community. I routinely ask the members of a group to reflect in silence, during a break period or overnight, on what they as individuals most need to empty themselves of in their own unique lives. When they return, their reports are as varied as the topography of our globe: "I need to give up my need for my parents' approval," "my need to be liked," "my resentment of my son," "my preoccupation with money," "my anger at God," "my dislike of homosexuals," "my concern about neatness," and so on, and so on. Such giving up is a sacrificial process. Consequently the stage of emptiness in community development is a time of sacrifice. And sacrifice hurts. "Do I have to give up everything?" a group member once wailed during this stage.

"No," I replied, "just everything that stands in your way."

Such sacrifice hurts because it is a kind of death, the kind of death that is necessary for rebirth.

Because the stage of emptiness can be so painful, there are two questions I am routinely asked with agony. One is, "Isn't there any way into community except through emptiness?" My answer is "No." The other question is, "Isn't there any way into community except through the sharing of brokenness?" Again my answer is "No."

As a group moves into emptiness, a few of its members begin to share their own brokenness—their defeats, failures, doubts, fears, inadequacies, and sins. They begin to stop acting as if they "had it all together" as they reflect on those things they need to empty themselves of. But the other members generally do not listen to them very attentively. Either they revert to attempts to heal or convert the broken members or else they ignore them by quickly changing the topic. Consequently those who have made themselves vulnerable tend to retreat quickly into their shells.

Sometimes the group by itself will soon come to recognize that it is blocking expressions of pain and suffering—that in order to truly listen they have to *truly* empty themselves, even of their distaste for "bad news." If they don't, it becomes necessary for me to point out to its members that they are discouraging the sharing of brokenness. Some groups will then immediately correct their callousness. But other groups toward the end of the stage of emptiness will wage their final last-ditch struggle against community. Typically, there will be a spokesman who will say, "Look, I have my own burdens at home. Why can't we talk about the good things, the things we have in common, our successes instead of our failures? I'd like this to be a joyful experience. What's the point of community if it can't be joyful?"

Basically this final resistance is an attempt to flee back into pseudocommunity. But here the issue at stake is no longer over whether individual differences will be denied. The group has moved too far for that. Instead the struggle is over wholeness. It is over whether the group will choose to embrace not only the light of life but also life's darkness. True community *is* joyful, but it is also realistic. Sorrow and joy must be seen in their proper proportions.

I have spoken of the stage of emptiness largely as if it were something that occurs solely within the minds and souls of the individuals who compose a group. But it is also a process of group death, group dying. The whole group seems to writhe and moan in its travail.

Just as the physical death of some individuals is rapid and gentle while for others agonizing and protracted, so it is for the emotional surrender of groups. Whether sudden or gradual, however, all the groups in my experience have eventually succeeded in completing, accomplishing, this death. They have all made it through emptiness, through the time of sacrifice, into community.

This is an extraordinary testament to the human spirit. What it means is that given the right circumstances and knowledge of the rules, on a certain but very real level we human beings are able to die for each other.

Community

When its death has been completed, open and empty, the group enters community. In this final stage a soft quietness descends. It is a kind of peace. The room is bathed in peace. Then, quietly, a member begins to talk about herself. She is being very vulnerable. She is speaking of the deepest part of herself. The group hangs on each word. No one realized she was capable of such eloquence.

When she is finished there is a hush. It goes on a long time. But it does not seem long. There is no uneasiness in this silence. Slowly, out of the silence, another member begins to talk. He too is speaking very deeply, very personally, about himself. He is not trying to heal or convert the first person. He's not even trying to respond to her. It's not she but he who is the subject. Yet the other members of the group do not sense he has ignored her. What they feel is that it is as if he is laying himself down next to her on an altar.

The silence returns.

Then the next member speaks. And as it goes on, there will be a great deal of sadness and grief expressed; but there will also be much laughter and joy. There will be tears in abundance. Sometimes they will be tears of sadness, sometimes of joy. Sometimes, simultaneously, they will be tears of both. And then something almost more singular happens. An extraordinary amount of healing and converting begins to occur—now that no one is trying to convert or heal. And community has been born.

What happens next? The group has become a community. Where does it go from here? What, then, is its task?

There is no one answer to those questions. For the groups that have assembled specifically for a short-term experience of community, its primary task may be no more than simply to enjoy that experience—and benefit from the healing that accompanies it. It will have the additional task, however, of ending itself. Somehow

43

there must be closure. Women and men who have come to care for each other deeply need time to say goodbyes. The pains of returning to an everyday world without community need expression. It is important for short-term communities to give themselves the time for ending. This is often done best when the community is able to develop for itself a joyous sort of funeral, with some kind of liturgy or ritual for conclusion.

If the group has assembled with the ultimate goal of solving a problem—planning a campaign, healing a division within a congregation, engineering a merger, for example—then it should get on with that task. But only after it has had the time to enjoy the experience of community for itself sufficiently to cement the experience. Such groups should always bear in mind the rule: "Community-building first, problem-solving second."

Or the task of the community may be the difficult one of deciding whether it will or will not maintain itself. This decision usually should not be made quickly. In the joy of the moment members may make commitments that they shortly discover they are unable to fulfill. The consequences of long-term commitment are major and should not be taken lightly.

If a community—or part of it—does decide to maintain itself, it will have many new tasks. Community maintenance requires that multiple major decisions be made or remade over extensive periods of time. The community will frequently fall back into chaos or even pseudocommunity in the process. Over and again it will need to do the agonizing work of reemptying itself. Many groups fail here. Many convents and monasteries, for instance, while referring to themselves as "communities," long ago allowed themselves to become rigid authoritarian organizations. As such they may continue to fill useful roles in society, but they do so without joy and fail to be a "safe place" for their membership. They have forgotten that maintaining themselves as a true community should take priority over all the other tasks of their community.

Because I have spoken so glowingly of its virtues, it worries me that some might conclude that life in community is easier or more comfortable than ordinary existence. It is not. But it is certainly more *lively*, more intense. The agony is actually greater, but so is the joy. The experience of joy in community, however, is hardly automatic. During times of struggle the majority of the members of a true community will not experience joy. Instead, the prevailing mood may be one of anxiety, frustration, or fatigue. Even when the dominant mood is one of joy, a few members, because of individual worries or conflicts, may still be unable to feel a part of the community spirit. Yet the most common emotional response to the spirit of community is the feeling of joy.

It was like falling in love. When they enter community, people in a very real sense do fall in love with one another en masse. They not only feel like touching and hugging each other, they feel like hugging everyone all at once.

It is only natural when a group of people fall in love with one another that enormous sexual energy should be released. Usually this is not harmful, but it is wise for communities to be aware of their great potential sexuality in order that it does not get out of hand. It may need to be suppressed. It should not, however, be repressed. And it is wise to remember that the experience of the other forms of love, "phila" and "agape" (brother or sister love, and divine love) can be even deeper and more rewarding than simple erotic or romantic bonding. The sexuality of community is an expression of its joy, and its energy can be channeled to useful and creative purpose.

If it is so channeled, life in community may touch upon something perhaps even deeper than joy. There are a few who repeatedly seek out brief experiences of community as if such episodes were some sort of "fix." This is not to be decried. We all need "fixes" of joy in our lives. But what repeatedly draws me into community is something more. When I am with a group of human beings committed to hanging in there through both the agony and the joy of community, I have a dim sense that I am participating in a phenomenon for which there is only one word. I almost hesitate to use it. The word is "glory."

CHAPTER 7

Duane Fickeisen

Skills for Living Together

Commitment of the heart is a necessary—nearly suffi-cient—condition for community building. People who are *seriously* committed to living together in community seem to rise to the challenges of differing goals, values, and strategies. There are some tools and skills that help develop community—but the best of them are of little use without that underlying commitment.

Honoring Diversity

Successful communities find ways to draw on the unique strengths of their members. Awareness that not everyone else learns, thinks, feels, senses, or is motivated to action in the same way that you do can be very helpful in developing effective ways of working (and playing) together.

These personal characteristics can be examined through many different lenses—books, ideas, models, diagnostic instruments, role-playing games, group processes, and the like—that can pro-vide insight into your own strengths as well as those of others.

In my experience, the primary value of such tools is in awak-ening awareness of the special abilities and talents each person brings to the community. From that you can seek complementarity among your combined skills.

Hero Archetypes

One of these windows on ourselves makes use of a model of the "hero's journey" and six archetypal heroes defined by Carol Pearson in her book *The Hero Within* (San Francisco: Harper and Row, rev. ed. 1989). The six archetypes are innocent, orphan, wanderer, warrior, martyr, and magician. This model suggests that during our lives we typically experience stages when different hero types are active. Each archetype has distinct goals and fears and approaches life differently.

There is no "best" archetype. Each has its unique strengths and weaknesses, and each faces special challenges and dangers. A community made up of one predominant archetype may experience itself overly focused on the tasks of that archetype. A community with people in many phases of their journeys may benefit from their various perspectives and strengths.

Personality Types

Personality differences can be viewed though the lens of the Myers-Briggs Typology.

According to this model, the way we *gain energy (introvert/ extrovert)*, *gather information* about the world around us *(sensor/ intuitive)*, *process that information (thinker/feeler)*, together with our comfort with *decision-making (judger/perceiver)* define sixteen distinct personality types. People tend to pick careers, avocations, and mates according to their type. Identifying and recognizing such differences in type can help build relationships and mutual understanding.

The typology may also help identify tasks and responsibilities that are aligned with your preferences or that will stretch your experiences beyond them.

Learning Styles

We also have different ways of learning. Harvard educator Howard Gardner proposes that there are at least seven different human intelligences (*verbal/linguistic, logical/mathematical, spatial, musical, kinesthetic, interpersonal,* and *intrapersonal*). We develop skills in each of them to different degrees, and group learning has been found to be enhanced significantly by use of all seven in teaching. In addition, we also exhibit *cognitive* style differences: some of us are *field independent,* preferring a learning path that leads from the details to the big picture, while others are *field dependent* and prefer to have the big picture first.

Another model of learning, developed by David A. Kolb, assigns preferred learning styles based on preference for *abstraction* or *concreteness* and preference for *action* or *reflection.*

Learners with a preference for concrete experience and active experimentation are *accommodators.* Accommodators learn from doing. They like to implement plans and get things done, and they tend to accept risk. Accommodators also rely more on other people for information than on their own independent analysis. They excel at getting things done and providing leadership.

Those who prefer concrete experience over abstract conceptualization, and reflective observation over active experimentation, are *divergers.* They tend to learn by integrating and synthesizing information from many sources. Divergers like group discussion but need quiet time for reflection. People with this style are innovative and imaginative and seek involvement in important issues. They excel at recognizing problems and understanding people.

Those with a preference for abstract conceptualization and active experimentation are *convergers.* Convergers have a need to know how things work and learn by testing theories. They value strategic thinking. People with this style have limited tolerance for uncertainty and need to know how things they are asked to do will help in "real" life. They are valuable in drawing a discussion toward completion and in bringing closure to an issue. Convergers excel at problem solving and decision making.

The *assimilators* are those with a preference for abstract conceptualization and for reflective observation. Assimilators have an appreciation for logic and tend to form theories and seek facts. They learn by thinking through ideas, value sequential thinking, and need details. People with this style want to know what experts think. They are enthusiastic group members. They excel at planning and creating models.

A community may find it valuable to examine learning styles and to draw on the unique characteristics of their members as needed for the issues at hand. For example, if the community finds itself to be predominantly divergers, it is likely that they will find difficulty in bringing closure to a discussion. In that case, it may well prove helpful to empower the divergers to make an intentional effort to move things along and to empower any convergers in the group to help focus on decision-making once several alternatives have been identified.

Motivations

Yet another window on diversity is the Strength Deployment Inventory®. This diagnostic questionnaire measures factors that "motivate" behavior. The underlying model is that we are motivated by desires to be *directive, helpful,* or *analytical,* and the instrument measures the importance of each of these three factors both when things are going well and when we experience stress.

These and other windows or lenses on diversity provide alternative ways of understanding and finding the *value* inherent in differences. None of them captures the whole truth, yet they each contain important elements of truth.

My advice is to explore several of them and use those that seem to fit for your group. Avoid assuming that the types are inflexible, or that they restrict your range of abilities. And don't get trapped into introspection to the exclusion of action!

Participation and Influence

The degree and quality of participation in the group is an indicator of the stage of development of the community and of its ability to use diversity and conflicting opinion constructively. There are many styles of participation, however, and the person who is actively listening and says relatively little may be engaged as much as the more vocal members of the group.

There is an important difference between *influence* and *participation*. Influence is not necessarily proportional to participation. For example, it may well be that the person who quietly listens, and occasionally offers a synthesis or summary of what has been said, will have more influence than those who are actively debating an issue.

Effective group leaders notice which members dominate the discussion and ensure that others have an opportunity to speak if they desire. This "gatekeeping" role is often shared among group members. A discussion leader may also ask if anyone can summarize the content of what has been said as a means of moving the group process ahead. This can serve to assure those who have expressed their views that they have been heard and thus enable the group to move on.

Task and Maintenance

Task functions are those that move a group toward a particular goal or solving a problem. *Maintenance* functions are behaviors that help the group build relationships and effective processes. Both are important for the long term, effective health of a group.

Task functions include initiating discussion, seeking and providing information and opinions, giving directions, evaluating options, summarizing the discussion, and diagnosing problems.

Maintenance functions include encouraging participation, harmonizing and compromising, facilitating communications, observing and commenting on process, building trust, and solving interpersonal problems.

Responsibility for these roles should be shared and flexible. While it may be helpful to designate a "process observer" from time to time, or someone to provide process directions, usually groups operate without such formal roles. However, leaders within the group should be aware of the two kinds of functions and monitor the group's progress for a balance between the two. When problems arise, it may be helpful to try to identify whether they are related to being stuck in working toward completion of the task or to ineffective relationship maintenance.

Communication Skills

Our sensory organs gather far more information than we are able to effectively process and use. To cope with the overwhelming amount of information, we have developed filtering mechanisms. Our filters enable us to hear or see only what we *want* to hear or see to a greater extent than many of us recognize.

Communications are further complicated by non-verbal factors. Perhaps as little as 7% of what is communicated face-to-face is contained in the verbal message; the remaining 93% is non-verbal.

High quality communication takes a lot of effort. But fortunately, communication skills are learned, and we *can* learn new ones. Begin with practicing *active listening*—really paying attention and affirming the speaker. Listen to understand, and don't get distracted by formulating your response. Instead, ask clarifying questions and check out your understanding.

One way to check out your understanding is to paraphrase—tell the speaker what you think they have just said, in your own words, and ask whether you have gotten it correctly.

Another important element in good communication is to be explicit about *describing feelings*. If you rely only on your non-verbal cues, you may not be understood, so describe your own feelings by identifying and naming them. Feeling statements have the form, "I feel angry" (or happy, anxious, calm, nervous, etc.). Note that statements beginning with "I feel that . . ." most often describe what you *think* rather than what you *feel*.

When you interpret another person's feeling or purpose, check out your interpretation. Start by describing the behavior you observe, giving your interpretation, and inquiring if you are correct. For example, "Your face is red and I suspect you are angry with me. Is that right?"

Don't give up on these new communication skills when they

feel awkward. With practice you will become more comfortable with them.

Decision Making

One of the most important decisions a group makes is deciding how to decide! Unfortunately, this most critical decision is often ignored or made by a default, at least until there is a critical issue involving high stakes at hand.

Decision-making methods range in the degree that those who will be affected by the decision are involved in the process. Decisions can be made by:

- a single decision maker without input from others
- an expert on the question of concern
- a single decision maker with input from others
- averaging of individual decisions or positions, without discussion
- a sub-group or committee
- majority vote
- consensus

No single method is ideal: the appropriate one to use depends on the situation.

With a high degree of participation in decision making, there will be more support for its implementation. Additional time and effort spent reaching the decision may be offset by reduced time and effort to implement it. It usually takes more time and energy to reach agreement with high participation methods. In some cases the issues don't merit this degree of involvement, and the process may become burdensome and inefficient unless alternatives are found.

When a group has reached the stage of development where differences are welcomed and there is a high level of trust, it may be appropriate to use consensus for decisions that require greater cooperation to implement and when the stakes are high. However, for those decisions that are less important, when group members lack relevant expertise, and when implementation does not require full cooperation, it may be appropriate to use one of the less demanding methods of decision making, for example, decision by an expert or by a committee.

Conflict Resolution

Conflicts are unavoidable in human relations. Our *approach* to them can be one that makes use of conflict as a means of building trust, creating innovative solutions to problems, and strengthening relationships. But unless serious attention is given to resolving conflicts constructively, they can generate distrust, destroy relationships, and stifle creativity.

Conflict is often approached as a zero sum game with the assumption that there must be a winner and a loser, and that the winner can only gain at the expense of the loser. Sometimes that's true—for example, when a limited resource must be divided between competing interests. But often a creative alternative can be found that meets the needs of both parties.

A key to conflict resolution is to identify the interests of all the stakeholders. Knowing clearly what your own interests are allows you to evaluate proposed solutions from the standpoint of meeting your underlying needs.

Interests are the underlying principles that are non-quantifiable and cannot be negotiated, as opposed to *positions* or *issues* which are measurable and can be bargained. For example, one's *interest* might be to have good nutrition. A related *issue* would be wanting to have access to a 400 square foot garden spot in which to grow vegetables in raised beds. It would be possible to negotiate for the location and size of the garden spot, but not over the desire to have good food.

In conflicts it is often helpful to make the interests of all of the stakeholders explicit and public. Clear understanding of everyone's interests may lead to creative ways to meet all of them.

Individual styles of dealing with conflict cover a range of behaviors that differ in their focus on the importance of the *stakes* and the importance of the *relationship*. If neither are important, it may be appropriate to avoid the conflict or flee from it. If the relationship is important but the stakes are not, it may be appropriate to accommodate the other party. Conversely, if the stakes are very important but the relationship is not, then compelling the other party to agree to your position may be the best strategy. A *collaborative* solution is called for when both the stakes *and* the relationship are important.

Leading and Managing

There is an important distinction between *leadership* and *management*. Leadership is involved in the process of creating new approaches and innovative ideas, envisioning a purpose, and enrolling others as co-creators. Management is the reactive process of maintaining the status quo, organizing resources to accomplish a goal, and solving problems that threaten to interrupt progress. Both are needed for effective community action.

Management roles in a community include *monitoring progress* and *tracking resources*. The manager translates plans into action, monitors progress against milestones, and finds ways to recover from setbacks or unexpected turns of event that threaten completion of the project.

In a group that is functioning effectively, leadership is a shared responsibility. Leadership qualities are not necessarily related to personality type, nor are they something we are born with. Rather, leadership involves a set of learned skills and behavior, and most of us are quite capable of learning these skills. Of course, there is also an art to applying leadership skills, but with practice that art can be developed.

Putting It All Together

Well, that sounds like a lot of work. It *is* a lot of work! And it can be frustrating to focus on process. But getting to know who you and your colleagues are, how you relate to each other, and how you work together is the most effective way I know to build and sustain a community. Even so, *knowing how* to do it isn't enough.

You must *do* it—*experience* community. That takes courage, creativity, and commitment as well as skills. It all starts with a simple decision to *be* in community—a decision of the heart that, once taken, creates its own fulfillment.

CHAPTER 8

Robert K. Greenleaf

The Leader as Servant

A fresh critical look is being taken at the issues of power and authority, and people are beginning to learn, however haltingly, to relate to one another in less coercive and more creatively supporting ways. A new moral principle is emerging which holds that the only authority deserving one's allegiance is that which is freely and knowingly granted by the led to the leader in response to, and in proportion to, the clearly evident servant stature of the leader. Those who choose to follow this principle will not casually accept the authority of existing institutions. *Rather, they will freely respond only to individuals who are chosen as leaders because they are proven and trusted as servants.* To the extent that this principle prevails in the future, the only truly viable institutions will be those that are predominantly servant-led.

Who is the Servant-Leader?

The servant-leader *is* servant first. It begins with the natural feeling that one wants to serve, to serve *first*. Then conscious choice brings one to aspire to lead. He is sharply different from the person who is *leader* first, perhaps because of the need to assuage an unusual power drive or to acquire material possessions. For such it will be a later choice to serve—after leadership is established. The leader first and the servant-first are two extreme types. Between them there are shadings and blends that are part of the infinite variety of human nature.

The difference manifests itself in the care taken by the servant-first to make sure that other people's highest priority needs are being served. The best test, and difficult to administer, is: do those served grow as persons; do they, *while being served,* become healthier, wiser, freer, more autonomous, more likely themselves to become servants? The natural servant, the person who is *servant first*, is more likely to persevere and refine his hypothesis on what serves another's highest priority needs than is the person who is *leader first* and who later serves out of promptings of conscience or in conformity with normative expectations.

My hope for the future rests in part on my belief that among the legions of deprived and unsophisticated people are many true servants who will lead, and that most of them can learn to discriminate among those who presume to serve them and identify the true servants.

Everything Begins with the Initiative of an Individual

The forces for good and evil in the world are propelled by the thoughts, attitudes, and actions of individual beings. What happens to our values, and therefore to the quality of our civilization in the future, will be shaped by the conceptions of individuals that are born of inspiration.

But the leader needs more than inspiration. He ventures to say, "I will go; come with me!" He initiates, provides the ideas and the structure, and takes the risk of failure along with the chance of success.

Paul Goodman, speaking through a character in *Making Do* has said, "If there is no community for you, young man, young man, make it yourself."

What Are You Trying to Do?

A mark of a leader, an attribute that puts him in a position to show the way for others, is that he is better than most at pointing the direction. As long as he is leading, he always has a goal. It may be a goal arrived at by group consensus; or the leader, acting on inspiration, may simply have said, "Let's go this way." But the leader always knows what it is and can articulate it for any who are unsure. By clearly stating and restating the goal the leader gives certainty and purpose to others who may have difficulty in achieving it for themselves.

The one who states the goal must elicit trust, especially if it is a high risk or visionary goal, because those who follow are asked to accept the risk along with the leader. A leader does not elicit trust unless one has confidence in his values and his competence (including judgment) and unless he has a sustaining spirit (entheos) that will support the tenacious pursuit of a goal.

Not much happens without a dream. And for something great to happen, there must be a great dream. Behind every great achievement is a dreamer of great dreams. Much more than a dreamer is required to bring it to reality; but the dream must be there first.

Listening and Understanding

One of our very able leaders recently was made the head of a large, important and difficult-to-administer public institution. After a short time he realized that he was not happy with the way things were going. His approach to the problem was a bit unusual. For three months he stopped reading newspapers and listening to news broadcasts; and for this period he relied wholly upon those he met in the course of his work to tell him what was going on. In three months his administrative problems were resolved. No miracles were wrought; but out of a sustained intentness of listening that was produced by this unusual decision, this able man learned and received the insights needed to set the right course. And he strengthened his team by so doing.

Why is there so little listening? What makes this example so exceptional? Part of it, I believe, with those who lead, is that the usual leader in the face of a difficulty tends to react by trying to find someone else on whom to pin the problem, rather than his automatic response being, "I have a problem. What is it? What can *I* do about *my* problem?" The sensible man who takes the later course will probably react by listening, and somebody in the situation is likely to tell him what his problem is and what he should do about it. Or, he will hear enough that he will get an intuitive insight that resolves it.

I have a bias about this which suggests that only a true natural servant automatically responds to any problem by listening *first*. When he is a leader, this disposition causes him to be *seen* as servant first. This suggests that a non-servant who wants to be a servant might become a *natural* servant through a long arduous discipline of learning to listen, a discipline sufficiently sustained that the automatic response to any problem is to listen first. I have seen enough remarkable transformations in people who have been trained to listen to have some confidence in this approach. It is because true listening builds strength in other people.

Acceptance and Empathy

If we can take one dictionary's definition: *acceptance* is receiving what is offered, with approbation, satisfaction, or acquiescence; and *empathy* is the imaginative projection of one's own consciousness into another being. The opposite of both, the word *reject*, is to refuse to hear or receive—to throw out.

The servant always accepts and empathizes, never rejects. The servant as leader always empathizes, always accepts the person but sometimes refuses to accept some of the person's effort or performance as good enough.

A college president once said, "An educator may be rejected by his students and he must not object to this. But he may never, under any circumstances, regardless of what they do, reject a single student."

We have known this a long time in the family. For a family to be a family, no one can ever be rejected. Acceptance of the person, though, requires a tolerance of imperfection. Anybody could lead perfect people—if there were any.

It is part of the enigma of human nature that the "typical" person—immature, stumbling, inept, lazy—is capable of great dedication and heroism *if* he is wisely led. The secret of institution building is to be able to weld a team of such people by lifting them up to grow taller than they would otherwise be.

Awareness and Perception

Framing all of this is awareness, opening wide the doors of perception so as to enable one to get more of what is available of sensory experience and other signals from the environment than people usually take in. Awareness has its risks, but it makes life more interesting; certainly it strengthens one's effectiveness as a leader.

The cultivation of awareness gives one the basis for detachment, the ability to stand aside and set oneself in perspective in the context of one's own experience, amidst the ever present dangers, threats, and alarms. Then one sees one's own peculiar assortment of obligations and responsibilities in a way that permits one to sort out the urgent from the important and perhaps deal with the important. Awareness is *not* a giver of solace—it is just the opposite. It is a disturber and an awakener. Able leaders are usually sharply awake and reasonably disturbed. They are not seekers after solace. They have their own inner serenity.

A leader must have more of an armor of confidence in facing the unknown—more than those who accept his leadership. This is partly anticipation and preparation, but it is also a very firm belief that in the stress of real life situations one can compose oneself in a way that permits the creative process to operate.

This is told dramatically in one of the great stories of the human spirit—the story of Jesus when confronted with the woman taken in adultery. In this story Jesus is seen as a man, like all of us, with extraordinary prophetic insight of the kind we all have some of. He is a leader; he has a goal—to bring more compassion into the lives of people.

In this scene the woman is cast down before him by the mob that is challenging Jesus's leadership. They cry, "The *law* says she shall be stoned, what do *you* say?" Jesus must make a decision, he must give the *right* answer, *right* in the situation, and one that sustains his leadership toward his goal. The situation is deliberately stressed by his challengers. What does he do?

He sits there writing in the sand—a withdrawal device. In the pressure of the moment, having assessed the situation rationally, he assumes the attitude of withdrawal that will allow creative insight to function.

He could have taken another course; he could have regaled the mob with rational arguments about the superiority of compassion over torture. A good logical argument can be made for it. What would the result have been had he taken that course?

He did not choose to do that. He chose instead to withdraw and cut the stress—right in the event itself—in order to open his *awareness* to creative insight. And a great one came, one that has kept the story of the incident alive for 2,000 years—"Let him that is without sin among you cast the first stone."

Persuasion—Sometimes One Man at a Time

Leaders work in wondrous ways. Some assume great institutional burdens, others quietly deal with one man at a time. Such a man was John Woolman, an American Quaker, who lived through the middle years of the eighteenth century and who almost singlehandedly rid the Society of Friends (Quakers) of slaves.

His method was one of gentle but clear and persistent persuasion.

————•————

Although John Woolman was not a strong man physically, he accomplished his mission by journeys up and down the East Coast by foot or horseback visiting slaveholders—over a period of many years. The approach was not to censure the slaveholders in a way that drew their animosity. Rather the burden of his approach was to raise questions: What does the owning of slaves do to you as a moral person? What kind of an institution are you binding over to your children? Man by man, inch by inch, by persistently returning and revisiting and pressing his gentle argument over a period of thirty years, the scourge of slavery was eliminated from this Society, the first religious group in America formally to denounce and forbid slavery among its members. Leadership by persuasion has the virtue of change by convincement rather than coercion. Its advantages are obvious.

Community—The Lost Knowledge of These Times

Men once lived in communities and, in the developing world, many still do. Human society can be much better than it is (or was) in primitive communities. But if community itself is lost in the process of development, will what is put in its place survive? At the moment there seems to be some question. What is our experience?

Within my memory, we once cared for orphaned children in institutions. We have largely abandoned these institutions as not good for children. Children need the love of a real home—in a family, a community.

Now we realize that penal institutions, other than focusing the retributive vengeance of society and restraining anti-social actions for a period, do very little to rehabilitate. In fact they *de*bilitate and return more difficult offenders to society. What to do with these people? It is now suggested that most of them should be kept in homes, in community.

There is now the beginning of questioning of the extensive building of hospitals. We need some hospitals for extreme cases. But much of the recent expansion has been done for the convenience of doctors and families, not for the good of patients—or even for the good of families. Only community can give the healing love that is essential for health.

The *school*, on which we pinned so much of our hopes for a better society, has become too much a social-upgrading mechanism that destroys community. Now we have the beginnings of questioning of the school as we know it, as a specialized, separate-from-community institution.

We are in the process of moving away from institutional care for the mentally retarded and toward small community-like homes. Recent experience suggests that, whereas the former provide mostly custodial care, the small community can actually lift them up, help them grow.

Now the care of old people is a special concern, because there are so many more of them and they live so much longer. But the current trend is to put them in retirement homes that segregate the old from normal community. Already there is the suggestion that these are not the happy places that were hoped for. Will retirement homes shortly be abandoned as orphan homes were?

As a generalization, I suggest that human service that requires love cannot be satisfactorily dispensed by specialized institutions that exist apart from community, that take the problem out of sight of the community. Both those being cared for and the community suffer.

Love is an undefinable term, and its manifestations are both subtle and infinite. But it begins, I believe, with one absolute condition: unlimited liability! As soon as one's liability for another is qualified *to any degree*, love is diminished by that much.

Any human service where he who is served should be loved in the process, requires community, a face-to-face group in which the liability of each for the other and all for one is unlimited, or as close to it as it is possible to get. Trust and respect are highest in this circumstance and an accepted ethic that gives strength to all is reinforced. Where there is not community, trust, respect, ethical behavior are difficult for the young to learn and for the old to maintain. Living in community as one's basic involvement will generate an exportable surplus of love which the individual may carry into his many involvements with institutions which are usually not communities: businesses, churches, governments, schools.

Out of the distress of our seeming community-less society, hopeful new forms of community are emerging: young people's communes, Israeli kibbutzes, and therapeutic communities like Synanon. Seen through the bias of conventional morality, the communes are sometimes disturbing to the older generation. But among them is a genuine striving for community, and they represent a significant new social movement which may foretell the future.

The opportunities are tremendous for rediscovering vital lost knowledge about how to live in community while retaining as much as we can of the value in our present urban, institution-bound society.

All that is needed to rebuild community as a viable life form for large numbers of people is for enough servant-leaders to show the way, not by mass movements, but by each servant-leader demonstrating his own unlimited liability for a quite specific community-related group.

CHAPTER 9

Michael Linton

Money and Community Economics

Let's look at the logic of the money game and see exactly how it affects community.

It all comes down to money in the end. The problems of the world come from our actions, and our actions, both as a society and as individuals, are largely determined by the way money works. Many trivial and even damaging things are happening—simply because some people have the money and the will to do them. In contrast, other things of real value, many essential to the survival of the planet, are not happening—simply because those who have the will, have not the money. People are working in ways detrimental to their personal health, to that of the environment, both locally and globally, and to the well-being of their community because they need the money.

For most of the planet, the money comes first, what we do to get it comes second. And this is so because money is our means of exchange—we need to earn it to keep in the game. This is a problem, since money is, both by design and in function, scarce and essentially difficult to come by. There are three reasons why money is hard to come by:

1) There is only so much money in circulation;
2) It can go virtually anywhere—and so it does;
3) You cannot print it yourself.

Notice that these conditions virtually ensure that some communities, indeed, some people, are "rich" while others are "poor." Notice that the flight of money from a community can leave it devoid of the means to trade within itself, even when resources are available. People are unemployed not because they lack skills or they are unwilling to work, but simply because the money to employ them has drained away from the part of the world where they live.

People are ready and willing, tools, materials, energy, land are often still available, and certainly need is still present. All that is missing is a method of coordinating the needs with the available resources.

But money is really just an immaterial measure, like an inch, or a gallon, a pound, or degree. While there is certainly a limit on real resources—only so many tons of wheat, only so many feet of material, only so many hours in the day—there need never be a shortage of measure. ("No, you can't use any inches today, there aren't any around, they are all being used somewhere else.") Yet this is precisely the situation in which we persist regarding money. Money is, for the most part, merely a symbol, accepted to be valuable generally throughout the society that uses it. Why should we ever be short of symbols to keep account of how we serve one another?

Any community suffering from unemployment of people or such other resources as land, equipment, or energy, simply because there is not enough money circulating in the community, can bring some, if not all, of those resources into effect by organizing a local money. We can eliminate unemployment and poverty in the community if we are willing to use our own money.

Hunger is a lack of food. Feed the hungry and they are hungry again tomorrow. Show them how to farm and they can feed themselves. Poverty is a lack of money. Give conventional money to the poor, and they are poor again tomorrow. Show them how to use their own money, and they can manage their own affairs. The argument to this point asserts that reliance on conventional money alone leaves the resources of the community underutilized, and that a local currency can "utilize" this spare capacity. But mere numeric growth in itself is often detrimental to real wealth.

The real issue is the quality of our work—what is it in fact that we are doing—planting trees or stockpiling arms? It is in this area that a localized currency can have its most important effects.

Consider the extent to which the economy of your own community is distorted at present by its need to import money—through the export of real resources, often at unrealistic prices. Communities will squander resources, pander to tourists, entice heavy industry, and accept questionable benefits from government programs simply to keep the wages rolling. And consider how your community exports money to bring in goods and services at the most "economical" prices, rendering local producers idle, at an incalculable cost to the infrastructure of the community. The world is round. In the real world, things circulate. Conventional money is often thought to go round and round—but for most communities it really just goes through and through.

Most regions are communities in name rather than reality. An effective community is a process, an ongoing collection of interactions and continuing relationships. It used to be that towns, villages, and regions were much more self reliant than now. When transportation was slow and expensive, when much had to be produced locally as it was too perishable to travel, when moving money was itself a risky business, most of the productive work in a community was addressed to meeting its own needs with what was available locally. With the advent of "cheap" energy and transportation, technologies of "preservation," and the present ease of monetary transfer, even across national boundaries, communities everywhere have been progressively drawn into patterns of cash crop specialization and the inevitable dependency relationship.

Establishing a local currency has the effect of creating a "skin" for the group that use it. Within that skin, the community will tend to develop patterns of trading that reflect a preference for using local money to employ local resources, for human scale, labor intensive options rather than high capital technologies. The community will be better able to make a positive contribution to global affairs when the local economy is working well.

It used to be difficult to organize a local currency with minted coinage or printed bills. Nowadays, since people are quite accustomed to bank accounts and paying by check or credit transfer it is quite straightforward to create a localized currency—merely by providing a set of accounts through which members can record their mutual trading. This is entirely legal and can generally be both easy and cheap to operate.

Spending money is how you really vote in the world. You do it every day and it determines how the world works. It is far more significant than how you cast your ballot. It is time that we use our own money in our own communities.

The Heart of the Matter

We are advised that we should love one another. Love needs to be expressed in action, not just felt as a warm inner glow.

The way we behave around money is not likely to support the development of loving relationships. Conventional money tends us towards competitive attitudes to one another and hence to the withholding of love.

Personal money is convivial money, supporting generosity, the growth of trust, mutual respect, and love.

Power and Consent

The common experience is that you get paid to work. Money is the reward for doing something you might not otherwise do. The carrot for the donkey—sometimes the stick. It's hard to get and easy to spend. And coercive—people with money exercise power over people without it. Who pays the piper calls the tune . . .

It is easy to earn in a personal money network. Everyone has money to spend. Nobody needs it, so things happen because people want them to happen. People serve willingly or not at all. Nobody gets to tell anyone else what to do. Rather than being paid for our work, we are acknowledged for what we give. Acknowledged in good money—good in our own community. After a while, most people come to realize that the greatest part of the reward is knowing that we are helping someone else.

The Role of Gift in Community

Really, a community is a persistent gift exchange cycle. Community exists to the extent that the pattern and quality of that which really happens is in some way serving its members. The reality is, that people give each other things, do things for each other. The mechanic fixes your car, the teacher gives your child an education, the salesman gives us the goods, you give your best at work. And in exchange for these real gifts—we confer symbols on each other. You give the mechanic $325, the teacher gets $2,184 per month, the price tag is $19.99, perhaps you get what you are worth at work.

Real actions and services in the world are acknowledged by placing monetary values on them. A symbol is attached to a reality. This raises two particular problems. One is well-known and needs little elaboration: Money itself becomes more important than real wealth. The symbol begins to seem real. Numbers that show on the balance sheet mean more than real costs that don't show—the depletion of unrenewable resources, the degradation of humanity. People become more interested in making money than the service they are offering.

The second problem is rarely noticed, but it is the most powerful determinant of our economy.

Patterns of Acknowledgement

Since real actions are compensated with money, the patterns of money flow determine the patterns of gift exchange. Actions take place *only* when money is available—no money, no deal.

Furthermore, as money flows in and out of the community, so do real gifts, goods and services, resources and energy. A "community" that uses only conventional money actually has very little gift recirculation in its local economy. Service of one by another in ongoing cycles is largely left to the informal economy—which is quite restricted and inefficient.

In contrast, in a local money network every action is naturally part of the cycle of gifts within that community simply because the way that the symbols are patterned determines the pattern of the economic world—to recycle money is inevitably to recycle goods and services—and love—within the community.

It makes little sense to be the witting victim of a symbol, simply the creation of the mind. Why not use money—just an arrangement of symbols—to keep account of our actions in a way that works?

Using personal money doesn't remove the need to spend it wisely, but it does lift the anxiety about ever running out of it. The focus returns to the goods or services being exchanged and the money becomes the secondary concern. This opens the opportunity to be generous, to give proper acknowledgement, as every dollar I spend circulates in the community and returns to employ me. It also enables me to fully enjoy the gift.

In our conventional economy we developed a particular set of symbols and we now allow them to dominate the reality of our lives. We attribute a significance to our accounts, our bits of paper, our pieces of silver that gives them more importance than the real wealth of the world. We need to recognize what is real and what is of our imagination, and we need to act on the knowledge of that difference.

CHAPTER 10

Amia Lieblich

The Economics of a Kibbutz

Presently I am the cost accountant at Makom and I understand that you wanted to learn about our economic state of affairs, but I want to tell you a little story first.

Several years ago I was arrested in Russia and was sentenced to fifteen years in a labor camp in Siberia. I don't want to go into the circumstances of my arrest, but, anyway, I was released after a few months and returned to Israel. I want to tell you one minor episode, however, which is of great significance from my point of view.

I was in a prison which served as a way station for convicts who were en route to Siberia. While most people stayed there for two or three days, my detention there lasted three months. I had the chance to meet hundreds, perhaps even thousands, of people and I tried to pass the time by listening to their stories and telling and retelling mine. So it happened that day after day I was telling prisoners about the kibbutz and how it works. I couldn't avoid it because there was always one prisoner from the day before who told the newcomers: "He's from a kibbutz in Israel; ask him to tell you about it."

Well, there were two reactions to my story. It's amazing how many times I heard these two reactions from so many different people. People would say: "We believe every word you say, of course, but tell us two things: Do you have a police station and a prison in your kibbutz? And can you buy a liter of brandy there?"

If I answered no to one of these questions, people frequently added, "Then your story must be just a fairy tale. You can't maintain a village without a prison and police and no one wants to live in a place where you can't buy brandy."

Well, let's forget about the brandy, but the first point gave me much to consider. I repeatedly ask myself whether they perhaps were right: How can we live without any formal law enforcement? My conclusion is that in the kibbutz the disciplinary tool is the atmosphere which is created by the total community. If a person cheats me once or twice, I don't care. But I wait until it becomes known and then the social atmosphere will take care of the matter, and the individual will either have to change his behavior or leave.

All this is to say that our economic success is just one part of the story, while the social and personal factors certainly play the more important role.

As cost accountant, I compile all our costs and profits.

Makom has two main productive branches, agriculture and industry. Our industry centers primarily on the cannery (what we call the "olive factory") and metal projects. These enterprises make much more money than the agricultural branches. Among our agricultural endeavors, the most profitable one is the cotton fields, but this area requires irrigation throughout the summer, which is a serious problem for us. The amount of land we allot to the cotton is in direct proportion to the amount of water we can spare in the summer.

Other agricultural branches are also problematic because the State sets certain production quotas, and, as long as the kibbutz stays within the limits of these quotas, it is subsidized by the State. This applies to our cattle and poultry farms; we try to stay within the limits because, without subsidies, these branches wouldn't bring in any profit. So, in all branches of agriculture, development is severely limited.

On the other hand, the kibbutz cannot depend exclusively on industry—no way. A kibbutznik doesn't like to work on the line in a factory; it simply doesn't agree with our mentality. The most valuable resource of the kibbutz is its people, and this cannot be ignored. One cannot take only purely economic factors into consideration and ignore the fact that most men want to work in agriculture. The human satisfaction is, from our point of view, at least as important as the profit we're making. Although these human factors cannot be conventionally calculated, they're nevertheless an important component in our general formula.

In practice, we try to help those people who do work on the assembly lines by allowing them one to three months of agricultural work per year. This works out well because agricultural work is seasonal and demands extra people for short durations; however, it still doesn't solve all the problems generated by routine industrial work.

For the same reason, we try to improve the technological efficiency of our factories, so that we can increase productivity without adding more workers. Another method we use is rotating personnel within the division. After two or three years of administrative work, we rotate, so that the chief administrator becomes a regular worker again and vice versa. Actually, we have no problem in filling the administrative and scientific positions in our industrial divisions; these jobs are indeed a challenge and many of our offspring have the degrees in engineering, economics, and other necessary fields of expertise. Our factories are also clearly different from urban ones in the way that all workers participate in the decision-making and planning processes, so they don't feel exploited by the system.

In spite of our problems of manpower we don't use any hired workers in our factories, with the exception of about ten experts who have been working on our metal project for years. The lack of workers is especially severe in the food industry, since our production depends on raw materials which have very short life spans. We produce pickles, for example, and have to treat all the cucumbers and onions within two or three weeks. In order to cope with such seasonal pressures we draft workers from all divisions of the kibbutz: School teachers (this season is during the school recess, anyway), secretaries, everybody is mobilized.

The harvest, although also seasonal, is somewhat easier to organize, for various reasons. Until recently, we used to buy a large portion of the vegetables that we preserved. Lately we have been growing most of the vegetables on the kibbutz, which increases our profits. Harvesting is done by sophisticated agricultural machines or, in the case of olives, by our schoolchildren. The important fact is that we avoid employing hired labor. I believe that this is one of the factors which keep our sons from leaving the kibbutz. People feel more at home and more involved in our autonomous economy; they would feel completely different if they met strange workers in every corner of the kibbutz.

Sixty percent of the adult kibbutz members work in the service divisions—education, administration, kitchen, laundry—and 40 percent work in the productive branches. Of that 40 percent, two-thirds are employed by industry and the remaining third by agriculture. Actually, very few people work in agriculture because we operate no branches that require any manual labor. With the aid of mechanical innovations, we've been able to increase production while using a smaller number of workers. We have excellent farmers here, I can assure you of that. It's incredible what we have been able to accomplish in such a short period of time. . . .

I still remember the Valley when I came to Molad in 1934. It didn't resemble the present place at all. Going out at night, for example, you now can identify all the settlements by their electric lights and it's impossible to get lost around the area. When I came, however, the Valley was completely dark at night. I used to drive our milk cart at night to the central dairy plant, which was situated in another village, and it wasn't unusual at all to lose the way, especially on rainy nights. . . .

Makom was built under particularly difficult conditions. When the group moved to its present location in 1936, it thought it could profit from the experience of the other settlements which had been living in the vicinity for several years. The early beginnings proved, however, that the climatic conditions of Makom, although so close to other settlements, were entirely different. The land needs artificial irrigation for almost every crop; the soil is heavy and somewhat salty, and the local water is salty as well. These conditions caused the settlers immense difficulties; in addition to the agricultural drawbacks, Makom's settlers had to support themselves independently from the beginning. Actually, agricultural experts who inspected the land greatly discouraged the settlers by concluding that the local conditions made it impossible to undertake any intensive farming. Add to this the fact that the more established neighbors refused to share their water with this intruding kibbutz—and what else do you need for failure? Pomegranate orchards, a textile factory, shoe making, and sheep raising were just a few of the abortive agricultural experiments. People who stayed here, and managed to achieve what you see now, must have had exceptional faith and dedication to overcome all these obstacles!

From 1952 on, several factors combined to contribute to the great economic success of this kibbutz. The first sons of Makom graduated from high school and returned from the Army and they were of immense help to the kibbutz. Also, we suddenly received a much greater water supply when several good wells were discovered in the Gilboa area and we reached an agreement to receive a fair share of any newly found water. A loan from the agricultural center was also granted for the first time at about the same period. (The agricultural center of the Jewish Agency had particularly taken upon itself to support five extremely poor kibbutzim, and Makom was amongst these five. This enabled us to get loans and credit under reasonable terms.) The German reparation money started to pour in at about this time. The original decision was to use this money only for special public purposes, such as memorial buildings and cultural projects, but later, due to the economic situation, it was decided to use it for the current budget of the kibbutz. Last among the contributing factors, I'd put ourselves— namely, the new group that arrived from Molad. It's true that we were experienced workers and our younger members bridged the generation gap in Makom, but I don't think that it's fair to say that it's due to us that the kibbutz suddenly started to flourish. All the factors I have mentioned were at least as important.

I want to complete my little economic history by returning to my story from the Russian prison. I don't think that our economic intuition is our secret charm; it's our social spirit which preserved us. I believe that our most profitable undertaking is rearing children. The core of people who first settled this location were an outstanding intellectual elite, much more intellectual than the average kibbutznik elsewhere. Every single one of them could easily have become an administrator or a branch coordinator, yet this kibbutz decided to allocate its best people to education and child care. Furthermore, whereas several years ago the average birth rate in the kibbutzim was .80 children per member, in Makom it was 1.25 children per member. So we have had many children (and still do), and, although people complain about the crowded children's houses, the difficult physical conditions and the number of adults who have to work in child care, I think that herein lies our success. We suffered a lot, we ate only half an egg, but we raised a lot of good children and provided them with the best possible education. This is our kibbutz talisman, our secret. As the result of all this, today 60 percent to 70 percent of the adult members are sons and daughters who were born or educated here (including their "imported" spouses), and it's this second generation who today carry the entire social and economic responsibility of the kibbutz. So, if you want the formula for our "economic miracle," our secret, it's all here in a nutshell, as formulated by an economically oriented accountant. . . . That's what we started with then: a personal-social factor which became a major determinant in our economic success story.

3

FINDING COMMUNITY:
THE SATISFACTION

I have perceiv'd that to be with those I like is
    enough,
To stop in company with the rest at evening is
    enough,
To be surrounded by beautiful, curious, breath-
    ing, laughing,
    flesh is enough,
To pass among them or touch any one, or rest my
    arm ever so
    lightly round his or her neck for a moment,
    what is this
    then?
I do not ask any more delight, I swim in it as in
    a sea.

                                        WALT WHITMAN

When people who actively make community a part of their lives are asked why they do it, the most common answers are "I like to be with people." "I feel like part of something." "I like the support I get."

Corinne McLaughlin and Gordon Davidson are co-founders of Sirius, an intentional community in Massachusetts. In their book *Builders of the Dawn: Community Lifestyles in a Changing World*, they echo the story of how modern society has lost the natural communities that existed before the industrial age and explore why these are beginning to be replaced by purposefully created community experiences. It is in this context that McLaughlin and Davidson describe the satisfaction that people all over the planet are experiencing by finding community.

"Community offers all the advantages of a caring family, without the loss of freedom often experienced in a blood family and without the authority and control often exercised by parents over children. In a community there is always someone to talk to or someone to share your excitement with when something wonderful happens. There are people who will really help you out when you need them. If you're sick, there's someone to care for you. If your car breaks down, there's someone to give you a ride. If you want to go to the movies or a party, there's usually someone to keep you company. If you're single and afraid of living alone, there's the safety of the group. And there are always community social events, like parties and special celebrations, that create a sense of belonging and of closeness, and group work projects where everyone pitches in.

"On the deepest level, community offers a safe and loving environment to allow individuals to develop their full potential and to discover greater meaning to life."

The point that McLaughlin and Davidson make, that we can replace a nonexistent or dysfunctional family with an extended family of people we choose, is an important one to keep in mind as we contemplate our own community building.

Equally powerful, however, is our strong biological drive to connect with our blood relatives. Sociobiologists have estimated that the drive to help relatives is directly proportional to the number of genes we have in common. Their research indicates that we automatically reach out to siblings more than to cousins, for example. With a drive as powerful as this at our disposal, it makes sense to think about kinship as the place to start in our community building activities. What if we found ourselves with the kind of fulfilling community experience described by McLaughlin and Davidson, but it included the blood relatives we already love?

In chapter 11, *Kinship and Friendship: The Flesh of Community*, psychologist Mihayli Csikszentmihayli describes the bond we feel for our blood relations and the pain we experience when our family uses this bond to control and manipulate. Csikszentmihayli focuses on the benefits of a family environment in which mother and father exhibit a mutual openness and caring that serves as a model for other family members. This can serve as a foundation for a family life that produces healthy individuals and a strong sense of community with relatives.

He also explores friendship, the "kinship" we feel with those who are not our blood relations. He describes the ways in which our usual patterns of socializing only mimic friendship and often can have a dangerous influence, particularly on young people who have no strong family ties to guide them in what is right and wrong. He emphasizes that it is important for us to actively seek friendships in which we can express ourselves, and feel whole as a result of communicating with someone who cares about us. Paradoxically, it is by being who we are while surrounded by those who love us that we truly develop our individuality. Thus, we serve as catalyst for one another in our personal growth, which, in the end, serves the community as well.

Usually we think of service to others only in its simplest form: the act of doing good deeds. But there is much more to service, as psychologist and spiritual teacher Ram Dass and political advisor and communications expert Paul Gorman point out in chapter 12, *Service: The Soul of Community.* They focus on the profound bond we can experience when we drop our masks and meet heart-to-heart in the mutually reassuring act of being present for one another. We experience a momentary unity together that helps us rise above the sense of isolation that is our normal state. We can derive great joy from doing small things for one another with no expectation of credit or recognition. We can protect the reputations of others by discouraging gossip. We can help someone to feel heard by truly listening. We can share the burdens of our family and friends, *and* allow ourselves to be served by others. When we do these things with a clear intention and a calm, quiet awareness, we are taking part in the discipline of service—the soul of community.

Dancing, singing, touching, laughing all give us pleasure in the company of others. Through celebration and ritual, we gain confirmation for our experiences. We have witnesses to our life. We join with those who have loved us and helped us, struggled with us shoulder to shoulder, encouraged us and pushed us to be the most we could be. We celebrate our passages from childhood, from puberty, into wedlock, through parenting, and finally to death. We create an identity for ourselves within the celebrations of community life. In chapter 13, *Celebration: The Spirit of Community,* peace activist and ecofeminist Starhawk presents a detailed description of the use of celebration and ritual to mark the passages of life and draw the members of a group together into a distinct community identity.

Our ability to respond to such celebration, and indeed, our entire ability to feel at home in a community, hinges upon our level of awareness. Too often in the company of others, we fall into a waking sleep in which we deny our real feelings in the interest of getting along. But a community that emphasizes awareness can overcome this tendency by granting us permission to recognize, communicate, and change the way we feel.

My grandmother once told me that she knew she would be

happy marrying my grandfather when she realized she didn't mind washing his socks. You can use a similar test to determine your own "fit" within a community. Do you hate doing the shared chores? washing the dishes? taking out the garbage? hosting the gatherings? mailing the invitations? attending the planning meetings? These can be early warning signals that you haven't found the right people to be with. But how can you be sure to notice these and the other small messages about your own happiness within your group? The simple answer is "by practicing awareness."

In chapter 14, *Awareness: The Consciousness of Community*, Vietnamese Zen monk Thich Nhat Hanh outlines ways in which we can practice awareness in our daily lives and especially in the context of a community. Nhat Hanh advocates the development of "communities of mindful living" to substitute for "our former big families." His modest proposal does not require us to leave our current situations and create a new home in some other setting. Instead, he advocates joining together with like-minded friends and families to create a country retreat where we can go to rejuvenate ourselves. In such a place, he suggests, we will find "aunts," "uncles," and "cousins" who can help us practice awareness, and support us through life's hard times.

Green Gulch Farm is one example of mindfulness in practice in a community setting. A part of San Francisco Zen Center, founded by Japanese Zen master Shunryu Suzuki, Green Gulch survived the trauma of losing its teacher to cancer, only to face the additional trauma of removing his successor for sexual misconduct. In the evolution of board, staff, and abbot leadership that followed, the community struggled with democratic processes to support and sustain the practice center. In chapter 15, *A Community of Awareness*, Green Gulch resident Stephanie Kaza describes life in this thriving community today. Here community is a matter of living attentively together in the rhythm of practices and place.

CHAPTER 11

Mihaly Csikszentmihalyi

Kinship and Friendship: The Flesh of Community

Many successful men and women would second Lee Iacocca's statement: "I've had a wonderful and successful career. But next to my family, it really hasn't mattered at all."

Throughout history, people have been born into and have spent their entire lives in kinship groups. Families have varied greatly in size and composition, but everywhere individuals feel a special intimacy toward relatives, with whom they interact more often than with people outside the family. Sociobiologists claim that this familial loyalty is proportional to the amount of genes that any two persons share: for instance, a brother and a sister will have half their genes in common, while two cousins only half as many again. In this scenario siblings will, on the average, help each other out twice as much as cousins. Thus the special feelings we have for our relatives are simply a mechanism designed to ensure that the genes' own kind will be preserved and replicated.

There are certainly strong biological reasons for our having a particular attachment to relatives. No slowly maturing mammalian species could have survived without some built-in mechanism that made most adults feel responsible for their young, and the young feel dependent on the old; for that reason the bond of the newborn human infant to its caretakers, and vice versa, is especially strong.

[But] no matter how strong the ties biology and culture have forged between family members, it is no secret that there is great variety in how people feel about their relatives. Some families are warm and supportive, some are challenging and demanding, others threaten the self of their members at every turn, still others are just insufferably boring. The frequency of murder is much higher among family members than among unrelated people. Child abuse and incestuous sexual molestation, once thought to be rare deviations from the norm, apparently occur much more often than anyone had previously suspected. It is clear that the family can make one very happy, or be an unbearable burden. Which one it will be depends, to a great extent, on how much psychic energy family members invest in the mutual relationship, and especially in each other's goals.

Until a few decades ago, families tended to stay together because parents and children were forced to continue the relationship for extrinsic reasons. If divorces were rare in the past, it wasn't because husbands and wives loved each other more in the old times, but because husbands needed someone to cook and keep house, wives needed someone to bring home the bacon, and children needed both parents in order to eat, sleep, and get a start in the world. The "family values" that the elders spent so much effort inculcating in the young were a reflection of this simple necessity, even when it was cloaked in religious and moral considerations. Of course, once family values were taught as being important, people learned to take them seriously, and they helped keep families from disintegrating. All too often, however, the moral rules were seen as an outside imposition, an external constraint under which husbands, wives, and children chafed. In such cases the family may have remained intact physically, but it was internally riven with conflicts and hatred. The current "disintegration" of the family is the result of the slow disappearance of external reasons for staying married.

But extrinsic reasons are not the only ones for staying married and for living together in families. There are great opportunities for joy and for growth that can only be experienced in family life. If the trend of traditional families keeping together mainly as a convenience is on the wane, the number of families that endure because their members enjoy each other may be increasing. Of course, because external forces are still much more powerful than internal ones, the net effect is likely to be a further fragmentation of family life for some time to come. But the families that do persevere will be in a better position to help their members develop a rich self than families held together against their will are able to do.

When a family has a common purpose and open channels of communication, when it provides gradually expanding opportunities for action in a setting of trust, then life in it becomes an enjoyable flow activity. Its members will spontaneously focus their attention on the group relationship, and to a certain extent forget their individual selves, their divergent goals, for the sake of experiencing the joy of belonging to a more complex system that joins separate consciousnesses in a unified goal.

One of the most basic delusions of our time is that home life takes care of itself naturally, and that the best strategy for dealing with it is to relax and let it take its course.

To play the trumpet well, a musician cannot let more than a few days pass without practicing. An athlete who does not run regularly will soon be out of shape, and will no longer enjoy running. In each case, without concentration, a complex activity breaks down into chaos. Why should the family be different? Unconditional acceptance, the complete trust family members ought to have for one another, is meaningful only when it is accompanied by an unstinting investment of attention.

Enjoying Friends

"The worst solitude," wrote Sir Francis Bacon, "is to be destitute of sincere friendship." Compared to familial relationships, friendships are much easier to enjoy. We can choose our friends, and usually do so, on the basis of common interests and complementary goals. We need not change ourselves to be with friends; they reinforce our sense of self instead of trying to transform it. While at home there are many boring things we have to accept, like taking out the garbage and raking up leaves, with friends we can concentrate on things that are "fun."

Because a friendship usually involves common goals and common activities, it is "naturally" enjoyable. But like any other activity, this relationship can take a variety of forms, ranging from the destructive to the highly complex. When a friendship is primarily a way of validating one's own insecure sense of self, it will give pleasure, but it will not be enjoyable in our sense—that of fostering growth. For instance, the institution of "drinking buddies," so prevalent in small communities all over the world, is a pleasant way for adult males to get together with men they have known all their lives. In the congenial atmosphere of tavern, pub, *osteria*, beer hall, tearoom, or coffee shop, they grind the day away playing cards, darts, or checkers while arguing and teasing one another. Meanwhile everyone feels his existence validated by the reciprocal attention paid to one another's ideas and idiosyncrasies. This type of interaction keeps at bay the disorganization that solitude brings to the passive mind, but without stimulating much growth. It is rather like a collective form of television watching, and although it is more complex in that it requires participation, its actions and phrases tend to be rigidly scripted and highly predictable.

Socializing of this kind mimics friendship relations, but it provides few of the benefits of the real thing. Everyone takes pleasure in occasionally passing the time of day chatting, but many people become extremely dependent on a daily "fix" of superficial contacts. This is especially true for individuals who cannot tolerate solitude, and who have little emotional support at home.

Teenagers without strong family ties can become so dependent on their peer group that they will do anything to be accepted by it. About twenty years ago in Tucson, Arizona, the entire senior class of a large high school knew for several months that an older dropout from the school, who had kept up a "friendship" with the younger students, had been killing their classmates, and burying their corpses in the desert. Yet none of them reported the crimes to the authorities, who discovered them by chance. The students, all nice middle-class suburban kids, claimed that they could not divulge the murders for fear of being cut by their friends. If those Tucson teenagers had had warm family ties, or strong links to other adults in the community, ostracization by their peers would not have been so intolerable. But apparently only the peer group stood between them and solitude. Unfortunately, this is not an unusual story.

If the young person feels accepted and cared for at home, however, dependence on the group is lessened, and the teenager can learn to be in control of his relationships with peers. Christopher, who at fifteen was a rather shy, quiet boy with glasses and few friends, felt close enough to his parents to explain that he was tired of being left out of the cliques in school, and had decided to become more popular. To do so, Chris outlined a carefully planned strategy: he was to buy contact lenses, wear only fashionable (i.e., funky) clothes, learn about the latest music and teenage fads, and highlight his hair with a blond dye. "I want to see if I can change my personality," he said, and spent many days in front of the mirror practicing a laid-back demeanor and a goofy smile.

This methodical approach, supported by his parents' collusion, worked well. By the end of the year he was being invited into the best cliques, and the following year he won the part of Conrad Birdie in the school musical. Because he identified with the part of the rock star so well, he became the heartthrob of middle-school girls, who taped his picture inside their lockers. He had indeed succeeded in changing his outward personality, and achieved control of the way his peers saw him. At the same time, the inner organization of his self remained the same: he continued to be a sensitive, generous young man who did not think less of his peers because he learned to manage their opinions or think too highly of himself for having succeeded at it.

One of the reasons Chris was able to become popular while many others do not is that he approached his goal with the same detached discipline that an athlete would use to make the football team, or a scientist would apply to an experiment. In other words, he transformed the daunting, vague monster of popularity into a feasible flow activity that he ended up enjoying while it gave him a sense of pride and self-esteem. The company of peers, like every other activity, can be experienced at various levels: at the lowest level of complexity it is a pleasurable way to ward off chaos temporarily; at the highest it provides a strong sense of enjoyment and growth.

It is in the context of intimate friendships, however, that the most intense experiences occur. These are the kinds of ties about which Aristotle wrote, "For without friends no one would choose to live, though he had all other goods." To enjoy such one-to-one relationships it is necessary not only to have common goals and to provide reciprocal feedback, which even interactions in taverns or at cocktail parties provide, but also to find new challenges in each other's company. These may amount simply to learning more and more about the friend, discovering new facets of his or her unique individuality, and disclosing more of one's own individuality in the process. There are few things as enjoyable as freely sharing one's most secret feelings and thoughts with another person.

While families provide primarily emotional protection, friendships usually involve mysterious novelty. When people are asked about their warmest memories, they usually remember holidays and vacations spent with relatives. Friends are mentioned more often in contexts of excitement, discovery, and adventure.

Just as with the family, people believe that friendships happen naturally, and if they fail, there is nothing to be done about it but feel sorry for oneself. In adolescence, when so many interests are shared with others and one has great stretches of free time to invest in a relationship, making friends might seem like a spontaneous process. But later in life friendships rarely happen by chance: one must cultivate them as assiduously as one must cultivate a job or a family.

CHAPTER 12

Ram Dass and Paul Gorman

Service: The Soul
of Community

What is it that so touches us about a single caring act or a life surrendered into service? Perhaps we see our deepest yearnings reflected in others, and this encourages us to believe in our own purity and beauty. These are no longer just ideals to strive for. We can reach them, we can be that way. Images of compassion beckon and encourage us onward.

Each time we drop our masks and meet heart-to-heart, reassuring one another simply by the quality of our presence, we experience a profound bond which we intuitively understand is nourishing everyone. Each time we quiet our mind, our listening becomes sharp and clear, deep and perceptive; we realize that we know more than we thought we knew, and can reach out and hear, as if from inside, the heart of someone's pain. Each time we are able to remain open to suffering, despite our fear and defensiveness, we sense a love in us which becomes increasingly unconditional.

We can see in this mosaic of limitations and strength a still deeper teaching. Common to all those habits which hinder us is a sense of separateness; we are divided within ourselves and cut off from others. Common to all those moments and actions which truly seem to help, however, is the experience of unity; the mind and the heart work in harmony, and barriers between us dissolve.

Separateness and unity. How interesting that these root causes, revealed in the experience of helping, turn out to be what most spiritual traditions define as the fundamental issue of life itself. Awakening from our sense of separateness is what we are called to do in all things, not merely in service. Whether these traditions speak of us as being cut off from God, Nature, Original Mind, True Being, the Tao, the Dharma—they call on us, in one voice, to undertake the journey back to unity.

Service, from this perspective, is part of that journey. It is no longer an end in itself. It is a vehicle through which we reach a deeper understanding of life. Each step we take, each moment in which we grow toward a greater understanding of unity, steadily transforms us into instruments of that help which truly heals.

Service not only reveals a larger vision of life, but steadily moves us along and supports us in our efforts to realize this vision. Each time we seek to respond to appeals for help we are being shown where we must grow in our sense of unity and what inner resources we can call upon to do so. We are constantly given, for example, the chance to experience the inherent generosity of our heart. Each time this happens, our faith in that part of ourselves which is intimately related to the rest of the universe is strengthened. So, too, approaching each act of caring with a desire to grow, we also meet our fears and resistances—but with the opportunity to see them for what they are, and, in so doing, to loosen their hold and ultimately to relinquish them. *On the path of service, then, we are constantly given feedback which helps us along the greater journey of awakening.*

We may start out to quiet the mind simply to hear the needs of others. To do so we learn to identify less with our own thoughts. Listening more, judging less, then, there is less divisiveness in our awareness. As we loosen our identification with personal motives and models of self, meanwhile, our awareness becomes more panoramic and inclusive; we're freer to take in more and more. Under these conditions, in turn, all our mental faculties can come into play as needed—memory, training, logic and analysis, intuition, wisdom. Unexpected connections become apparent. We may recognize deeper patterns in the events which are unfolding. As we continue, we may even begin to gain insight into a larger order of lawfulness we cannot understand rationally but which nevertheless resonates within. We come to sense the Way of Things (Tao) of which our actions are but a part. The hold of separateness is thus being broken at its source, in our own mind.

These practices open us up to an awareness within ourselves *which is itself unitive*. Not only do we see and hear more, but our very openness and spaciousness dissolve opposition and discord.

Through these practices, and our efforts to keep our hearts open in the presence of suffering, we find ourselves more available to whoever we are with. Compassion is increasingly an automatic response. We find a deep quality of love infusing our actions with others. The expression of this love, in turn, becomes increasingly our goal, whatever the circumstances. The more unconditionally we share it, the more helpful it is to all.

One enters into the helping act not only because there is a need to be met. Service gradually becomes an offering, first to those we are with, but eventually to that greater truth or source of being in which we are all joined in love. Helping becomes an act of reverence, worship, gratitude. It is grace merely to have the chance to serve.

Mother Teresa, for example, bending to hold a dying leper, sees there only "Christ in a distressing disguise." She's not "helping a dying leper," she's loving God, affirming in whomever she's with universal qualities of perfection and beauty. One can imagine how it might feel to be held in this spirit during one's final moments of life.

The Hindu deity Hanuman offers a similar example of devotional service. Every act he performs becomes an offering to Rama (God). His service brings him to the very edge of unitive love. How powerful his vision: "When I know who I am, I *am* you," he says, kneeling before Rama, "when I don't know who I am, I *serve* you."

For both of these inspirational figures, and for any of us, the smallest acts of caring—making a sick friend's bed, filling a bowl on a soup line, welcoming a stranger, comforting a frightened child— can be a means of affirming the greater unity of life in love. As real as this spirit is in us, we have to communicate it to others, in addition to everything else we are doing on their behalf.

Placing service in a spiritual perspective in no way diminishes what we have to offer others through training, experience, individuality, special skills, or sense of humor. Quite the reverse. Our particular talents and unique qualities are likely to come forth more reliably when we have a richer and more spacious sense of who we are—the very promise of all spiritual practice.

To the question, "How can I help?" we now see the possibility of a deeper answer than we might once have expected. We can, of course, help through all that we *do*. But at the deepest level we help through who we *are*. We help, that is, by appreciating the connection between service and our own progress on the journey of awakening into a fuller sense of unity.

We work on ourselves, then, in order to help others. And we help others as a vehicle for working on ourselves.

CHAPTER 13

Starhawk

Celebration: The Spirit of Community

Ritual affirms the common patterns, the values, the shared joys, risks, sorrows, and changes that bind a community together. Ritual links together our ancestors and descendants, those who went before with those who will come after us. It helps us face together those things that are too painful to face alone.

A living community develops its own rituals, to celebrate life passages and ease times of transition, to connect us with the round of the changing seasons and the moon's flux, to anchor us in time. When we attempt to create community, ritual is one of our most powerful tools.

A culture of life would be filled with ritual: personal rituals, birthday parties, family and household celebrations, neighborhood rituals, street fairs, promenades, processions, fiestas, vigils, carnivals. As we begin to create rituals of community, we encounter new challenges and arenas of creativity.

Celebrating Passages

Ritual affirms the value of any transition. When we celebrate life changes together, we create strong bonds of intimacy and trust that can generate new culture.

When we undergo a change uncelebrated and unmarked, that transition is devalued, rendered invisible. If we wish to restore value to the body, we can celebrate its changes with ritual. If we value a new relationship, we can publicly celebrate our commitment. When we finish a major project, such as writing a book, we can let it go with ritual.

We can create rites of passage for any transition. To give one example, my women's coven created a ritual for Bethany, the daughter of one of our members. We celebrated her first menstruation, her first blood. First, we discussed the ritual with her to be sure she would feel comfortable with every aspect of it. This is a vitally important step for any ritual, especially one such as this: many young women would die of mortification at the very idea of such a celebration.

We prepared for months, making her a special robe upon which each of us embroidered some symbol of power. On the appointed day, we took her and her mother down to the beach. We tied them together with a silver cord, and asked them to run. They ran together as far as the mother could run; then we cut them apart and the daughter ran on alone.

We then went to a friend's house and joined other women in a hot tub. Thirteen of us, all women, spent the afternoon telling Bethany the stories of how we had become the women we were. Each of us gave her a special gift. We dressed her in her robe, formed a circle around her, and chanted her name to empower her.

Afterward, we went into the house, where the men in our community had prepared a special feast of red foods in her honor. We had wanted the ritual to be a women's mystery, but we also wanted Bethany to experience her womanhood being celebrated and affirmed by men. The men also gave her gifts, and we ended, as usual, by eating and drinking and enjoying each others' company.

In later months, some of the same men, who are in a men's ritual circle together, created a rite of passage for one of their sons when he reached puberty. The completion of his ritual was his celebration by both the women and men in the community.

A group of women in British Columbia celebrate a Croning ritual for each woman who reaches menopause. The ritual marks a woman's passage into a new stage of life: the Crone stage, in Witchcraft considered the time of life when experience and wisdom bring a woman into her full power. On one woman's farm stands an old, weathered gate. During the ritual, the woman who is becoming a Crone passes through the gate, and her circle sings, chants, and celebrates her reaching the other side.

Sophia created a ritual for her daughter Vanessa when she weaned her at the age of two. Sophia's mother had given Vanessa a special cup at her birth, in keeping with a long-standing family tradition. At weaning, Sophia gave the cup to Vanessa within a sacred circle. She poured dairy milk into the child's cup and her own ritual chalice, saying, "Now this will be your cup, and I will no longer be your cup. Now we can be sisters, and drink together."

Small groups can build intimacy and trust that lend a ritual power and intensity. Large group rituals have a different function. They bind a larger community together; they introduce new people to the concepts and values the ritual represents; and they generate excitement, energy, and a wild beauty.

Large rituals are logistically demanding. Processes that are powerful in a group of ten are tolerable in a group of thirty and impossible in a group of a hundred. Passing a bowl of salt water around the circle for a cleansing meditation may take twenty minutes for five people and hours for fifty. Give careful thought to the physical problems of moving people in space, of passing objects around, of hearing and seeing. You can always multiply ritual objects: provide ten bowls, and someone to collect them. Or break into small groups, or groups of three, to share more intimately. Then find some way to come back together.

Keeping energy focused in a large group can also be a challenge. Especially if many people are new, or shy, energy tends to dissipate. You might:

- Learn to drum. The drum is the single most useful ritual object you can have.

    Drumming is an art, and fine drummers practice for many years. Fortunately, you can be a very minimally skilled drummer and be quite effective in ritual. Being able to keep a simple, steady beat is more important than being able to drum elaborate patterns or syncopated rhythms. Most important, however, is the drummer's sensitivity to energy. The drum must follow the energy of a ritual, not fight it. If the drum tries to override the energy's movement, if the drummer gets so lost in self-expression that she or he becomes oblivious to the flow of the ritual, a drum can destroy a ritual instead of unifying it. Also, once a drumbeat begins in a chant or story, it carries the energy. If the drum stops, the energy drops.

- Seed the ritual with more experienced people who know what to expect, can move energy, and can be models for others. When they get wild, others will follow. And when they ground the energy, it will bring the energy of newcomers back to earth with it.
- Appoint Graces, people to help greet newcomers, explain aspects of the ritual, teach songs, and make people feel welcome.
- Appoint Dragons, who will guard the boundary of the circle and deal with disruptive drunks, fundamentalists talking in tongues, police, and other distractions.
- Designate a few Crows, to keep the overall plan of the ritual in mind.
- Make sure that whoever leads the ritual is also a good Snake, who can watch the energy and be aware of the undercurrents.
- Choose a clear focus, a clear central image, and keep the plan simple.
- Try to avoid using terms or symbols that will make people feel uncomfortable, uneasy, or confused.
- Elements of performance work especially well in larger groups. Be dramatic, write poetry, compose music, create culture.

When we face a collective task or undertake a new direction, ritual can help strengthen us and clarify our path.

Ritual can also help us make a collective transformation, to confront problems and issues as a community that are too big for us as individuals.

The Spiral Dance

Halloween is the Witch's New Year, the time for honoring the ancestors, the beloved dead, for turning the wheel of the year.

Three hundred people are gathered in a hall in San Francisco. Around the walls are built altars of crates, hung with old lace, holding dolls and skulls and ancient Goddesses, plates heaped with food for the dead, pumpkins, deer horns, pomegranates, candles.

The space has been made sacred, marked off from the circles of the world. The boundary has been drawn with wand and candles, with a procession of masked figures and beating drums.

We have called the Goddess and God as the great pattern of the mystery that runs through us and beyond us, as the powers that begin, sustain, end, as the green, the wild, the animal, the wise. In the repetition of this naming, ritual after ritual, year after year, we begin to restore that power within that knows itself to be bound to the pattern of birth, death, and regeneration, to be animal and wise, to grow and fade. Naming that self as sacred we restore its value and know its depths.

> For you can see me in your eyes,
> When they are mirrored by a friend—
> There is no end to the circle, no end,
> There is no end to life, there is no end.

We are sacred, within sacred space. And so we begin the calling of the dead. For Halloween, it is said, is the time when the dead walk, when our ancestors return, when the veil is thin that divides the world of the seen from the unseen. It is the time of mourning and reunion, when year after year we must remember the limits of control, remember that we, too, must die in time, and yet know that death is not an ending of the cycle but a part of the pattern that turns and turns around again.

The litany of the dead names our common ancestors of struggle, those whose names we do not know. In the Yoruba tradition, when you do not know your ancestors' names, you name them by the ways they died. And so we call them: those who died of hunger, who died on the slave ships, who were burned. Every year the litany grows. Now one person after another goes to the microphone (for this mystery does not disdain technology), and cries out a section, while we keen, tear cloth, rub ashes on our faces, and chant the response to the call "What is remembered lives."

We name the tribes who once called this place home, the dead of Auschwitz, Hiroshima, the disappeared of El Salvador, those gunned down in South Africa, the assassinated dead, the tortured, the poisoned, the AIDS dead, the war victims, the suicides, the burned Witches. With each section of the litany the moans become cries of anger and sorrow, rising together in a collective outpouring of rage and grief. In a city caught in the grip of the AIDS epidemic, as we each face fear and grief for our friends and our loved ones, this sacred space becomes a place where we can cry together, where the sound of our voices binds us together in the snaring of our hurt, our despair at the wounds and the immense task of healing.

Then we name our own dead. "I remember my grandfather who fathered eight children in India and dreamed they would come to America." "I remember my aunt, a closeted lesbian who loved me as her own child." "I remember my mother who died when I was too young to know her." The naming goes on and on: we hear the tragic deaths, the suicides, the car crashes, and the peaceful deaths. "My grandmother May, who died at eighty, the last of the great housekeepers." We cry together, hold each other, even laugh. "I remember Wally—he was my lover." "I remember Wally—he was my lover, too." I name my friend Anne, who would be thrilled by the ritual. And my father, wondering what he would think of it all, old leftist secular Jew that he was—would he prefer a Yizcar, or nothing? But he was an actor, too; if nothing else, he would have loved the drama of it. For this is the essence of theater: each death we name, each person we describe in a phrase or two, is another story, comic or tragic, and in the telling of these stories we become, all three hundred of us, one community, weaving together the different strands of these ancestors with those we have named in the litanies, so that they become our common ancestors, different races and religions and viewpoints not erased but linked. For in the public naming of our dead, we assert their value, which has not been destroyed by death. And in valuing them we value each other, the true histories of our lives, where we come from, who we are.

Morgan, who is only five, has a voice too soft to be heard above the crowd. I motion to her mother and whisper "shhhh" through the microphone. Her mother brings her up, and her voice sounds clear: "We remember Grandma Claudia." And I know, watching her, that this ritual has come alive, become a living tradition that for her will be how things are done, how the dead are mourned, a touchstone for her own identity. Months later, she tells a child in her preschool that she is a Witch. "You're not really a Witch," he says. "I am a Witch!" she asserts. "I called my Grandma Claudia at the Spiral Dance."

We grieve until we are empty. Then we let the ritual take us on a journey to the land of the dead, which is the place of beginning, the seed place of all potential.

The journey takes place by drum and voice and imagination; we form a ship, we sail, we arrive at the shining isle, we dance, we call into being all we envision for the new year:

> A year of beauty,
> Let it begin now
> A year of plenty
> Let it begin now . . .

As deep as we have gone into our grief, we go now into a great roaring wildness that leaps up and sends us whirling and singing and dancing together. The energy runs loose beyond our ability to contain or direct it—always it surprises us—breaking out into clapping and stomping and shouting rhythms, winding in crazy spirals that always go wild, into snakes and chains and free-form whirls and eddies of ecstasy; and the people dance, building power, building a vision that never confines itself to the poetry of the litany, but takes on a form of its own. Until at last the power peaks, in one rising cry of open throats; all our voices become one voice, one rising cone, carrying the vision and the wildness and the closeness out into a world where our rage and grief have opened a space to be filled by the passion for life.

When we let go, there is silence. We fall to the ground, returning the power to the earth. For the ritual, too, has its pattern, which is the mystery pattern, the cycle. The power we draw from the earth must return, what we raise must fall if it is to rise again. So we enact the cycle of the mystery, and, enacting it, we become united in it.

What the earth needs for her healing may be something we cannot see or even imagine, something that can only be brought to being by the unleashing of the wildness, the rising of the animal in us all.

When we return to the world of the living, we sing the names of the babies born this year. We give them a public welcoming, we acknowledge the sacred value of each one of them, for they are the continuance of life. The wheel of the year has turned. Halloween is the Witch's New Year, and now the lament for the dead gives way again to the song of life.

CHAPTER 14

Thich Nhat Hanh

Awareness: The Consciousness of Community

We can make people happy. One person has the capacity to be an infinite resource of happiness for others. The more we practice the art of mindful living, the more we become a source of happiness and joy. This is possible.

But we need a place, such as a retreat center or a monastery, where we can go to renew ourselves. The features of the landscape, the buildings, and the sound of the bell should be designed to remind us to return to awareness. Even when we cannot actually go to the retreat center, we can think of it, smile, and feel ourselves becoming peaceful.

The community does not need to be big. It is enough to have ten or fifteen permanent residents who emanate freshness and peace, the fruits of living in awareness. When we go there, they care for us, console and support us, and help us heal our wounds.

From time to time, the residents can organize large retreats so that we can learn the arts of enjoying our lives more and taking good care of each other. Mindful living is an art, and this community can be a place where joy and happiness are real. They can also offer Days of Mindfulness, so that people can come and live one happy day together in community. And they can organize courses that teach *The Sutra on the Four Establishments of Mindfulness*, *The Sutra on the Full Awareness of Breathing*, and other courses on Buddhist psychology and healing in a Buddhist way. Most retreats will be for preventive practice, practicing mindfulness before things get too bad. But some retreats should be for people who are undergoing a lot of suffering, although even then two-thirds of the retreatants should be healthy, happy people. Otherwise it may be difficult to succeed.

Practice has a lot to do with the happiness of the people in a family or a community. We practice not only in the meditation room, but in the kitchen, the backyard, the office, and in school as well. How can we incorporate practice into our daily lives, so that our daily lives can be joyful and happy?

The *sangha* is a community that lives in harmony and awareness. When you are with your family and you practice smiling, breathing, recognizing the Buddha in yourself and your children, then your family becomes a *sangha*. If you have a bell in your home, the bell becomes part of your *sangha*, because the bell helps you to practice. If you have a cushion, then the cushion also becomes part of the *sangha*. Many things help us practice. The air, for breathing. If you have a park or a river bank near your home, you can enjoy practicing walking meditation. You have to discover your *sangha*. Invite a friend to come and practice with you, have tea meditation, sit with you, join you for walking meditation. All these efforts can help you establish your *sangha* at home. Practice is easier if you have a *sangha*.

The foundation of a community is a daily life that is joyful and happy. In Plum Village, children are the center of attention. Each adult is responsible for helping the children be happy, because we know that if the children are happy, it is easy for the adults to be happy. In old times, families were bigger. Not only nuclear families, but uncles, aunts, grandparents, and cousins all lived together. Houses were surrounded by trees where they could hang hammocks and organize picnics. In those times, people did not have many of the problems we do now. Today, our families are very small. Besides Mom and Dad, there are just one or two children. When the parents have a problem, the whole family feels the effects. The atmosphere in the house is heavy, and there is nowhere to escape. Sometimes a child may go to the bathroom and lock the door just to be alone, but still there is no escape. The heavy atmosphere permeates the bathroom too. So the child grows up with many seeds of suffering and can never feel truly happy and then transmits these seeds to his or her children.

Formerly, when Mom and Dad had some problems, the children could always escape by going to an aunt or an uncle. They still had someone to look up to, and the atmosphere was not so threatening. I think that communities of mindful living can replace our former big families, because when we go to these communities, we see many aunts, uncles, and cousins, and that can help us a lot.

You know that aged people are very sad when they have to live separately from their children and grandchildren. This is one of the things in the West that I do not like very much. In my country, aged people have the right to live with the younger people. It is the grandparents who tell fairy tales to the children. When they get old, their skin is cold and wrinkled, and it is a great joy to hold their grandchild, so warm, so tender. When a person grows old, his or her deepest hope is to have a grandchild to hold in his or her arms. They hope for it day and night, and when they hear that their daughter is pregnant, they are so happy. Nowadays the elderly have to go to a home where they live only among other aged people. Just once a week they receive a short visit, and afterwards they feel even sadder. We have to find ways for old and young people to live together again. It will make all of us very happy.

A community of mindful living should be in a beautiful location in the countryside. In many cities today, you do not see a lot of trees, because so many trees have been cut down. I imagine—and I believe it is very close to reality—a city which has only one tree left. (I don't know what kind of miracle helped preserve that one tree.) Many people in that city have become mentally ill because they are so alienated from nature, our mother. In the old time, we lived among trees and we sat in hammocks. Now we live in small boxes made of concrete. The air we breathe is not clean, and we get sick, not only in our bodies but in our souls.

I imagine that there is a doctor in the city who understands why everyone is getting sick, and every time someone comes to him, he tells them, "You are sick because you are cut off from Mother Nature." And he gives them this prescription: "Each morning, take the bus and go to the tree in the center of the city and practice tree-hugging meditation. Hold the tree and breathe in, 'I am with my mother.' Then breathe out, 'I am happy.' And look at the leaves so green and smell the bark of the tree that is so fragrant." The prescription is for fifteen minutes of breathing and hugging the tree. After doing it for three months, the patient feels much better. But the doctor has many patients, and he gives each of them the same prescription.

So I imagine a bus in the city going in the direction of the tree, while people are standing in line, waiting their turn to embrace the tree and breathe. But the line is several miles long, and the crowd is becoming impatient because they have to wait for such a long time. They demand new laws which will limit each person to just one minute of tree-hugging. But one minute is not long enough to be effective, and then there is no remedy for society's sickness. I am afraid we will be close to that situation very soon, if we are not mindful of what is going on in the present moment.

When we practice mindful living, we know what is going on in every moment of our daily lives. When we throw a banana peel into the garbage, we know it is a banana peel, and that banana peels decompose quickly and become flowers. But when we throw a plastic bag into the garbage, we have to know that it is a plastic bag. This is a practice of meditation: "I am throwing a plastic bag into the garbage can." If we practice mindfulness, we will refrain from using things made of plastic, because we know that they take much more time to degrade into soil and become flowers. And we know that disposable diapers take four or five hundred years, so we refrain from using them. Nuclear waste, the most difficult kind of garbage, takes 250,000 years to become a flower. We are making the Earth an impossible place for our children to grow up.

Practicing mindfulness with friends allows us to get in touch with the healing aspects of life. Breathing mindfully the clean air, we plant seeds of healing within ourselves, our friends, and society. Smiling, we realize peace and joy. Communities of mindful living are very important for us to cultivate these practices.

CHAPTER 15

Stephanie Kaza

A Community
of Awareness

Communitas, communis—the Latin root for "community" means *common* or what is held in common, shared by many. At Green Gulch Farm and Zen Center, where I lived for three years, what is held in common is the place, the time together, and the teachings of Zen Buddhism. The community is mutually created by those who stay in this place for a period of time, whether for a few hundred years (as a redwood might) or a single day.

What is the shape of this place? Green Gulch Farm lies in a beautiful coastal valley in the flood plain of Green Gulch Creek, which empties out into the Pacific Ocean at Muir Beach, just north of San Francisco. It is surrounded by open space protected by the Golden Gate National Recreation Area and Mount Tamalpais State Park. The valley is flanked on the north and south by sedimentary rock and open grassland ridges. It is blessed with fertile soils, mild and foggy summers, windy springs, and warbling songbirds.

Many people come to Green Gulch Farm in search of community, but it is elusive in definition. It is not defined by the experienced Zen priests who have been here 10–20 years; it is not the people who come for lecture on Sunday; it is not the rolling hills dropping down to the ocean, nor the plant and animal communities known as grassland, coastal scrub, oak savanna, and stream or riparian. It is the *interaction* of all the various parts in any single moment. The task of this community is to offer room for all beings to grow and flourish within the limits of the landscape.

Given the volume of traffic through Green Gulch, this is no easy task. Retreat centers often suffer from overuse of the land and the staff, and from projections of need for human community. Green Gulch serves thousands of people over the course of a year. A residential staff of 25–30 assisted by 10–20 guest students serves class and conference groups of 25–50 people each day, plus Sunday crowds of 200–300 visitors. Without some clear structure for human traffic flow and behavior, the capacity to offer spiritual and psychological nourishment would quickly erode. Over time, it is the structure which shapes the community and the practice of being together.

Rhythms and Reference Points

The focus of Zen practice is to develop attention or mindfulness in relation to all beings and all activity. Over and over again we ask: Where am I? What am I doing right now? What is guiding my actions? Typically our decisions reflect personal preferences and an orientation to ourselves as enduring entities. Buddhist practice, however, is the constant stripping away of false references to the self to reveal the larger patterns of interconnection and interdependence. One finds one's bearings through temporal and spatial reference points beyond the false sense of self. Thus the schedule and the landscape provide the structure of both community and practice.

The daily schedule shapes the rhythm for the whole human community. Sitting meditation and service in the morning is followed by breakfast and morning work period. After lunch is another work period, with meditation before and after dinner. Through changes in abbots, directors, and water levels, this schedule has remained a constant shaping force, an experience held in common by those who visit or live at Green Gulch. Meditation and meals are announced by specific rolldown patterns on the wooden *han* and bells. Though apparently consistent in form, the soundscape reflects the quality of mind and attention of those who sound the instruments. These sounds in the empty silence of dusk or dawn are for some people the most powerful impressions of place and community. They represent the possibility of sustainable human relationships in the context of spiritual practice.

The weekly rhythm is marked by Friday—a day off, before the heavily attended events of the weekend. The monthly rhythm is focused around the Full Moon Precepts and Founders' Memorial ceremonies—services that are the same each month and help in developing a kind of community consciousness of the moon cycle and respect for the lineage of teachers through time.

We also mark the four turning points of the year. Spring Equinox service is set up on the east-facing side of the valley where we chant to the rising sun of the new year; Summer Solstice is marked at mid-day; Autumn Equinox with an altar facing west in a service at dusk; Winter Solstice at midnight. Always the chanting is the same; only the timing, location, and dedication vary, grounding the changes of the year in our bodies through a sense of seasonal rhythm and place.

The yearly temporal reference points are Arbor Day in February, Buddha's Birthday in April, and Thanksgiving. The whole community participates, including the wider group of children and families from around the Bay Area. For both residents and those who visit infrequently, these celebrations are important patterns that form a sense of human community in relation to the land. On Arbor Day we plant 300–500 tree seedlings, restoring the lost forests of the hillsides and creating windbreaks for crop protection. On Buddha's Birthday, we survey the local wildflowers and chant the names of all in bloom as a part of the joyful service giving thanks to the baby Buddha. And on Thanksgiving we offer abundant gifts to the altar of the year's harvest of potatoes, squash, lettuce, pumpkins, beets, and herbs. Each of these ceremonies contributes to the group sense of place, the traditions of honoring the valley and our interdependence with it. They work and are effective because people want to participate in them; they want to reconnect with the land in a spiritual context.

A Sense of Place

Just as temporal reference points form a framework for community experience, so do spatial reference points serve to contain and shape each person's journey through this particular landscape. At Green Gulch the four directions are conveniently aligned more or less with the landforms, making it easy to find one's bearings in the larger universe. The creek flows south to the ocean from the lip of the watershed a few miles inland. The ridges run north-south, so the rising sun and moon shift along this axis as the seasons turn. We know the high winter moon of the Solstice will rise at the high end of the hill when the low winter sun shifts to the south. Several times each year on a full moon night, we walk the big loop up to Coyote Ridge on the south flank, along its spine, down by the ocean and back through the valley. This is a way of incorporating the landscape into our bodies, of knowing community through knowing place.

The low points of water also mark the shape of this place, and the limits to human, plant and animal activity as well. At the end of a long summer, the creeks are virtually dry and the water tank fills much more slowly from the hillside spring. The nature of this water determines how we exist here, the size of the community, and the necessary mindfulness practices for water.

The strongest sense of place and spatial reference at Green Gulch lies in the farm and garden areas. Two acres at the head of the valley are planted in organic perennial and annual flowers; 20 acres down the valley support potatoes, squash, and 16 varieties of lettuce. Zen students and staff tend flowers and vegetables as part of mindfulness work practice, reinforcing a sense of connection with the land that generates their lunches and altar arrangements. The garden is often used for walking meditation practice during retreats. Here students can breathe deeply and enjoy the efforts of gardeners and plants in realizing beauty.

As poet and Zen student Gary Snyder suggests, "There is strength, freedom, sustainability, and pride in being a practiced dweller in your own surroundings, knowing what you know." For many people who come to Green Gulch, the *place* is the draw. Their sense of community, of *communing*, is being at a place that is beautiful, that is cared for, that is a container for spiritual practice. It is not the same as a park or a backyard; it is a place to find orientation in the context of landscape and schedule. It offers the possibility of finding one's self by joining the flow of life through this community of time and place.

To Benefit All Beings

A Zen practice center is distinct from other country retreat spots because of the shared intention to practice certain guidelines and teachings. Here community is sustained not just by external spatial and temporal reference points, but by cultivation of internal reference points for choices of action. The central Buddhist teachings naturally encourage an ecological awareness and thus serve as ethical criteria for community practices. "An ethical life is one that is mindful, mannerly, and has style." (Gary Snyder) In Soto Zen tradition, the emphasis is very much on ethical or mindful acts in everyday practice. The simple, repetitive acts of eating, breathing, walking, and greeting others become opportunities for deepening a sense of interdependence and community. Each moment in place reflects myriad causes and conditions that all contribute to the particular experience of community at that instant for that person.

In the Zen tradition one way to cultivate strong intuition is through the use of vows. For example, one vows not to abuse the Three Treasures—the *Buddha* or teacher, the *Dharma* or truth, and the *Sangha* or practice community. The act of saying vows is a practice that shapes the internal landscape, the realm of choice and intention. It is also a practice that bonds people into a community. Vows represent an agreement to behave well together, with human as well as plant, animal, and landscape beings. They acknowledge the impacts of our actions and encourage awareness and restraint.

Community as Teacher

As a visible public practice place, Green Gulch is in a position to serve as a model for ecological community living. In this regard, consistency is important—consistency between the teachings, the place, and the practice. With the inspiration of various staff members, Green Gulch has made great strides over the last two years in its efforts to recycle everything from incense ash to batteries. The 1991 winter practice period focused on tree planting for its daily work, including public work days every Saturday. Meals have always been vegetarian, thus reducing the impact on animals as well as the consumption of grain, water, and energy that support meat production. In the last year, the officers have undertaken the task of "eco-monitoring" Green Gulch, Tassajara, and the San Francisco City Center for environmentally effective and ineffective practices.

Still, there are many areas open to improvement. Though many of the practices I've described here are now seen as traditional (in the short space of 10–15 years), not everyone who spends time at Green Gulch becomes environmentally enlightened. We do not always make sure people see the landscape outside the zendo. I would, for example, be tempted to require a ridgetop hike and introduction to the water system for all incoming guest students. But the practices are evolving, and they are guided by the traditional monastic model of restraint, simplicity, and moderation. People keep coming in large numbers to learn from the land and the teachings and to participate, at least for a time, in this elusive event called community. They come to taste, as Gary Snyder puts it, "a life that is vowed to simplicity, appropriate boldness, good humor, gratitude, unstinting work and play, and lots of walking to bring us close to the actually existing world and its wholeness."

4

LIVING COMMUNITY: A WIDE RANGE OF CHOICES

Diversity is a necessity, not just the spice of life.

EUGENE P. ODUM

Many people fear that joining a community means giving up their individuality and privacy, turning over all they own to the group, retreating from the rest of the world, and living a "simple life" that is really no more than poverty in disguise. But living in a formally organized community is not the only way you can experience the "sense of community" that is explored in this book. Any time a group of people comes together, the opportunity for creating that deeply felt sense of community exists. Sometimes we make it happen and sometimes we don't, but the opportunities are still there.

There are many forms of community experience that arise from mutual interests and ideologies. In the end, what makes them communities is a feeling of belonging and sharing. Even the so-called "intentional" communities range from those in which everything is jointly owned, all income and expenses are pooled, and all work is divided equally to a much more individualized arrangement in which the members' only ties are their collective values and activities.

You can begin your own community experience simply by gathering your friends to do something together. A man I know invited friends to help him build a boat. While the boat project was certainly what brought the men together and kept them coming back for the first eighteen months, the camaraderie they created continued to draw them closer to one another long after launch day.

Several other friends have become deeply involved in a community that interacts more than half of the time by using a computer/telephone link up. Support groups, team sports, communal gardens, neighborhood improvement, house building, boat building, church groups, the work place, our children's schools, all of these and more present opportunities for living in community. The only requirement is that we take the actions necessary to create a sense of connectedness, to make each other feel welcome. If our time together makes us feel somehow enriched, we *are* a community.

No single book could ever list all the alternatives. But in this section we introduce a large sample to give you an idea of the possibilities.

American history has seen a number of periods in which interest in community building has peaked. The most recent occurred in the 1960s and early 1970s, spurred by the same dissatisfactions that caused the political and social movements of those times. Contrary to popular belief, the movement to create intentional communities didn't start in the 60s. In chapter 16, *Intentional Communities*, educator and community advocate Geoph Kozeny clears up this misconception and gives us a fascinating history of the intentional community movement in this country and internationally.

The 60s and 70s *were* important, of course. The key movements to emerge from the protests and social ferment of that time are those for civil rights, women's rights, world peace, and ecology. It is not widely recognized, though, that a successful men's movement also arose from that time because, until recently, this movement has not received as much media attention as the others. In the early years, the men involved interacted mostly in the same ways that people in other movements did: through affinity groups, consciousness-raising groups, action-oriented groups, basic support groups, and therapeutic or "process" groups.

In the past few years, however, a new form of men's group has emerged, the so-called "ritual men's group," in which participants draw from ancient mythology and native cultures to explore their own masculinity and to forge a connection between the inner, individual part of each man's life and what is universal in the lives of all men. Because of the power of ritual to evoke feelings and emotions, many participants in ritual men's groups feel a deep bonding that they experience as a very strong sense of "community." Physician Wayne Liebman has been active in ritual men's groups for many years. In chapter 17, *Ritual Men's Groups*, he takes us inside such a group to help us understand what they are, how they work, and how we can join or create our own ritual groups.

Most of us spend one-third or more of our adult life at the workplace. It would stand to reason, then, that we might find a rewarding group experience there. While many observers doubt that the workplace can ever be anything more than an environment for extracting the value of labor from the worker, a new model of "corporate community" is emerging that belies these doubts. " 'Corporation' conjures up images of authority, bureaucracy, competition, power, and profit. 'Community' consistently evokes images of democracy, diversity, cooperation, interdependence, and mutual benefit," explains management consultant Juanita Brown. In chapter 18, *The Corporation as Community*, Brown draws on her own experiences with corporations around the world to show us that it is possible to experience community where we work.

We can also find community where we live. In Denmark, experiments in housing designs that encourage community have been going on for many years. The Danes have built more than 100 shared living environments which they call "living communities." Two American architects, Kathryn McCamant and Charles Durrett, have studied these communities and coined an English term, "CoHousing," to describe them. In chapter 19, *Collaborative Housing*, McCamant, Durrett, and associate Ellen Hertzman describe how CoHousing reestablishes many of the advantages of traditional village living in a modern context.

Even if you don't live in a CoHousing development, you can still bring people together in your home, to break bread and share ideas. Bringing people together to share common interests is as viable a form of community as any. In chapter 20, author and editor Stephanie Mills describes one of the oldest forms of social discourse—*salons*. Mills believes that salons enrich and elevate the level of communication among their participants and, by extension, in society as a whole. Whenever we gather to talk about ideas, she says, we bring our cultural forms into being and encourage the artistic and the unexpected, which we need if we are to survive as a democratic society.

Twentieth-century communications technology offers yet another opportunity to gather people together, but with the difference that we don't even have to leave our own homes to meet. The first conversations between computers, over telephone lines, through a central, "host" computer took place in the 1960s at the New Jersey Institute of Technology. Today, electronic mail and computerized bulletin boards have become the nexus of what authors Kristin Anundsen and Carolyn Shaffer call *Electronic Communities,* in chapter 21. Anundsen and Shaffer take us "online" to show us that we don't need to stand face to face with one another to be together in community.

Nothing strengthens the bond of community like shared adversity. In chapter 22, *The Castro: Building Community in the Face of AIDS,* Pulitzer Prize winner Frances Fitzgerald describes the evolution of the first openly gay community in America. In this inner-urban community, sexual preference was the initial binding force, but the efforts of those who lived and died in the Castro during its formative period provided one of the strongest experiences of community in recorded history.

CHAPTER 16

Geoph Kozeny

Intentional
Communities

An "intentional community" is a group of people who have chosen to live together with a common purpose, working cooperatively to create a lifestyle that reflects their shared core values. The people may live together all under a single roof or clustered together on a piece of land in the country or in an urban neighborhood.

Intentional communities can include communes, student cooperatives, land co-ops, collaborative housing groups, monasteries, or farming collectives. Although incredibly diverse in philosophy and lifestyle, each of these subgroups places a high priority on fostering a sense of community, the feeling of belonging and mutual support that is increasingly hard to find in mainstream America.

A Time-Honored Idea

Mainstream media typically promotes the popular myth that shared living began with the "hippie crash pads" of the 60s and died with the advent of "yuppies" in the late 70s and early 80s. Nothing could be further from the truth. Today there are literally thousands of groups, with hundreds of thousands of members, that live in intentional communities and extended families based on something other than blood ties. And this type of living has been around for thousands of years, not just decades.

It is well documented that early followers of Jesus banded together to live in a "community of goods," simplifying their lives and sharing all that they owned. That tradition continues to this day, particularly through many inner-city Christian groups that live communally—pooling resources and efforts in their ministry to the homeless, the poor, orphans, single parents, battered mothers, and otherwise neglected and oppressed minorities.

Yet shared living goes back much farther than that, predating the development of agriculture many thousands of years ago. Early hunter-gatherers banded together in tribes, not just blood-related families, and depended on cooperation for their very survival. The advent of the isolated nuclear family is, in fact, a fairly recent phenomenon, having evolved primarily with the advent of industrialization, most notably with the development of high-speed transportation. As transportation has become cheaper and faster, we've also witnessed an increase in transience, and the demise of the traditional neighborhood.

Roots and Realities

Although many contemporary community visions emphasize the creation of neighborhood and/or extended family ties, their philosophic roots are amazingly diverse. They range from Christians, Quakers, and Eastern spiritualists to 60s dropouts, anarchists, psychologists, artists, and back-to-the-land survivalists. The scope of their primary values is equally broad, including ecology, equality, appropriate technology, self-sufficiency, right livelihood, humanist psychology, creativity, spirituality, meditation, yoga, and the pursuit of global peace. However, even among groups that base their philosophy on "achieving a holistic view of the world," it would be quite surprising to discover a community that has achieved "perfection" amidst the fast-paced chaos of modern life.

Communities draw their membership from society at large, and those members bring with them generations of social conditioning. The problems we see "out there" in the mainstream—greed, dishonesty, excessive ego, lack of self-esteem, factionalism, inadequate resources, poor communication skills, you name it—all manage to find a significant role in alternative cultures as well.

What is encouraging about many intentional communities is their tendency to be open to new ideas, their willingness to be tolerant of other approaches, and their commitment to live in a way that reflects their idealism. Although communities exist that are close-minded and bigoted, they're the exception, not the rule.

Some Key Issues

Spirituality or religion, regardless of the specific sect or form, is probably the most common inspiration for launching a new community. Such groups bear a striking resemblance to their centuries-old predecessors, despite current developments in technology, education, psychology, and theology. Many of North America's leading centers for the study of meditation and yoga, for example, were established by intentional communities based on the teachings of spiritual masters from the Far East.

Among secular communities, the inspiration is sometimes isolationist (wanting to escape the problems of the rest of the world, creating instead a life of self-sufficiency, simplicity, and serenity), though, more typically, such experiments are based on bold visions of creating a new social and economic order, establishing replicable models that will lead to the peaceful and ecological salvation of the planet.

Most members of intentional communities share a deep-felt concern about home, family, and neighborhood. Beyond the obvious purpose of creating an extended-family environment for raising a family (typically within a broader context of cooperation), many communities also afford the opportunity to leave doors unlocked, any time day or night. For some, merely having that kind of security is reason enough to join.

Dozens of intentional communities, alarmed by rising student/ teacher ratios and falling literacy rates in public schools, have opted to establish alternative schools and to form communities as a base of support for that type of education. Intentional communities comprise a sizable chunk of the membership of the National Coalition of Alternative Community Schools, an organization of

119

private schools, families, and individuals who share a commitment to create a new and empowering structure for education. Coalition members publish a quarterly newsletter and organize an annual spring conference for sharing resources and skills for social change.

Other groups, usually smaller, have created rural homestead communities where they can pursue home schooling without fear of legal pressure from local school officials. Many state laws favorable to home schooling have been promoted, and sometimes initiated, by members of intentional communities.

Another popular issue these days is ecology. Perhaps as many as 90% of contemporary intentional communities, even those located in urban areas, practice recycling and composting. Many serve as model environments or teaching centers for sustainable agriculture and appropriate technology, and feature such concepts as organic gardening, grey-water systems, and passive-solar home design. Eco-Home, a small cooperative household in Los Angeles, is an inspiring model of how to live ecologically in an urban environment. "The Farm," an intentional community involved in agriculture, ecology, and the peace movement, has launched a wide range of environmentally-focused projects including the development of radiation-detection equipment; a solar car company; and a publishing company.

The Franchise Approach

Some communities find a combination of philosophy and lifestyle that enables them to thrive, and occasionally one will embark on a program to spread its message and its influence. During the Reformation, a group of German Anabaptists decided to pool their goods and unite in Christian brotherhood. Jakob Hutter became their leader five years later, in 1533. The community prospered, and subsequently cloned itself repeatedly. Today there are nearly 400 colonies of the Hutterian Brethren in Canada and the USA, as well as communities in South America and Europe. When a Hutterian community reaches its optimum capacity (100–150 members), it acquires a new piece of land, builds a new set of structures (homes, schools, barns, etc.), then divides the population into two groups. One group stays at the original site, and one moves on to the new one. Neighboring colonies support each other with backup labor and various resources, an approach that yields a very high ratio of success for the new colonies. Each colony has common work and a common purpose, and most have an economic base of large-scale agriculture with an organizational structure resembling that of a producer cooperative. They have been so successful in their endeavors that in the 80s some of their neighbors initiated lawsuits to prevent Hutterites from acquiring more land, claiming that their communal economy amounted to "unfair competition." The Hutterites have retained many of their native customs, including dress, family structure, a simple lifestyle, and the German language. To many outsiders, Hutterites seem quite out of place when compared to their contemporary neighbors.

In contrast, members of the Emissaries of Divine Light, another spiritually-based network, manage to fit right in. The Emissaries, founded in the mid-40s, have a network of twelve major communities plus a number of urban centers that span the globe. Their overall focus is directed toward achieving a more effective, creative life experience and developing spiritual awareness without rules or a specific belief system. Their lifestyle would be described by many as "upper middle class," and business-oriented. Nuclear family units, though not mandated, are the norm. Emissaries pride themselves on being on good terms with their neighbors. One longstanding resident was elected mayor of a neighboring town for fifteen consecutive years, and members of their business staff are well respected, so much so that government tax officials in British Columbia regularly consult Emissary personnel before deciding on strategies for implementing new tax laws and regulations. The connections between and among the communities in this network are maintained in many ways. Inspirational talks and special events are always recorded, and transcripts are kept on file at each Emissary center. Some events are recorded on video, with copies distributed by mail within a couple of weeks. On a weekly basis, several centers link up via satellite for instantaneous transmission of related presentations originating from multiple locations.

Network Alliances

There is also growing interest among independent communities to be in closer contact with like-minded groups in their region and around the world. Many community groups have suffered a lack of contact and support due to their mistaken impression that they are among the few survivors of a bygone era. Alliances for the sharing of ideas, resources, and mutual support are gaining support and visibility. Hopefully, these new linkages will enable groups to learn from each others' failures as well as successes.

One network of more than fifty Catholic Worker Houses publishes a periodic newspaper and organizes occasional gatherings for the sharing of ideas, skills, rituals, friendship, and solidarity. Another values-based network is the Fellowship for Intentional Community (FIC), a North American network created to promote shared living in whatever forms it may take. The Fellowship regularly handles hundreds of inquiries from seekers hoping to find a community to join, from communities looking for new members, from academics doing research, and from media people gathering material for stories. Major FIC projects include the initiation of research to document the broad-based movement, publication of a thick Directory of Intentional Communities, creation of a fledgling Speakers Bureau, and the organization of an International Celebration of Community. To encourage participation in its work, the Fellowship rotates its semiannual meetings among different regions of the country, seeking out host communities sympathetic to its mission. The FIC's core organizers, many of whom are leaders in their home communities, find these meetings a source of inspiration and support for their own "life's work" which, not surprisingly, is geared toward making the world a better place.

A third organization of note is the Federation of Egalitarian Communities (FEC) established to promote and develop democratically-run communities based on the concept of equality. FEC encourages the identification and elimination of the "isms" (racism, sexism, classism, ageism, etc.), and emphasizes such practices as non-violence, cooperation, ecology, and sustainability. Member communities are required to hold all land, labor, and other resources in common. The FEC communities tax themselves $200 per year plus one percent of net revenues and use this fund to finance joint recruitment campaigns, fundraising, and travel to meetings and between communities. They also have created a voluntary joint security fund for protection against the economic strain of large medical bills. This fund has now grown to about $100,000, and is used in part as a revolving loan fund which provides low-interest loans to projects and community businesses compatible with FEC values. Member communities also participate in a labor exchange program which allows residents of one community to visit another, receiving labor credit at home for work done away. This is especially handy when one community's peak workload occurs during another's off season, and the labor flows back and forth when most appreciated. The exchange of personnel also offers a wonderful opportunity to take a mini-vacation, learn a new skill, make new friends, maintain old ones, and share insights about common experiences.

A Contemporary Wave

Historically, participation in shared living communities has come in cycles. One major wave came just ahead of the U.S. Civil War. Other notable waves followed, one at the end of the past century, one immediately preceding the First World War, and another during the Great Depression. The most recent wave came out of the counter-culture in the 60s. And the 90s is experiencing a new wave. The most recent *Directory of Intentional Communities* documents more than fifty new communities started during the past five years. The *Directory* also lists 160 that have survived at least a decade, and eighty others that have been in existence for more than two decades.

Although shared living does not appeal to everyone, ongoing social experiments will inevitably lead to new developments in a wide variety of areas, developments that will eventually find useful applications in other segments of society. It's hard to predict just when an intentional community will come up with something new that will be assimilated by mainstream culture—but if social experimenting results in a product, a process, or a philosophy that makes life a little easier or a bit more fulfilling, we'd be well advised to keep an open mind as we monitor the progress.

CHAPTER 17

Wayne Liebman

Ritual Men's Groups

The Nature of the Ritual Group

The focus of a ritual men's group is mythological. The group enables its members, for a limited time in a protected space, to enter what some have called the mythological world. Through their interaction with this world, men feel an authenticity in their place as men.

Myths are universal and impersonal, yet they touch us individually by articulating some invisible theme or drama that goes on under the surface of seemingly routine life. When we perceive an event mythologically, that event cannot be seen as insignificant or foolish. Rather, any experience (viewed from a mythological perspective) is a meaningful drama with a purpose and a message.

The ritual group builds on the work of what are known as "process" or "therapy" groups. Both the ritual and process group invite deep feeling. Both are receptive to the concerns that men have, seek to heal the emotional numbness men often feel, and attempt to validate their inner lives. The two groups differ in the way they deal with feeling. The process group emphasizes the feeling life of men as individual human beings; the ritual group emphasizes the feeling life of men *as men*, pointing to something deep within and yet greater than their individual selves.

Working Mythologically

An hour after sunset ten men gather in a dark room. They sit in a circle on the floor in the center of which is a lit candle. Next to it lies a bowl of burning sage. The odor of sage surrounds them, washes over them, recalls them to a time when the land on which this house was built was a vast prairie. No one speaks. The only sound is the measured breath of one man, then another, then another. They inhale the sweet smell of sage and breathe it out again, and in their mingled exhalation a shadowy outline forms. Some nights it is the shadow of a raven, or coyote, or feather. Some nights it is nothing at all.

The ritual men's group is a vessel which clears a place for the extraordinary in my life and so awakens my imagination to it. When this happens, my life is no longer just my life, but the characterization of a larger story telling itself through me. Every man has a story to tell. For example, one man may tell a story of heartache about his relationship with his father. This may stir the other men to tell their stories about how it is for them with their fathers—what are the pitfalls, the challenges, the rewards. Out of the group sharing comes a sense of how men encounter "father" in their lives. The group may go on to note parallels between their stories and some myths and fairy tales which are thousands of years old, and which link them to a community of men over time.

So the story moves from the individual to the group to the universal. The story becomes about what fathering means and is, what the maleness in the relationship between father and son is. Each man feels himself living out part of the theme of maleness, and the theme living itself out in him. He is thinking about himself mythologically rather than psychologically, and the significance of this is not that it gives answers to problems, or even that it compels creative responses to problems, but that it fosters a sense of partnership with the mysterious forces of the universe.

If a man finds a myth or part of a myth that is telling his story, then he looks for ways to get closer to it, to bring it down into his life and his body. Memorizing and telling the story is one way to do this. Another way is to act a part of it out ritually; using his imagination, a man creates an action which opens him even more to the story, allowing it to resonate more sharply in him.

Building a Container

Since the group's relationship with the mythological world is both precious and vulnerable, it becomes important for them to safeguard it by considering certain details of containment. When I first began to think about the idea of a container for the group, I thought it odd. The image of containment is distinctly feminine— something which holds, nourishes, encloses, and protects. It's very different from the kind of constructions we usually associate with men and boys—edifices, towers, swords. Yet by the enigmatic act of men creating a container the group perpetuates itself. I'm sure that something deeply unifying happens inside each man as he grapples to develop this shepherding, caretaking function in the absence of women. I believe he learns something that he can only learn from other men, and which is vital for his life and relationships.

The need for lodge or sanctuary should be given some attention and thought. A private, indoor, permanent home for the group seems to help harness and center the force of the mythological world. When a group meets in the same place time after time that place becomes special to them and contributes to the power of the group.

The way membership is defined also influences the container. Some men's groups (often called "councils" or "lodges") are open each time to all comers. Usually these are fairly large gatherings (ten to fifty men or more) which meet once a month or so in a public facility. These groups seek to re-create the atmosphere of a men's conference and give the participants a feeling of community. This environment is necessarily less intimate than that of the small ritual group. The small group has about ten members, plus or minus two or three, and meetings are open only to members.

The Form of a Meeting

Early in the life of a ritual group, the men may worry about what to do at a meeting, and whether they're doing it right.

Though ideas and guidelines are often helpful, I want to stress again the importance of a group's developing its own form out of its feelings, needs and preferences. There is no "proper" way for a meeting to unfold, nothing required of the men beyond attending to the quality of their experience. If things go well on a given night, then the group will be in touch awhile with how the mythological world is manifesting in them. If not, and the group feels out of touch with their purpose, then it will be important for them to review what they are doing and consider changes.

Although the ritual group is leaderless it needs direction. I've spent a lot of time in groups shooting the breeze, everyone secretly hoping the meeting would somehow start itself. One way to help the group fix its bearings is to designate in advance one man each meeting to "hold the container." This man functions as the "ritual elder" who orchestrates the evening, protects its structure and keeps the group on track. It's his job to say "It's time to start," "Is everyone finished with this?," etc.

"Holding the container" impels a man toward a sense of stewardship for the group. It encourages him to take the development and preservation of the container seriously. It's not only the group's container, it's his container, and his work and the group's work are tied together. One simple way is to move through the group roster in alphabetical order. This gives each man time to think about what he wants to lead the group in and permits him to notify the others in advance if, for example, he wants them to come prepared with a dream or poem.

A few minutes before the formal start of the evening, some groups take time to socialize over coffee or tea. Someone (the man holding the container, if there is one) might signal when it's time to begin. There may be announcements ("There's a good article in this or that journal") and logistics ("Next meeting falls on a holiday so we need to talk about changing the date"), followed by a check-in.

A check-in is a quick once-around in which each man tells the others what's happening in his life—I'm having a good week, my girlfriend and I are fighting, etc. (It's a good idea to apply a fairly strict time limit, say two or three minutes, to protect against the evening getting consumed in this way.) The check-in is a means of honoring the natural concern and affection that the members have for one another.

The next step is to edge away from the outer world. It helps if each man can take a step down into his feelings. Some groups have a second round, an "inner" check-in, expressly for that purpose. Usually once the anecdotes are out it's easier to get to the feelings. You can do it in a word, better yet a sound.

To help shift the mood out of ordinary time, it's useful to make a physical change at some point—stand up and stretch, dim the lights, sound an instrument, etc. This is also a good moment for an opening ritual. In many groups the ritual elder smudges everyone with burning sage. Smudging is a Native American tradition, in which smoke is wafted (usually with a feather) over each man. The intent is that as the smoke washes over you it momentarily cleanses you of your outside cares. After the ritual elder has smudged everyone the last man smudges him. Some groups sit in silence awhile afterward, others chant or drum. The attempt here is to feel sacred time, and there is no hurry.

Throughout the meeting, the ritual elder holds an awareness that the group needs a sense of where it is, although he himself may not always know. So he doesn't simply present what he's planned. He asks, "Would it feel right if we did this now?" The group proceeds by consensus. Maybe something unexpected has come up—for example, a death in one man's family. The ritual group is an ideal place to take a personal event of this magnitude and use it as a vehicle for all the men to strengthen their connection. The men choose whatever form feels best—pass the talking stick, improvise a ritual of healing, etc.

There is often a ritual to close, such as the "naming" ritual that ends some larger conferences: The men rise and stand in a circle with their arms around one another. When the first man is ready he says, "My name is ———." The group responds "Your name is ———," and repeats the name twice more. Then the man next to him says his name in the same way, the group responds to him, and so on. Sometimes you feel apprehensive leaving the intimacy of sacred space to reenter ordinary time. The naming ritual reaffirms your identity in the outer world as you move away from the inner one.

Being Lost

It's said that we've lost all hope of contact with the old ways. That is, whatever rituals of initiation were practiced by the elders on young men in ancient and primitive times are forever beyond our knowing; that even if we did know them they probably would not do us much good since the mythology behind them has ceased to be our mythology, if it ever was. Yet I believe there is a congruency between the men in the modern ritual group and the boys who were led off into the bush by the old men. The ancient experience of initiation surely entailed some element of chaos and terror, some component of being picked out of a safe environment and thrown into alien territory, not knowing what to expect, unable to go back to the familiar ways of doing things, unsure of the new ones. This is precisely the experience of uncertainty we choose in a ritual group.

The group that meets for ritual purposes asks its members to surrender something of themselves. They surrender to the discipline of the ritual, to the space where the ritual is performed, to the force in the mythological world which the ritual honors or appeals to. With the surrender comes fear: fear of uncertainty, fear of chaos, fear of buried pain, fear of being vulnerable in front of other men, fear that the group itself will be a failure.

In a strange way, fear is the only guide to be completely trusted. The next step seems always to come out of a place of darkness, out of the tension of not knowing. The crux of "what now?" lies in your own experience, in containing the apprehension of uncertainty and being willing not to know and not to be told.

Not having a leader, not being part of any formal men's organization or set of beliefs, being left to glean your way, is the contemporary experience of maleness. In the heat of the small groups you build a local community to discover and learn to sustain pieces of your manhood.

When a group of men sit in silence and darkness together, when they drum by candlelight . . . We are looking to live our sacred connectedness and we can take heart that men of all times have agonized and asked the same question, "Is this right? Is this the way to be men?"

CHAPTER 18

Juanita Brown

The Corporation
as Community

We have asked senior executives and line personnel
from corporations throughout the United States, Europe, and Latin
America to share their images of "corporation" and "community."
No matter what sector of the organizational world participates in
the dialogue, the responses are surprisingly consistent. "Corporation" conjures up images of authority, bureaucracy, competition,
power, and profit. "Community" consistently evokes images of
democracy, diversity, cooperation, interdependence, and mutual
benefit.

If this is the case, then we may want to ask ourselves if the
images, associations, and feelings that are implicit in many contemporary views of the corporation are the ones we want to guide and
motivate our everyday actions in today's changing world. *This is
not a philosophical issue, but a pragmatic one.* The answer to this
question is fundamental to achieving the business results and financial returns that will ensure the survival and health of corporations in a fiercely competitive global marketplace.

Modern organizations and the promise of the "good life" have
separated us from traditional ties to the land, to our families, to the
community, and perhaps most importantly, from the connection to
our own spirit.

These developments have been unintended consequences of
the Industrial Age. Not only are the human and social costs stag-
gering, but their impact on the corporation is *undercutting its*

ability to compete in the marketplace.[1] Is this where we intended to go? We think not. Today, business is at a crossroads, faced with an unprecedented challenge:

> Built into the concept of capitalism and free enterprise, from the beginning, was the assumption that the actions of many units of individual enterprise, responding to market forces and guided by the "invisible hand" of Adam Smith, would somehow add up to desirable outcomes. But in the last decade of the 20th century it has become clear that the "invisible hand" is faltering. It depended on a consensus of overarching meaning and values which is no longer present. So business has to adopt a new tradition which it has never had throughout the entire history of capitalism. This is, as the most powerful institution on the planet, to take responsibility for the whole.

This perspective offered by Willis Harman, noted futurist and a founder of the World Business Academy, may seem like an overwhelming burden for today's corporate leader, already concerned with rising costs, intense competition, and unpredictable changes in the larger environment.

Whether it is difficult or not, modern organizations need to confront this challenge.

Frankly, we do not believe the transformation we are considering is as complex as it may seem. If what the current research suggests is true—then adopting the positive image of corporation as community may become a key factor in revitalizing corporate life.[2]

What if we were to consciously choose to think of the corporation as a community and its managers as community leaders? Is it possible to create a merger between these apparently paradoxical ideas? In fact, they are actually quite compatible and complementary. The Swedish word for *business*, "narings liv," literally means "nourishment and life" when translated into English, and the word *corporation* refers to "any association of individuals bound together into a *corpus*, a body sharing a common purpose in a common name."[3] *Community* has the root meaning "with unity." This suggests an evocative question. What if we were to think of the Corporate Community as being "a body of people sharing a common identity and purpose, acting with unity, to provide nourishment and life both to its own stakeholders (including stockholders) and to the larger society"?

What would such a corporate community look like? What are the principles by which it would operate? The "Merger Tale" we share below is a vehicle for stimulating further dialogue about the possibilities of designing organizations that can create a merger between the strengths of the corporation and the vitality of a healthy community. The Merger Tale is a composite creation. A fully functioning corporation-as-community does not yet exist. However, the examples of practice we describe are occurring already in corporations across the globe.

The Corporation as a Community: A Merger Tale

It was a difficult executive meeting. The reports showed that trend lines were flattening. Nothing alarming in the short term, nothing Wall Street would notice yet, but several of the executives in the room seemed concerned.

"The international situation is shifting. Our brands are facing stiffer competition abroad as well as at home," one said.

"The consumers' needs seem to be changing as well," another added. "You know, they are more health and quality conscious than ever, and I don't know what R&D has in the pipeline that will meet that demand."

Another added, "Frankly, getting new products developed and out the door, as well as producing and delivering the ones we have already is a complex process involving a lot of departments. The whole way we are organized and managed has promoted a type of corporate arthritis. I'm an old timer and even I'm getting concerned about the bureaucracy and turfdom around here. Everyone's working independently to be the best without thinking how it all fits together to achieve our real purpose."

The one female member of the team raised a series of issues that had recently come up in the Employee Attitude Survey:

"Our employees don't think we are listening to their creative ideas, so they keep quiet. They want a piece of the action when they help us succeed. They are no longer willing to compromise their family life in return for a base salary and the knowledge that we hit the quarterly targets. They want to contribute to a purpose that has value beyond the numbers. It's a different work force than we had ten or fifteen years ago."

Another member, respected as a strategic business thinker whose ideas had paid off handsomely over the years, challenged those sitting around the conference table:

"What is our real purpose, anyway?" he asked.

That started it!

In the discussion that followed, the group re-examined their corporate purpose, which focused solely on maximum financial returns and competitive supremacy. They realized something was missing. The CEO and his executive team decided not to wait until crisis hit, but began to actively chart the appropriate role and future direction for the business. They expanded their Strategic Planning Department to include not only business and financial analysts but also specialists in organizational strategy and large-system change. Their organizational strategy specialists assisted in the design of a series of "good conversations," based on the traditional concept of the New England town meeting. The corporate community meetings focused on what kind of business approach was needed to thrive in the last decade of the 20th century. What kind of corporation would be responsive to the needs of constituencies whose support they required for their continuing success?

The senior leadership group began a series of community meetings with representation from all levels within the organization as well as with external constituencies including employees' families, government agencies, local school systems, and key stockholder groups. They soon realized that their corporation was actually like a bustling community that included not only employees and their families but hundreds of thousands of customers, suppliers, and stockholders.

The leaders asked themselves, "What if we thought of ourselves as leaders of a corporate community? How would this affect our overall strategy?" Things looked very different from this perspective. A new Statement of Purpose developed, reflecting their emerging perception of themselves as corporate community leaders:

The purpose of our Corporate Community is to meet the needs of our customers for high-quality goods and services, to serve the needs of our employees and their families for an enhanced quality of life, and to be a responsible corporate citizen in the larger society of which we are an integral part.

"What happened to 'competitive advantage' or 'return on investment'?" they were asked. "Profitability is only one measure of our success," they replied. "We believe that in serving this enhanced purpose, our corporation and its stockholders will be richly rewarded financially as well as in other relevant performance measures."

With their purpose clear, they identified the values they were willing to commit to—values that would serve to guide decision making and daily behavior at all levels. The acronym I STATE was used to help people remember the core values:

I ntegrity

S upport
T rust
A ccountability
T eamwork
E mpowerment

The enthusiasm spread. Employees at all levels volunteered to be members of TAQ (Take Action Quickly) Teams to speed up the transition. They brainstormed action plans and began implementation. Some of their key contributions were to:

- Develop a *Bill of Rights and Responsibilities* for members of the corporate community.
- Analyze the *business situation*, proposing creative strategies, and suggesting "stretch objectives" that were both challenging and fun.
- Understand *customers' needs* in order to create quality partnerships.
- Identifiy *high leverage business and organizational processes* that needed redesign or streamlining.

- Develop *clear performance standards* and a performance feedback system that supported goal setting and self-development.
- Create a performance-based *reward and recognition system* that would reinforce the I-STATE values, including incentives for intrapreneurship and profit sharing based on business results.
- Re-think the *design of the organization* to create a "human-scale architecture" of smaller-size units focused on meeting customer needs.
- Review the corporation's key *policies and procedures* to see if they were consistent with both the I-STATE values and the Bill of Rights and Responsibilities.
- Figure out how to make *continuous learning for improvement* a way of life at the company.
- Explore *leadership development* and encourage new leadership competencies based on service, coaching, and mentoring.
- Develop methods for *broad information sharing and communication* about business issues, financial results, and other dimensions of corporate community life.
- Understand *diversity* and honor individual contribution while encouraging an environment of teamwork.
- Create a *corporate responsibility* policy and recommend projects that would benefit the health, education, and welfare of company employees, their families, the larger community, and the environment.

What began to happen was fascinating. Decades of pent-up energy began to be released, tentatively at first. Employees at all levels wondered, "Do they really mean it? What will happen if for some reason the numbers go south for a quarter or two? Is our management in this for the long haul? Will my job be affected?" People were scared and excited at the same time.

The CEO assured his senior group that he was in this for the long term. He made himself personally available to communicate this message broadly. He used the "old paradigm" reward system to nurture the "new paradigm" into existence. He held his managers accountable for acting in accordance with the Statement of

Purpose and I-STATE values. Management performance bonuses that year were derived in large measure from leaders' success in fostering widespread participation at all levels in the corporate community in the service of the corporate purpose.

The CEO helped get the resources (money, time, people, and technology) needed to respond to the TAQ Team recommendations and other initiatives that sprang up. While maintaining his and the Executive Team's prerogatives to define the shape and boundaries of the playing field, the coaches gave their players a great deal of room to create the plays and manage the game.

Cross-functional Community Improvement Teams were formed to work on immediate as well as longer-term challenges and opportunities. All were supported by "community organizers," employees and managers who were trained in designing meetings for results.

Learning became the key to success. "Learning to learn" groups were started across the company. The firm's information systems were redesigned to enable creative problem solving and business planning at the local level. The Great Game of Business seminar helped employees learn about financial planning so they could begin to think of themselves as owner/managers of the business.

The Family Wellness and Employee Assistance Program attracted widespread participation. Company retirees joined the Caring Companion project, volunteering their time to help in the Corporate Kindergarten and to tutor and coach children at higher grade levels who were interested in being part of a college scholarship incentive program. The Loan-a-Resource project enabled executives and other employees to share their talents with local nonprofit organizations. The employees created the "Corporate Community Today" show, an interactive video program in which they shared successes in every area of community life as well as provided up-to-date information on business performance and results.

And what were the results? Here are highlights of what happened during the first three years:

- Cycle time for new product development was reduced by 40 percent.

- Productivity increased 33 percent.
- The company received the National Environmental Award for reducing plant emissions to 50 percent less than the required government standards.
- The accident rate was reduced by 50 percent.
- After the new Corporate Kindergarten started, absenteeism declined by 30 percent, and the employee turnover rate dropped almost 10 percent.
- Divisions that instituted Wellness and Employee Assistance programs for employees and their families paid 30–60 percent less in health care costs than those that chose not to participate.
- Customer complaints were reduced by more than 60 percent.

What about the bottom line? The above statistics begin to hint at what occurred. Since the corporate community development process began, operating profits more than doubled and they are still breaking records.

Change itself is hard, and not without its critics. The corporation has had to be sensitive to those who argue that, in serving as a catalyst for the re-creation of community in people's lives, it is returning to the paternalism of an earlier age clothed in new garments. It has needed to balance the universal needs for individual achievement with those for joint effort—the desire to stand out while staying in. It has had to meet the formidable challenges of nurturing shared culture and values in a community that is not geographically based. It has struggled with how to design integrated systems, processes, and structures consistent with its purpose and values, while at the same time remaining flexible and responsive. Even with all these dilemmas, the corporate community continues its journey because its people have decided that the destination is worth the trip.

The elected employee representative to the Board of Directors summed it all up when he was asked why the employees had become such committed partners in creating a positive future and in sustaining outstanding results. He paused for a moment and then commented thoughtfully, "You know, I think it's because we are becoming value-led rather than market-driven."

CHAPTER 19

Kathryn McCamant, Charles Durrett,
and Ellen Hertzman

Collaborative Housing

It's 6:45, and people are starting to congregate in the common sitting room and dining room. Joan pulls into the lot and ducks into her house to change from her office clothes. Jon has been outside playing a version of basketball with Bren and Katherine's 2-year-old. Judy glances up from her magazine from time to time. Fran's 11-year-old daughter comes in, proudly carrying the chocolate cake she baked for her mother's birthday. Nome is trying out the paper he will deliver the next day at a conference in Seattle on a small group of listeners in the corner. His wife Janis (who's already heard it a dozen times) is still up in their home, wrapping presents for their granddaughter whom they will be visiting. The tables are set and Katherine and Gary, the evening's cooks, put finishing touches on the meal. In the Doyle Street CoHousing Community dinner is about to start.

The meal is delicious, a Hungarian stew from a recipe of Katherine's grandmother's. At dinner, the upcoming local election is the primary topic of conversation. The common house telephone rings; it's Chris saying she'll be home late and could someone please save her something to eat.

By 9:30, dinner has been over for some time. Gary and Katherine are finishing up the dishes. They won't have to cook and clean again for another month. A few people are still drinking coffee and chatting in the dining room. Judy is back at her magazine; she could take it home to read but she prefers the swirl of life

138

in the common house. Chris dashed in to grab dinner, then headed home for a late night of desk work. The little ones have reluctantly been persuaded away from the children's room and home to bed. These individuals, who didn't know each other two years earlier, have become a community.

———•———

Dramatic demographic and economic changes are taking place in our society, and most of us are feeling the effects of these trends in our own lives. Things that people once took for granted—family, community, a sense of belonging—must now be actively sought out. Contemporary households—characterized by smaller families, women working outside the home, and growing numbers of single parents, elderly, and singles living alone—face a child care crisis, social isolation, and a chronic time crunch, in part because they are living in housing which no longer suits them. At the same time, an increasingly mobile population has distanced many Americans from their extended families which have traditionally provided social and economic support. Traditional forms of housing no longer address the needs of many people, and they find themselves mis-housed, ill-housed or unhoused because of the lack of appropriate options.

A new approach to housing which we have termed "CoHousing" addresses such questions. Pioneered twenty years ago primarily in Denmark, where now over 140 such communities exist, the CoHousing concept is being met in the United States and Canada by a groundswell of popular enthusiasm because it speaks to the realities of late twentieth-century life. As of early 1993, four CoHousing communities have been built in the United States—in California, Washington and Colorado—with more than 100 others under construction or in the planning stages.

CoHousing communities differ from typical housing developments on several levels. They can be defined by four basic principles:

- They are designed by the residents, in conjunction with architects, developers, and other professionals, to address the needs of the residents, and specifically the desire for community.

- Communities are designed to have a pedestrian-oriented layout, with cars kept to the periphery.
- Individual dwellings—complete with kitchens—are complemented by extensive common facilities such as kitchen, dining room, children's play room, workshop, and guest room, providing residents with the option for shared dinners, child care, and other resources.
- Finally, CoHousing communities are resident-managed, generally by a homeowner's association made up of all the households.

Typically, residents do not know each other at first, but come together seeking an alternative to the isolation of current housing options, or because they wish to create for themselves a neighborhood in the old-fashioned sense, with its mix of generations and family types who interact and depend on each other. They express the need for a better place to raise children and a desire for a spontaneous social life that doesn't require making appointments with friends. CoHousing communities can offer an economically and ecologically sound alternative to conventional housing, balancing the need for privacy with the need for community.

In many respects, CoHousing communities are not a new idea. In the past, most people lived in villages or tightly knit urban neighborhoods. Even today, people in less industrialized regions typically live in small communities. Members of such communities know one another's families and histories, talents and weaknesses. This kind of relationship demands accountability, but in return provides security and a sense of belonging. To expect that today's small households, as likely to be single parents or single adults as nuclear families, should be self-sufficient and without community support is not only unrealistic but absurd.

CoHousing Communities in the United States

Since our book, *CoHousing: A Contemporary Approach to Housing Ourselves*, was first published in the fall of 1988, we have encountered tremendous interest in this type of housing from a wide variety of Americans. People of all ages, incomes, and lifestyles are attracted to the social and practical aspects of CoHousing communities, as well as to the potential for shared resources and services.

The first American CoHousing communities are inspiring many individuals to re-examine their current housing alternatives. Muir Commons, in Davis, California, is a community of 26 town houses and a 3600-square-foot common house that opened in summer 1991. The residents live in one-, two-, and three-bedroom homes, and share common facilities including a kitchen and dining room, a children's play room, a workshop, a guest room, and an exercise room. They take turns cooking for each other about five nights a week, and cooperate to provide informal child care.

The Muir Commons residents spent many hours before construction started determining the design and policies that would best address their needs. They hired The CoHousing Company to facilitate this participatory design process and to draw the preliminary designs. By the time the residents were ready to move into their new homes, almost three years after they first began meeting, they were functioning as a cohesive community and making all decisions by consensus. Community-building takes place as the group encounters and overcomes hurdles in the development process. Working through the details of creating the physical community, residents build trust, history, and friendship.

CoHousing communities planned or built in a variety of settings across the country indicate that the CoHousing concept makes sense to a lot of people. Urban, suburban, small-town, and rural environments now boast CoHousing communities, with many more to come. Unit prices are generally comparable to other local housing options and include the individual dwelling plus a portion of the common house and community outdoor areas. The dwellings are typically owned as condominiums or cooperatives with a homeowner's association overseeing management of the common areas.

The Doyle Street CoHousing Community in Emeryville, California, provides city-dwellers with a safe and inviting place to come home to. The conversion of a brick industrial building to a twelve-unit CoHousing community allows residents to combine a fast-paced urban life with an old-fashioned sense of neighborhood. Meals are served in the common house several times a week, and residents don't hesitate to exchange tools, rides to the airport, or plant- or baby-sitting. Community work days provide a chance for residents to complete special projects such as building planters or installing a hot tub. But what residents seem to value most is the casual interaction that can take place so easily. The key is the balance—always having a choice between privacy and community. Gary, a longtime community member, comments:

> If I want privacy, I can always come in and close the door, but for the times I want community, I just step outside and it's right there. Sometimes I head down to do a load of laundry in the common house and I get into a half-an-hour conversation.

As a warehouse conversion, the Doyle Street development adds to the diversity and life of the neighborhood. The location—in a transitional neighborhood of residences and light industry—provides round-the-clock activity which is a sure deterrent to crime. The intergenerational community benefits everyone. By directly speaking to the desire of its residents to create a community in which they feel secure, the Emeryville project faces the pressing question of how to create a comfortable and safe urban home for those who have most to fear in the city—women, children, and seniors.

People need community at least as much as they need privacy. We must reestablish ways compatible with contemporary American lifestyles to accommodate this need. CoHousing communities offer one alternative for recreating a sense of place and neighborhood based partly on the village or small town of the past and partly on the needs of the future.

CHAPTER 20

Stephanie Mills

Salons

It was really a salon that my friend Joan and I attended at the Neahtawanta Inn near Traverse City, Michigan, the night after Thanksgiving, although in these parts they tend to be called potlucks. Joan was up visiting from Washington, D.C., taking a break from prosecuting drug fiends. Our hosts, Sally and Bob, are longtime ecology and peace activists and organizers. Sally teaches yoga and also sometimes works in classrooms with developmentally disabled kids. Bob was once a high school science teacher and ran a small screen printing business for a while. As a citizen activist he now teaches science to his county commissioners, constantly nudging local public policy toward ecological literacy. Jeff, who manages a local computer store, and his wife Leigh, a high school librarian, were part of the group around the two tables.

Three other couples rounded out the party. As we enjoyed the heaps of good food we all had brought, our conversation was general, a mix of news and opinion, giggles and commiseration. When it came to national politics, our repartee, it must be admitted, was a little cynical, but it all strengthened our local sense of community and improved our knowledge of one another. It was fun and—even better—it was nourishing to be talking about the things that matter, seeing old and new friends at particular moments in their lives. We were mutually interested, and caring in appropriate degree, fostering our little subculture's vision of peace and sustainability.

Could an evening like that change the world? Not all by itself, certainly, but a thousand widely scattered variations on it would be a respectable beginning. Small groups have always been the locus of change. What they do, in a sometimes offhand way, is constellate new cultural forms and give birth to the unexpected. Sometimes the talk is the thing, sometimes the feeling. When we risk talking about something we really care about it's infectious. Like any good infection, such talk can produce heat, a fever of intellectual excitement. People seem to enjoy participation in a group that's known to be making a creative contribution. Word gets around and Hey! Presto! You are hip for real.

Hankering to be hip has long been a basic incentive to salon participation. However frivolous the glitter of wit, it holds an undying fascination, as evidenced by the enshrinement of the Algonquin Round Table. One of America's most famous salons, it was a brilliant, boozy writers' luncheon of the 1920s. Convened daily at the cozily handsome Algonquin Hotel, just across the street from the offices of *The New Yorker,* the Round Table was a salad-days confab for the likes of Dorothy Parker, Edna Ferber, Alexander Woollcott, George S. Kaufman, Franklin Pierce Adams, Ring Lardner, and many of Broadway's leading lights. It was their conversational playground before they and it became legendary, which is probably why they felt free enough to be so witty.

For most of human history it's been like this, people banding together in little social units, larger than the family, smaller than the tribe. In earlier times, the nature and propriety of every form of relationship were well understood. People knew how to be together in groups like lungs knew how to breathe. Indeed, some hold that the Neolithic era marked a high point in the development of human culture, that cavewomen and cavemen were riffing around their campfires, sharing tales of children's antics, and gathering expeditions in the bush in new songs that took shape over needles and sinew.

Ever since the Renaissance, salons have been under the aegis of women, if not their exclusive domain. Women set the tone, perhaps of a basic receptivity; they established an attitude of listening and responding that evoked significant conversation. The salons of the Renaissance, Enlightenment, and modern eras were hothouses of intellectual activity, where the most brilliant authors and philosophers would gather to present their latest poem or chapter, to meet patrons and other influential folk, and just to do some freestyle scintillation. Given the evanescence of conversation, all of this activity has never been, strictly speaking, *productive*. Nevertheless—or perhaps as a result—salons have been enormously influential. William Doyle writes in his *Origins of the French Revolution*, "The aristocratic ladies of the salons were the midwives of the Enlightenment."

In descriptions of great salonieres, one reads of their social prowess, charm, wit, and force of personality. Clearly, the ability to orchestrate a great salon is as distinctive a human gift as perfect pitch. Hosting a salon takes finesse, intelligence, and respect. It's a dynamic art of composition.

The word *salon* is French for *drawing room,* and a place to hold a salon is indeed essential. That, plus a willingness and ability to commit the time, are really the only external conditions to be met.

These days, our large-scale institutions don't seem to be doing famously well at educating, legislating, healing, employing, producing, governing, or even entertaining, so the ardor for meaningful conversation remains unquenched and is worth fanning.

Certainly there's good thinking going on everywhere. But thought can easily get trapped in its particular realm. Community leaders and local organizers need theoretical expertise. Visionaries need to confront the discipline that implementation demands. The dreamers, the leaders, and the theoreticians may be members of separate circles that need to intersect to be useful to society as a whole. So we need to become acquainted, to share information, to develop trust in one another, and to challenge, correct, and synthesize. The tradition and courtesy of the salon afford a setting in which all that can happen. A salon is a thought-traders' rendezvous.

It seems clear that for groups to remain benevolent, there must be respect and courtesy among participants. Some kind of covenant, even an undertone of sacrament, needs to be established. In the wildly proliferating 12-step groups, the passion is for staying alive by helping others do so, too. Their unofficial etiquette often is: No leaders, allow and address the silence; no dialogue, no cross-talk, no advice-giving, just "I" statements. The result is not what you could call conversation, exactly, but there is an extraordinary quality of reflection and candor in many meetings that sparks fellowship and healing.

All forms of discourse, which foster community, empower their participants, and are conducive to grass-roots democracy, represent a liberation of the salon from the confines of economic, intellectual, and artistic aristocracy, and even from the limitations of space and time. All this social invention attests to people's irreducible need for the small group.

One such intimate situation, in San Francisco, is A New American Place—"an open house for reflection on human spiritual maturity, responsible life governance, and our emerging creation story." First convened a few years ago by Sidney Lanier, a former Episcopal priest and founder of an off-Broadway theater, A New American Place is a monthly gathering, by invitation, of 50 to 75 Bay Area intellectuals, preponderantly from the field of humanistic and transpersonal psychology, and from academe.

"It's an intuitional community," says Lanier. A New American Place began literally as an open house given by Lanier and his wife, Jean, when they took up permanent residence in San Francisco. Thirty-some guests from the Laniers' circle attended, and they so enjoyed what was too rare an opportunity to see one another that they wanted more.

"Being somewhat of a convivial soul," says Lanier, "I responded, 'Well, let's make it a *thing.* "

The *thing* loosely revolves around Lanier's concern with the fate of the Republic and his dream of "conscious democracy as a global spiritual path." In his manifesto for A New American Place, Lanier writes, " 'America's destiny,' said Benjamin Franklin, 'is not power but light.' I believe we are meant to be an exemplary community of light—even world servers, not simply another transient structure of empire. How can we recover our destiny?

"By coming together as Americans and confronting penetrating existential questions ["Where are we Who are we Who are we together What are we to do" reads the running foot of Lanier's stationery], we may learn how to play our assigned part."

The intuitional community ("postgraduates of everything") that shares these noble sentiments has grown to 80 and shows no sign of losing energy. The structure of these gatherings is a continuing experiment, but Lanier is adamant about the value of physical presence. It is important "to get together in the same time and the same space," he says. "Electronic media are bloodless and passive. But when you're with people you can't turn them off."

So the people gather, have light refreshments, and then enter the salon, where they listen to someone's short presentation. Then they break up into smaller groups for three-quarters of an hour to discuss what they've heard, and then reconvene for conversations between the groups and presenters. Their general conversation is kept flowing by the use of a talking stick—a Native American custom that entitles the person holding some designated object to speak without interruption.

"We have a lot of fun," says Lanier. And some of the "fun" is friendly contention and downright serious argument. "The discourse is at a pretty high level." And it seems to be influential. Because the participants are all leaders of other communities, the energy moves outward through them. Artifacts of A New American Place are books, articles, a theater called the Earth Drama Lab, and other spin-off groups that have developed a separate existence.

When I first encountered the idea of salons back in 1972, I likewise had a high purpose—saving the world. I began by throwing dinner parties in Stockholm for renegade environmentalists in the vicinity of the United Nations Conference on Human Environment. From time to time afterward, I was subsidized to do more. My last official salon was more than a decade ago, in Bernal Heights, San Francisco, where the Trust for Public Land set me up in a nice old Victorian house to play innkeeper to their executives-in-training and to throw the odd dinner and tea party as well.

The single most luminous anecdote I can recall from that salon was an evening when David Brower and Margaret Mead kissed and made up after a fight they'd had a few years before at a previous salon of mine. The setting for that earlier encounter had been the UN Conference on Human Habitation in Vancouver, British Columbia. Friends of the Earth provided the auspices. The Brower-Mead dispute had been over the question of whether accommodating human needs by providing low-cost housing would not ultimately remove the check that misery exerts on the expansion of human population. Brower thought possibly so, Mead thought it indecent even to contemplate withholding such fundamental care for any reason, and she let Brower know this in classic, ranting, Meadian style.

In addition to the charming image of the reconciliation of this rift between two great souls, the other memory that I cherish from that soirée in Bernal Heights is Margaret Mead's complimenting me on the quality of my ironing of the thrift store damask table-cloth, and of my *crème caramel*.

I reminisced about that evening while stacking this year's firewood at my modest domicile outside of Maple City, Michigan. Despite the fact that I have settled in a land where the heady thrills of conversation are less endemic than the quieter pleasures of rural solitude, I find myself spending more time than ever before in groups, with more varied participants, and wiser intentions. A sign of the times perhaps, heartfelt response to a planetary—and spe-cies—need.

As Margaret Mead herself put it: "Never doubt that a small group of thoughtful committed citizens can change the world. In-deed, it's the only thing that ever has."

CHAPTER 21

*Kristin Anundsen and
Carolyn Shaffer*

Electronic
Communities

Computers can open the door into community for people who might otherwise have been shut out. One of these people is Wanet Miller, who became paralyzed from the neck down as a result of an automobile accident in 1974. "Everything changed in that moment," he recalls. "My marriage fell apart, I fell apart." Lacking a family support system, he decided to move with a colleague from Phoenix to Berkeley, where people from the Mormon church became his first new friends.

Still, he felt isolated. "I became a hermit except for visits from church people," Miller explained. Then, despite the fact that he'd hated computers for years, he was so bored he decided to purchase a Commodore. With the aid of a friend, he figured out how to rig it up so he could work it with a stick held in his mouth. From then on, his world began opening up.

First, he helped his church community by preparing computerized mailing lists. Eventually the church committees began holding their meetings at his house, bringing dinner along to add a social dimension. When he bought a modem so that he could communicate with a friend who had one, he was suddenly presented with new possibilities for connectedness.

One by one, he joined computer networks. Not only did he meet a variety of new acquaintances—including other disabled people—he was able to enhance his own feelings of self-esteem by using the computer for activities that had formerly been problematic, such as shopping and banking. In fact, he now assists his growing circle of friends by helping them make airline reservations, do research, and shop online for electronic equipment.

Today, Miller spends at least three hours a day online. For him, the computer is his link not only to electronic communities but also to the wider community. "The world," he says joyfully, "is interesting again."

Networking by computer usually supplements and even encourages what network users call meeting "f2f" (face to face). However, the process of developing closeness evolves differently. As several users have observed, in traditional place-based communities we meet people and then, if we choose, get to know them; with electronic communities, we usually get to know people first and then decide whether to meet them f2f.

Some network communities set up regular gatherings for their participants. The WELL (which stands for Whole Earth 'Lectronic Link) holds monthly get-togethers in the San Francisco area, although many WELLites hail from other parts of the country—the world, even. Members of ECHO (East Coast Hang Out), a smaller, cozier network composed mostly of New York City residents, arrange picnics, dances, bowling parties, members' art shows, and other events.

What happens when online acquaintances meet f2f? Neesa Sweet, a video scriptwriter in Chicago who belongs to several online groups, recalls the first time she attended a convention of the Electronic Networking Association. "We looked at each other's name tags and started hugging and kissing as we recognized each other."

It's not uncommon for a couple to meet on the network, then get together in person, and finally marry. It's a bit like marrying your pen pal, except that the getting-to-know-you stage progresses more quickly and more multidimensionally. Courting couples can have private conversations by exchanging electronic mail, and they can also join each other in public conferences on issues as general as Culture or as intimate as Sexuality.

The line between network community and traditional, place-based community is often blurred. A few years ago, the City of Santa Monica launched the world's first teleconferencing network operated by a municipal government. Called PEN, an acronym for

Public Electronic Network, its purpose was to link residents to City Hall.

All residents of the city were offered free use of PEN, where they could read city information, send messages to their representatives in City Hall, and join teleconferences to debate issues. To participate, they could either use a home computer or drop into a library or school and use one of PEN's 19 public terminals. This meant that, for the first time, all kinds of formerly disinterested or disenfranchised people had a chance to influence city government. And they did.

Online comments from homeless individuals spurred some PENners to form a PEN Action Group that met not only via computer, but also in person in a local library. When a few people with scraggly hair and shabby clothes showed up for one of these f2f meetings, they were recognized for the first time as the homeless whose cause the group had been championing. They had been so articulate online that most of the others had been unaware of, or had forgotten, their status.

The homeless people explained how lack of early-morning showers, access to clean clothing, and storage space for belongings was an obstacle to finding jobs. So the PEN Action Group developed a proposal called SHWASHLOCK—a system for providing SHowers, WASHers, and LOCKers for homeless people—that was later adopted by the Santa Monica City Council.

Network habitues are fond of comparing their online conferences to gatherings in a neighborhood café hangout. But unlike actual café conversations, you don't physically see your friends, rub elbows with them, or absorb the visual and tactile ambience of a favorite hangout.

In at least one major city, however, those who enjoy both online hangouts and the physical café variety can experience both at the same time. In certain coffee houses in and around San Francisco, you can plunk down your cappucino next to a tabletop terminal and log onto SFNet for a bull session or a foray into the Love Connection, a computerized personals column. In fact, SFNet has become such a conversation piece that people have met standing next to each other over the terminal.

Group support and group rituals are becoming as common in online communities as in families and neighborhood social circles.

Life passages from birth to marriage to death are celebrated together. One poignant event was The WELL's reaction to the news that one of its members had committed suicide. Before he killed himself in the "real" world, he had committed "virtual" suicide by erasing almost all his old WELL postings. After struggling with shock, denial, grief, and anger online, his fellow WELLites pulled together for a memorial service. Screenfuls of heartfelt comments and tributes poured in from all corners of the network. Networkers even managed to create a new file of the man's old postings, which had been saved on a backup disk.

Despite the many similarities between networks and traditional communities, it would be a dangerous mistake to assume that the two behave in exactly the same way. Take, for example, the lack of visual and aural cues in electronic interactions. On a network, we can get to know each other's minds and spirits without considering age, education, ability, race, physical appearance, or other potential barriers. But by the same token, we are vulnerable to deception, intentional or unintentional, and misperception. It's possible to build up a complex picture of another person in our mind and then have to do a lot of mental rewiring after an f2f meeting. A balding, rotund man can represent himself as a sex god—or even as a woman.

When we can't see facial expressions or body language and can't hear tone of voice, it's easy to misinterpret someone's words. It's also easy to go off on a tangent and sweep other communicators along. A pervasive issue is the typical communication glitch that can cause what network users refer to as "flaming": a rash of anger or general craziness (sparked by a miscommunication) that spreads through the conversation like wildfire.

Networkers have evolved several ways to mitigate misunderstandings. Online hosts or moderators for a particular conference keep track of conversations and try to nip communication problems in the bud. And, individuals take personal responsibility for making sure their communication is clear by using typed signals to amplify their words. For example, participants type "just kidding" or, abbreviated, "j/k." Network language includes a range of "emoticons," symbols composed of punctuation marks that indicate subtle emotions and body language and look like stylized faces turned on their sides. These include the smiley face :-), the wink ;-), and the frown):-(. Some users are careful to type "hmmm" to show that they have heard what another participant has just said and are considering their reply.

Like living organisms—and unlike our old notion of machines—network communities emerge spontaneously in response to diverse, intrinsic needs for connection—political, social, emotional, intellectual. Self-creating and self-regulating, they tend to spurn hierarchy, resist control, and expand amoeba-like in all directions, crossing physical borders and psychological boundaries.

Sometimes, to be sure, reliance on electronic communication can go too far, actually inhibiting community. Craig Brod tells the story about a newspaper journalist who called to interview him and ended up complaining about her own workplace. "They're making us use electronic mail," she said, "and now I can't even talk to Sally in person." "And where is Sally?" Craig wondered aloud. "Five desks from me," was the reply.

More encouraging is a 1991 RAND Corporation study of two groups of employees at the Los Angeles Department of Water and Power. Both groups were able to meet in person and talk on the phone, but one group also exchanged messages on an electronic network. That group, the study found, worked together more closely and became better friends than the other.

What does the future of electronic community look like? It's a moving picture. Certainly, as technology becomes cheaper and public access more widespread, the phenomenon will grow and become more powerful.

Electronic technology can turn people into machines and suck the lifeblood out of human interaction, but only if we forget that it's a tool rather than an end in itself.

Used with wisdom and compassion, computer networks help us adapt to the sometimes frightening new world that technology itself has helped to create.

From experienced networkers, here are a few suggestions for creating healthy online community:

- Don't be too intimidated by the technology; there are also people who are willing to help you.
- Be open and honest. Type in your phone number, a brief biography, and your full name even if these are not required.

- Be courteous and sensitive, and express yourself clearly so as not to be misinterpreted.
- Log on and participate regularly.
- For each conference you join, identify your host, moderator, and/or process observer. If there is none, suggest someone experienced in facilitation and conflict resolution.
- Remember that, although network communities save time by making your participation so convenient, it's easy to get hooked into spending hours a day online that might be better spent in face-to-face bonding. Don't read everything—learn how to select what interests you most—and don't waste time in frivolous online banter.
- Discuss your community's goals, ethics, liabilities, and communication style.
- Celebrate online and f2f. Connect by phone also.
- Keep asking, "What should we all be doing together?" "How can we link up with other communities (electronic and non-) to produce positive change?"

CHAPTER 22

Frances Fitzgerald

The Castro:
Building Community
in the Face of AIDS

"Don't worry," said [journalist] Armistead Maupin. "We're on gay time, so the parade won't have started yet."

He was right, of course. Rounding a corner, we came upon a line of stationary floats. The balloons were flying—the lavender, pink, and silver bouquets crowding the sky—and the bands were just warming up. People in costumes milled about amid a crowd of young men and women in blue jeans. The Gay Freedom Day Parade had not yet begun.

That summer—it was 1978—estimates of the gay population of San Francisco ranged from 75,000 to 150,000. If the oft-cited figure of 100,000 were correct, this meant that in this city of less than 700,000 people, approximately one out of every five adults and one out of every three or four voters was gay. A great proportion of these people—half of them or more—had moved into the city within the past eight years. And most of these new immigrants were young, white, and male. There were now some 90 gay bars in the city and perhaps 150 gay organizations including church groups, social services, and business associations. There were 9 gay newspapers, 2 foundations, and 3 Democratic clubs. While the gay men and women had settled all over the city, they had created an almost exclusive area of gay settlement in the Eureka Valley, in a neighborhood known as the Castro.

At first glance it was much like other neighborhoods: a four-block main street with a drugstore, corner groceries, a liquor store, dry cleaners, and a revival movie house whose facade had seen better days. Here and there upscale money was visibly at work: a café advertised Dungeness crab, a store sold expensive glass and tableware, and there were two banks. But there was nothing swish about the Castro. The main street ran off into quiet streets of two- and three-story white-shingle houses; the main haberdashery, The All-American Boy, sold clothes that would have suited a conservative Ivy Leaguer. In fact the neighborhood was like other neighborhoods except that on Saturdays and Sundays you could walk for blocks and see only young men dressed as it were for a hiking expedition. Also the bookstore was a gay bookstore, the health club a gay health club; and behind the shingles hung out on the street there was a gay real-estate brokerage, a gay lawyer's office, and the office of a gay psychiatrist. The bars were, with one exception, gay bars, and one of them, the Twin Peaks bar near Market Street, was, so Armistead told me, the first gay bar in the country to have picture windows on the street.

Armistead and his friends liked to take visitors to the Castro and point out landmarks such as the Twin Peaks. But in fact the only remarkable-looking thing on the street was the crowd of young men. Even at lunchtime on a weekday there would be dozens of good-looking young men crowding the café tables, hanging out at the bars, leaning against doorways, or walking down the streets with their arms around each other. The sexual tension was palpable. "I'd never live here," Armistead said. "Far too intense. You can't go to the laundromat at ten A.M. without the right pair of jeans on." The Castro was the place where most of the young gay men came. Fifty to a hundred thousand came as tourists each summer, and of these, thousands decided to settle, leaving Topeka and Omaha for good. New York and Los Angeles had their Polk Streets and Folsom Districts, but the Castro was unique: it was the first settlement built by gay liberation.

Gay liberation was, more than anything else, a move into consciousness. The movement "created" some homosexuals in that it permitted some people to discover their homosexual feelings and to express them. But its main effect was to bring large numbers of homosexuals out of the closet—and into the consciousness of others. Its secondary effect was to create a great wave of migration into the tolerant cities of the country. All the gay immigrants I talked to said that they had always known they were attracted to the same sex; their decision was not to become a homosexual but to live openly as one and in a gay community.

By the time our truck turned onto Market Street, I was in fact too late to see the head of the parade: the Gay American Indian contingent followed by Disabled Gay People and Friends, followed by a ninety-piece marching band and the gay political leaders of the city. But leaving my truck to walk along the sidelines where a crowd was now gathering, I was able to make my way up to number forty-one: the Gay Latino Alliance, or GALA, a group of young men dancing down the street to mariachi music. Just behind them was a group representing the gay Jewish synagogue. The Local Lesbian Association Kazoo Marching Band led a number of women's groups, including the San Francisco Women's Center, UC Berkeley Women's Studies, and Dykes on Bikes.

The 1978 Gay Freedom Day Parade marked the ninth anniversary of gay liberation. The event heralding its birth was a riot on Christopher Street in Greenwich Village, New York. On June 27, 1969, the New York City police raided the Stonewall Inn, a bar that catered to effeminate young street people and drag queens among others. Instead of acquiescing, the customers and onlookers fought back with beer bottles and paving stones. The scene was iconic, and as the rioting continued for a second night, there appeared graffiti on the walls and sidewalks announcing the birth of a revolutionary new movement. Extraordinarily, a movement came into being that summer and was an immediate success. In the first year it spread like wildfire across the campuses—from Columbia to Berkeley and Ann Arbor to colleges across the nation.

"We're the first generation to live openly as homosexuals," said Randy Shilts, who would later write *And the Band Played On.* "We have no role models. We have to find new ways to live."

In San Francisco these young men had not only changed their lives but they had found a community, a cause, and an intellectual endeavor all in one. The homophile leaders had been engaged in a civil rights struggle, but gay liberation had widened the task, for it, like feminism, offered a new perspective on the whole culture. The taboo against homosexuality went, after all, to the heart of it; to deny the taboo was therefore to throw into question the traditional family structure, traditional gender roles, and sexual mores.

Homosexuals had always been marginal to the culture—anomalies within it; thus, liberated homosexuals—that is, gay men and women—had, as they saw it, a privileged position from which to observe it. In changing their own lives they would provide a model for other gay men and women in the generations to come; in breaking sex and gender taboos they would change the whole society. Gay liberation was, of course, a national movement, and its theorists lived largely in New York, but what was a matter of theory elsewhere seemed a matter of imminent realization here. The Castro was, after all, the first gay settlement, the first true "gay community," and as such it was a laboratory for the movement.

To a great degree gay men—and to a lesser degree gay women—were building themselves a world apart from the rest of the city. Gay men, after all, could spend days, or an entire week, going to their offices, to the cleaner, the bank, and the health club, dining in restaurants, attending political meetings, and going to church without coming into contact with anyone who was not gay. While the density of gay institutions gave them a good deal of power and influence in the city, it also, paradoxically, had the effect of separating them from it. The gay community thus evolved according to its own logic and became more and more articulated and distinct. It now had not only its own political leaders but its own habits and customs and its own holidays: Gay Freedom Day, Halloween, and the Castro Street Fair. As for the Castro, it was a great hive where everyone knew everything that happened that day. To an outsider it seemed self-preoccupied and claustrophobic. Gay activists might argue among themselves, but they presented a united front to the outside world. In the Castro gay men even presented a uniform appearance.

Looking back, Randy Shilts felt that 1978 was the year when the Castro clone style reached an almost Platonic perfection. In the early seventies, the look had been unisex hippie: the green fatigues and the pea jackets snatched from military surplus stores and added, willy-nilly, to items found on the racks at the Salvation Army. Now "the Castroids," as they sometimes called themselves, were dressing with the care of Edwardian dandies—only the look was cowboy or bush pilot: tight blue jeans, preferably Levi's with button flies, plaid shirts, leather vests or bomber jackets, and boots.

Accessories included reflecting sunglasses and keys dangling from leather belts; in the hot weather there were muscle T-shirts. The counterculture style had been loose and flowing, concealing of gender differences; the new look was male to the point of what the psychologist C. A. Tripp called "gender-eccentricity." Short hair was now the style—very short hair cut far above the ears; mustaches were clipped, and there wasn't a beard or a ponytail to be seen anywhere. And the new gear was cut to show off bulging deltoids, slim hips, and rippling stomachs. The muscles seemed to belong to the uniform—as did the attitude. Men would swagger slightly walking down the street and watch each other from under lowered lids, a slightly hostile air about them. Bellied up to a bar, they would look around them with a studied casualness and with one foot on the rail, communicate with their neighbor in grunts. The look, Shilts wrote, was supermacho. . . .

That the whole bar and sex culture of the Castro might be harmful to gay men themselves was not at the time given any serious consideration in the gay community. And yet it clearly was unhealthy in many respects. "In the seventies you used to go into someone's refrigerator and see no food, only dope," one gay activist told me years later. The bar scene involved a great deal of alcohol and various sorts of drugs, including amyl nitrate, which was stressful to the heart. Alcoholism was prevalent—as were a good many sexually transmitted diseases. Syphilis and gonorrhea were epidemic in the Castro. Some gay leaders, including some of the bar owners, worried about the casualties from alcoholism—to the extent at least of raising money for treatment centers and outdoor activities. No one worried about the sexually transmitted diseases because they were curable. "Clap was a big joke," Shilts told me years later. "Going to the city clinic was part of the routine. There would be all this camaraderie, and people would tell each other how many times they'd been there."

Of all the epidemic diseases AIDS was in many respects the most terrible. In San Francisco, one of the cities where the disease was first noticed, there were 24 cases in December 1981, 61 cases six months later, and 118 cases the following December—and so on. Proportional to the population, the numbers advanced the most rapidly in the close-knit community of Castro. In March 1983 it was estimated that 1 out of every 333 gay men had AIDS; a year or so later, it was 1 out of 100. An epidemiological survey published in 1985 indicated that 37 percent of gay men in San Francisco had been exposed to the AIDS virus; the figure later climbed to over 50 percent. How many men would end up contracting the disease, no one could predict with any certainty, but AIDS researchers thought it possible that the Castro would be literally decimated in the course of the next decade: 1 out of 10 men would die. The gay carnival with its leather masks and ball gowns had thus been the twentieth-century equivalent of the Masque of the Red Death.

In fact the Castro had become something like the Algerian city of Oran that Albert Camus described in *The Plague*—a city separated from the outside world, where death and the threat of death hung over everyone. By 1984 there were few gay men who did not know someone, or know of someone, who had been struck by AIDS. Most of the victims were in their twenties, thirties, and forties—men in the prime of their lives. Very often they were athletic, ambitious, good-looking men who one day found a purple spot somewhere on their body. The purple spot was the nightmare that haunted the sleep of the Castro.

Quite early on in the epidemic it became clear that gay men could affect the course of the disease: they were responsible for their own lives and for those of others in a way that the citizens of Camus's city were not. The only certainty was statistical: if a sufficient number of gay men refrained from high-risk sex with new partners, then the spread of disease would abate. Thus, beyond the individual dramas going on in the Castro, there was also a collective moral drama which involved all of its inhabitants.

In the gay community the initial reaction had been one of incredulity. "A disease which killed only gay white men? It seemed unbelievable," one gay doctor told me, remembering the period. "I used to teach epidemiology, and I had never heard of a disease that selective. I thought, they are making this up. It can't be true. Or if there is such a disease, it must be the work of some government agency—the FBI or the CIA trying to kill us all."

It was impossible to think about AIDS without strong feelings, and in the face of disaster, communities, like emperors, have often preferred to blame messengers rather than to take responsibility— and action. But the form gay anger took still had to be explained. Jerry Berg [one of the founders of the Stonewall Gay Democratic

Club] had suggested an answer to this when I asked him about the impact of AIDS on the community. "Generally speaking," he said, "there was a lack of personal definition of what it meant to be gay. Those who think that what binds us together is sex and not broader human qualities are very threatened by the disease. To them AIDS looks like a great threat to everything gay." Gerry Parker [a downtown San Francisco lawyer and close associate of San Francisco Mayor Dianne Feinstein], for example, said: "The AIDS crisis has gotten people to come together and look at themselves in the mirror and ask critical questions about their lives. In the irresponsible seventies you used to see a lot of refrigerators with drugs in them but no food. Now people are concerned about health; there's a realization that we're all interdependent. People look for an inner purpose, and there's a lot of interest in Taoism and Buddhism. There was a time when we were cutting the edge of commercialism and fashion—that was a part of our being—but it's no longer true. Now we're into backpacking and wholesome relationships. The lesbian community is far ahead of us in many ways, particularly in its sense of cooperation and interdependence. There's a feminization process going on in the gay community now, and it's very healthy."

By April 1985, the looks of the Castro had changed once again. On a weekday morning or afternoon the people on the main street included numbers of older people and women with children. These people had not just moved into the area; rather, they had taken up doing their shopping and socializing on the main street again. The tourists had vanished, and with them a number of the most expensive gift stores and clothing boutiques. The Castro was a neighborhood once more. The gay bars were still there, and on Saturday mornings the street would fill up with young men. But now the only remarkable thing about these young men was their numbers. Very few—perhaps one or two in a crowd—wore leather or one of the other sexual costumes. Most looked like all other men of their age, and most were clearly doing Saturday errands, having been at work all week. The Castro was still a gay neighborhood, but it had lost its "gender eccentricities."

An era was over, and yet the Castro seemed much as it had been in the very old days when Armistead and his friends had thought of it as their stamping grounds and a small fraternity. It was now the pattern in the Castro for men, whether they were living with someone or not, to have a number of very close friends with whom they spent the holidays, in whom they could confide, and who would take care of them if necessary. This was the family the Castro had developed, and it was stable and domesticated. But then the people of the Castro had grown up together, and they had a great deal more in common now than the fact of being gay. Indeed, the people they had very little in common with were gay men in their twenties—for whom the clone style [was] as antiquated as high-button shoes. There was only ten years' difference between them, but when men of the Castro generation talked about the younger men, grumbling that they took "gay" for granted and were not pulling their weight, they sounded like codgers talking about the decline of the work ethic. Steve Beery, Armistead's friend, who himself did not look much more than thirty, told me his revelation about the generation gap. One day, when he was at home sick, he looked out on the steps and espied a beautiful young man taking a lunch break with his shirt off in the sun. The young man looked with great interest at Steve, so the next day when he came back at lunch hour and looked in Steve's direction again, Steve invited him up to the apartment. "I was thinking . . . well, you can imagine what I was thinking," Steve said. "But the guy just kept sitting there in the chair talking about one thing and another. As he was leaving, he asked me for a date. A date! I was shocked. He was, I gathered, looking for commitment. He was looking for a lifelong partnership."

5

THE DARK SIDE
OF COMMUNITY:
FACING AND
OVERCOMING
THE PITFALLS

*I say beware of all enterprises that require new
clothes, and not rather a new wearer of clothes. If
there is not a new man, how can the new clothes
be made to fit? If you have a new enterprise before
you, try it in your old clothes.*

HENRY DAVID THOREAU

*The only real alternative to hierarchy, submis-
sion, and unquestioning obedience is a passion
for freedom and a belief in the true community of
equals, one in which every member is acknowledged as a possible source for truth or meaning,
and in which truth and meaning are forever being
formed, never fully given—always opening up,
ahead, in the future, never fully attained.*

PETER MARIN

*One of the gravest indictments of our society is
that it has made deep and lasting friendships,
love affairs, and marriages so difficult to achieve.*

As social life becomes more and more warlike and barbaric, personal relations, which ostensibly provide relief from these conditions, take on the character of combat.

CHRISTOPHER LASCH

We cannot change the world alone. To heal ourselves, to restore the earth to life, to create the situations in which freedom can flourish, we must work together in groups. For a group to become a place of liberation, its structure and process must foster freedom. The ways in which we structure groups and perceive power determine what can happen in a group, how conflicts can be resolved, and how creative energies can be manifested.

STARHAWK

It was as a child that I first encountered the conflict between what I wanted to do with each moment of my life and the expectations that others had of what I "should" do. Because I was vulnerable and dependent upon those older and bigger, I tended to do what pleased them. This set up a powerful emotional conflict within me, which I sometimes responded to with frustration and anger and sometimes by pushing my personal desires aside.

This is how most of us cope with the tension between dependence and independence. Think of the "terrible twos," when our children begin to "act out" this conflict by energetically exploring their world and responding to adult supervision with the words "my," "me," "mine," and "No!" Later, in adolescence, we again act out in response to our repressed desires, often against our own wills. This is what contemporary psychologists call "shadow behavior." Once we've grown up, it shows up most often as exaggerated feelings about others ("How could he dare treat me that way?"), negative feedback from those close to us ("Why are you always late?"), impulsive or inadvertent behavior ("I'm not usually like this. I don't know why I said that."), or exaggerated anger about other people's shortcomings ("Look at the way that idiot is driving!").

These manifestations are mild compared to the shadow behavior we see reflected in the news. Author and editor Connie Zweig and psychotherapist Jeremiah Abrams, in their anthology

Meeting the Shadow: The Hidden Power of the Dark Side of Human Nature, give us a vivid image of the shadow's pervasiveness: "It shouts from newsstand headlines; it wanders our streets, sleeping in the doorways, homeless; it squats in X-rated neon-lit shops on the peripheries of our cities; it embezzles our monies from the local savings and loan; it corrupts power-hungry politicians and perverts our system of justice; it drives invading armies through dense jungles and across desert sands; it sells arms to mad leaders and gives the profits to reactionary insurgents; it pours pollution through hidden pipes into our rivers and oceans, and poisons our food with invisible pesticides."

Anger, paranoia, greed, deception, and the abuse of power all rise up from our repressed shadow side. And if that weren't enough cause for concern, our personal shadows can join together in a collective shadow, which can masquerade as the "chosen people" and attempt to make everyone else conform to rigid beliefs about what is right and wrong, repressing and abusing those who are different. The behavior of this collective shadow can lead to scapegoating and war.

Communities as large as whole countries or as small as a single church can be affected by the shadow. The Muslim fundamentalists of Iran and the Christian militants of Serbia leap to mind, as do the massacred members of Jim Jones' Peoples Temple. Other examples include the disenfranchised devotees of Indian guru Bhagwan Shree Rajneesh, the lock-step disciples of Sun Yung Moon, or the millions of followers of the "one true way" of the multitude of television evangelists. And religion is not the only organizing force. In the political arena the effects are equally noticeable, from the German Nazis and the Italian fascists of World War II to the intolerance and racism of the political movements behind George Wallace or Pat Buchanan. More recently, a minority of religious fundamentalists and political conservatives who temporarily captured control of the Republican Party created the national platform of 1992. There hasn't been a clearer example of the "chosen people" attempting to force conformity to their values since the brownshirts came to power in Germany prior to World War II.

In its more benign manifestations, the collective shadow is most commonly exhibited as mindless conformity. Many communities exist today in which members conform to the expectations of the group, rather than taking the inner journey of self-discovery, including the recognition and reowning of the shadow, which could make them much better contributors to the common good. Fears and superstitions keep us locked into acceptance of standards of behavior that are determined by someone else.

When your community determines your personal identity without allowing you the opportunity for self-discovery, it not only inhibits your individual potential but also reduces the likelihood that the community will survive for very long. And it doesn't offer much of a positive contribution to the world either. True community is made up of true individuals, people who have done the hard work of looking inward and growing from the experience.

Many people feel safe only when they are with those who appear to be like them. Fear of the new or different causes them to cluster together with others whose appearance and actions fall within narrow, subjective boundaries of what is acceptable. This behavior is probably a remnant of an evolutionary strategy that ensured the safety of the species by causing individuals to avoid others who might be potentially threatening to their survival. But most of us have evolved beyond the need for this precaution. The differences between one race and another are insignificant compared to the differences between two species.

However, when we exaggerate our differences and perceive those who are different from us as a threat, we take the first step in creating the Other. A belief in the Other is a belief in "them or us." It is an experience of separateness, of being alone in the world. It ignores the contrary evidence that we are inseparably related to all of nature and to each other. If we allow ourselves to indulge in these perceptions of fear and danger, we can never live in peace and harmony. In chapter 23, *The Other: Community's Shadow*, Charlene Spretnak describes the effect of this most common manifestation of the collective shadow.

The Other is also at work when you say one thing while thinking something else (a subtle form of submission) or when you repeatedly interrupt someone to get your own opinion across (a not so subtle form of domination). When a man's advice is taken with more credence than the same advice from a woman, we see sexism in action, part of the cultural shadow that devalues women's authority. These patterns of power have so permeated our culture that it is not easy to escape them. We need to recognize these patterns and be willing and able to talk about them if we want to build communities that endure. In chapter 24, *Domination and Submission: The Subjective Side of Power,* ecofeminists and educators Margo Adair and Sharon Howell point out what it takes to understand and overcome our powerful cultural patterns of domination and submission, a process they believe is necessary if we are to build communities that are life-affirming.

There is a widespread tendency to label any group of people living or working in a way different from the norm as a "cult." But this is an oversimplified, reactionary stance. In Chapter 25, *The Cult: A Mirror of the Times,* psychiatrist Arthur Deikman gives us a more in-depth look at what cults are and how they can act as a mirror to reflect our assumptions about what is normal. As Deikman points out, people who join cults are very much like the rest of us. "They have two kinds of wishes. They want a meaningful life, to serve God or humanity; and they want to be taken care of, to feel protected and secure, to find a home." When we understand that others are not really much different from us, we understand that Socrates was right: We must know ourselves, especially our shadow selves, if we want to overcome the dangers of cult behavior, and build communities that enrich, rather than harm, their members.

The single best indicator of when a community has become a cult is the presence or absence of blind obedience by student or follower to the teacher or leader. There are many other valuable indicators and in chapter 26, *On Cults and Organizations,* you will find a simple "consumer checklist" to help you evaluate a group or community that you want to join to see just how cult-like it really is.

Finally, in a story of horror, stranger than fiction, we see what can happen when the individuals of a community give up personal responsibility to a charismatic leader. Chapter 27 is made up of excerpts from journalist Tim Cahill's classic piece in *Rolling Stone* magazine, in which he describes the most terrifying example of the horror and power of the collective shadow that society has known in modern times, the Jonestown massacre.

CHAPTER 23

Charlene Spretnak

The Other:
Community's Shadow

All being on our planetary home is descended from the supernova that gave birth to our solar system. The birth date of our particular species, the evolutionary "moment" at which we differentiated our being from that of other primates, is unclear. Paleoanthropologists believe we became human about 5 million years ago, spreading out from Africa more than a million years ago. A group of biochemists, however, have deduced from studies of mitochondrial DNA, which is passed only from mothers to offspring, that all humans now living are descended from one womb, from a woman who lived in Africa about two hundred thousand years ago. Their findings are known as "the Eve hypothesis." Whether or not the entire human family is literally one clan, the fact of our amazing diversity (no two faces exactly alike, except for identical twins, out of 5.3 billion manifestations!) can mask our internal relatedness.

The inflated "I" becomes the informing reality, while that which lies beyond the self is perceived to be less than fully real. For the narcissistic "I," the only valued collective is the tightly proscribed "we." People outside the "we" group are seen as deserving of less concern, or no concern at all, being merely "the Other."

Why, in a society where there is so much suffering, where 5 million children under age six, the most vulnerable Other, live in poverty, is it not a matter of shame to have far more money than a person or family could possibly need? Since abusing the environment (nature as the Other, posterity as the Other) has gradually come to be perceived as shameful behavior, is it too wildly unrealistic to expect that harmful hoarding might come to be regarded as a rending of communion? Only in a culture desperately estranged from its own depth of being could maximizing one's income be embraced by so many people as the major goal in life. One of the brokers convicted in the insider-trading scandals on Wall Street in the late eighties, Dennis Levine, recalled the teaching of his favorite business professor: "Greed is a nice religion. If you are greedy, you are going to keep your shoes polished, you won't run around on your wife or get drunk. You will do whatever it takes to maximize your lifetime income, and that doesn't leave time for messing up."[1] In the drive to keep on increasing one's assets far beyond what is needed to fulfill reasonable desires of living comfortably, having enough retirement income and medical coverage for old age, and leaving some money to one's children, the magic number identifying one's financial net worth becomes a label of one's personal worth for all those "major players" who simply cannot bear to stop playing.

While it is true that some wealthy individuals give generously to charities and other worthy causes, the ideal of sharing, of caring deeply for community, has little place in an atomized culture. Since various studies indicate that the richest 1 percent of American families own between 28 and 40 percent of the net worth owned by all American families, is not a sharply graduated income tax necessary to adjust the extreme maldistribution? Such tax revenue could be used to restructure the economy by building up community-based economics, providing training and seed grants for ecologically sound worker-owned businesses of appropriate scale that serve a regional market. Even in a community-based economy with no banks (replaced by non-profit, county-level credit unions), however, the kind of callous attitude expressed in instructions to employees selling junk bonds in Charles Keating's now-defunct Lincoln Savings and Loan—"Remember the weak, meek, and ignorant are always good targets"[2]—would still be with us unless we can cultivate awareness of the communion inherent in community. Structural change alone cannot save us from estrangement.

During the past decade we have seen just how tenuous a sense of community is when it is based only on proscriptions against base behavior as understood in the social contract. Once the tone of sacrificial community went out from the highest levels of government, minorities and women gradually became targets of harassment and attack with increasing frequency. By the closing years of the decade college students, who had come of age during the Reagan years, widely used racial and ethnic slurs and cheered comedians who expressed contemptuous, degrading views of women, people of color, gays, and the disabled. White supremacist groups are now a presence even in many of our high schools. As of this writing, the incidents of harassment are increasing, and history shows us that frenzied hatred of the Other, once cultivated, does not necessarily dissipate when employment levels rise again.

Perceiving differentiation while failing to perceive communion can be a deadly error for a society. When there is seemingly nothing but difference, everyone outside one's group is alien, odd, and of lesser value. College students today "are separating themselves in unhealthy ways" as old prejudices deepen, according to a report issued in 1990 by the Carnegie Foundation for the Advancement of Teaching, "Campus Life: In Search of Community." I suspect we are witnessing the effects not only of adult-induced bigotry, but of the breakdown of various community institutions that used to mix up various groups of children in pleasant situations. Some of the happiest memories of my youth are from the portions of eleven summers spent at a Camp Fire Girls camp in the Appalachian foothills of southern Ohio that drew girls from every part of Columbus. Many of the girls were from families who could not afford the $25-per-week fee. They were there on "camperships," but no one, not even the counselors, knew who they were, as that was all taken care of by the countywide office. Nature's bounty and a challenging, loving program revealed to us the dynamics of differentiation, subjectivity, and communion among ourselves in ways that we made our own. Today, however, the opportunity for such formative experiences is dwindling. Around the country, much of the middle class, who provided the base of financial support for such programs, has pulled out of Scouting and Camp Fire in favor of tennis camps and the like. My own camp's annual season has been reduced to only a few weeks, and the Fourth of July parade in my hometown suburb, which used to feature four Camp Fire floats plus a couple each from the Girl Scouts and Boy Scouts, now often has not a single one. (Even worse, military planes buzzing over the parade route have been added. A telling, if disheartening, swap.)

The after-school and weekend youth programs existed because certain adults, usually mothers, had the time and caring inclination to help children develop their unique potentials. In most families today both parents must hold jobs, as must nearly all single parents. In addition, the real purchasing power of many family incomes is less now than it was twenty years ago, so parents are stretched thin. The "extra" time available for community commitments is largely gone. Professional programs to fill the gap have often proven unsatisfactory, but indictments of such efforts sometimes embrace nostalgic yearning without acknowledging the labor that traditionally sustained community. For example, several years ago I listened to a lecture by a "hip" professor of public policy who mocked the idiocy of a hypothetical young woman who had trained in college to be a "bereavement counselor" and had set up shop in a small town to aid the community in psychologically helpful modes of grieving for their dead. His theme was that community functions are being devalued and pushed aside by the new helping professions and that we were better off with the old ways. The first of the invited respondents to his lecture, the feminist author Elizabeth Dodson Gray, walked up to the microphone, looked out over the audience, and asked in stately tones, "How many men . . . in this hall . . . have ever made a casserole . . . and taken it . . . to a grieving family?"

Expecting a rich community life to flourish once again through women's now taking on the equivalent of three jobs—employment outside the home, most of the housework and child-rearing, and nearly all the caring work to nurture community bonds—is neither a realistic nor appealing vision. Perhaps the thirty-five-hour workweek, recently won by some major unions in Germany, will be widely adopted in time. Jobsharing is also making more part-time work available for those who can afford the reduction. The additional free time, along with a perception—on the part of both sexes—of labor as a gift to one's community, could fuel the growth of community-run food co-ops, service-trade networks, child care, youth programs, senior programs, literacy programs, and so forth.

The fragmentation and weakening of community by economics and bureaucracy has proven damaging but not irreversible. Among the most ambitious attempts to restore community today are several "beyond development" efforts in the Third World in which people focus on their community needs, often drawing from precolonial cultural constructions to restructure the social dynamics, with economics reduced to a support service. They insist they are not "doing community-based economics"; they are "doing community."

An Italian priest, Prosperino Gallipolli, who has worked with rural co-ops in Mozambique for more than thirty years, explains, "The economic part is only a way to help people gain self-esteem. Underdevelopment is a spiritual problem; it's a lack of active, critical thinking, initiative, self-confidence. People here still have complexes left over from colonial days."[3] The diminishment of the person in every disadvantaged community in the world is violence against the sacred. Differentiation is scorned rather than celebrated; everyone must try to look and act like the oppressor group. Communion between the oppressed and oppressors is profoundly denied. Social justice, then, restores the possibility for fundamental life processes to flourish.

The process itself can yield joy ("subversive joy," as Cornel West has suggested) and graced communion. Yet a sense of spiritual hunger sometimes dogs activists in church-based social-change projects. Jim Wallis, editor of *Sojourners* magazine and an activist minister, suggests that "works righteousness" arises whenever one mistakes actions for grace or whenever "Christian ministry or leftist ideology" use the poor "to make capital out of their suffering," rather than desiring to be their friend.[4] He believes that grace helps us overcome the temptation to believe we are better than those who need convincing and converting: "The marks of grace are gentleness, hope, and faith. The most dependable sign of its presence is joy."[5]

No matter what spiritual path one prefers, the core teachings of the Semitic traditions remind us that our spirituality is always tested: If you allow injustice, you fail to grasp the depth of communion. If you cannot honor and cherish the face of ultimate mystery in every being, your sense of the sacred is a pale imitation. If you deny interrelatedness and mutual humanity with people considered the Other, you have detached yourself from communion. To know—deeply know—the nature of the sacred web of life is to live a life of cosmological integrity.

CHAPTER 24

Margo Adair and Sharon Howell

Domination and Submission: The Subjective Side of Power

Nobody talks about power. Those who have it spend a great deal of effort keeping it hidden. Those who don't rarely risk raising the issue.

Power is the ability to do what one chooses—the more power one has, the more options one has. Those without power are led to believe this is a personal failing; those with it come to consider it a sign of personal success.

Instead of talking about power, we have learned to talk in terms of "freedom": the right of an individual to do what s/he chooses. This emphasis on individual freedom obscures the power arrangements. It hides the fact that the options available to some are made possible only at the expense of others and of the earth. It is no wonder that freedom is the only word we hear. Naming power is taboo. *To raise the question of power is to threaten the freedom of those who have it.*

We live in a culture in which the measuring stick for normalcy is defined as white, male, Protestant, middle-class, heterosexual, able-bodied, and serious. The narrowness of this measure leaves most of us feeling that we never quite belong. We must prove we are just as good as the white, male, Protestant, middle-class, heterosexual, able-bodied, serious person in order to be considered competent. We have to trivialize or hide the particular aspects of who we are that don't fit the mold. "Passing," usually thought of in terms of blacks pretending to be whites, is something we all do to have access to privilege. The price we pay is the fragmentation of ourselves.

Because mass culture devalues and marginalizes the lives and experiences of everyone except those who fit the "norm," claiming the power to define oneself is the beginning of liberation. This involves acknowledging all the different aspects of who we are, the ways in which each of us has experienced both privilege and oppression. For example, a gay, white, working-class man experiences privilege by virtue of being white and male, *as well as* oppression by virtue of being gay and working-class. Privilege on one power axis does not negate oppression on another.

The Dual Reality

The force necessary to maintain power is not acknowledged. But power means control of physical survival—income, jobs, homes, education, food . . . When acting alone, people dependent upon those in power cannot afford to alienate those in power. Therefore, the exploited, dehumanized, trivialized, and dispossessed are forced to live hypocritically—thinking one thing and saying another.

Everyone has experienced this dual reality in the workplace when they say or do what they need to for the boss, despite what they are thinking. If they were to say what they thought, it would only get them in trouble. This gives rise to a dual reality which creates the subjective climate that holds power in place: the visible one for which there is supposedly a social consensus, and the invisible one, which is the experience of those who, in any given situation, are locked out.

Only by making all realities visible can we break the imposed consensus. The narrow, dehumanizing context is transformed. For instance, at the workplace, if people begin a conversation about their families—which are assumed to be heterosexual—and a lesbian is present, she will be identifying with her inner thoughts rather than the sanctioned view of reality. So to change the power dynamics, the invisible lesbian experience must be acknowledged.

Our willingness to grapple with different experiences enables us to create a common context for relationships and true community.

People in the dominated group have always had to know more about the dominators than those at the top have had to know about the experiences of those at the bottom. For example, it is not uncommon to hear progressive people talk about Native Americans in the past tense, as if their cultures no longer existed. Nor is it uncommon to watch a differently-abled person treated as if s/he were incapable of any independent activity. When we are in a dominant group we need to become aware of the assumptions we have that result from our socialization and privilege.

When experiences kept from view are addressed, people are no longer forced to deny themselves. We no longer have to choose between self and other. Experiences, no longer invisible, become part of what everyone grapples with and not just "their problem." The boundaries of the situation expand, our humanity is enriched, and the basic assumptions of the power structure have to be re-examined. Naming power begins our process of reclaiming it.

Patterns of Power

Frequently, the behavior we aspire to, the most accepted and normal in our society, is that of the dominators. They are our most visible role models. Even those of us who have lived with enforced submission find ourselves capable of dominating others. Oppression does not make us immune from hurting others. All too often, it serves as a lesson in how to behave once we get whatever power we can. The following are generic patterns which apply to any situation of domination and submission. The hierarchical and competitive nature of our society gives everyone plenty of opportunities to experience both sides.

Behavioral Patterns that Perpetuate Relations of Domination

Individual of the Dominant Group

Projects an aura of authority.

Defines parameters, judges what is appropriate, patronizes.

When in disagreement with status quo is seen as, and feels, capable of making constructive changes.

Assumes responsibility for keeping system on course. Acts unilaterally.

Self-image of superiority, competence, in control, entitled, correct.

Views self as logical, rational. Sees others as too emotional, out of control.

Disdains nature.

Believes certain kinds of work below their dignity.

Presumptuous, does not listen, interrupts, raise voice, bullies, threatens violence, becomes violent.

Seeks to stand out as special.

Assumes anything is possible, can do whatever s/he wants as an individual, assumes everyone else can too.

Individual of the Oppressed Group

Projects an aura of subservience.

Feels inappropriate, awkward, doesn't trust own perception, looks to expert for definition.

When in disagreement with status quo, is seen as, and feels, disruptive.

Blames self for not having capacity to change situation.

Self-image of inferiority, incompetent, being controlled, not entitled, low self-esteem.

Often thinks of own feelings as inappropriate and a sign of inadequacy.

Disdains own nature.

Believes certain kinds of work beyond their ability.

Finds it difficult to speak up, timid, tries to please. Holds back anger, resentment, rage.

Feels more secure in background, doesn't want to betray peers, feels vulnerable when singled out.

Feels confined by circumstance, limits aspirations.

In whatever ways we have access to privilege, we have been carefully socialized to accept, protect, and maintain it. In whatever ways we are likely to be oppressed, we are socialized to accept it, protect ourselves and one another. This patterning is why we duplicate the very relations we are trying to transform. As we become aware of the impact of domination on ourselves and others, we are appalled by how we have somehow participated in its perpetuation and how much it permeates our every interaction from the intimate to the occasional.

Precisely because these patterns are so deep within us, the process of identifying them creates tremendous anxiety. The question is not whether we behave based on these patterns—we all do. The issue is our willingness to change them. Altering either side forces change on the other. Power exists as a relationship. Changing our own tendencies toward domination or submission cultivates a context of trust and cooperation that includes everyone's contribution.

The process of breaking out of these patterns necessitates reflecting on how they apply in our own lives by asking such questions as:

- Is the humanity, intelligence, sensitivity, and contribution of each person respected?
- Am I taking up more or less time than others?
- Do I interrupt others?
- Do I censor myself?
- Is information available to everyone?
- Are people dismissed for making mistakes or supported in changing?
- Are differences minimized or is pride encouraged in each of our ethnicities and struggles?
- Are decisions about the use of resources shared?
- Is there an awareness of the differences in our access to resources?
- Is there a generosity of spirit or are guilt and blame operating?

Healing in a Troubled Time

Replacing the unconscious and silent assumptions that have governed our relationships for so long with new principles of respect, accountability, and harmony must become the core of our efforts to create change collectively. Evaluating whose interests are being served, and whether or not we are moving away from domination and control should be the basis of decisions.

Because behavior patterns that perpetuate the status quo are so deeply ingrained in us, it is inevitable that we'll feel awkward, inappropriate and disruptive when we raise questions of power. To do so necessarily means breaking the power taboo and making the struggles visible. Though it may make us uncomfortable, this process will profoundly alter the context of our interactions. Trust begins to emerge, blame and guilt dissolve, it becomes possible to create an atmosphere where everyone is important.

In our efforts to build new ways of living together, we'll make mistakes with one another. Our challenge is to create contexts where we can support each other to change. When we listen, share and respect diversity, we create an expansive atmosphere, one in which we can honestly express what we are experiencing and make principled decisions.

By breaking the power taboo and naming the power dynamics that are operating, bringing the invisible realities to the surface, by reclaiming our heritages and our integrity, and by placing principles in the center of our relationships, we can build new ties and ways of being together that heal us and reestablish communities that are once again sustained by the sanctity of life.

CHAPTER 25

Arthur Deikman

The Cult:
A Mirror of the Times

A few years ago I took part in a research seminar on new religious movements, the religious and utopian groups which sprang up in the sixties and seventies and made the term *cult* familiar to all newspaper readers.

In reading about cults, most of us in the seminar felt repulsion and fear, but also fascination. Cults present us with images of surrender, violence, sex, and power. We respond to them with avid interest because they speak to unconscious wishes. Moreover, we can watch at a seemingly safe distance because the cults of which we are aware usually have foreign trappings or unusual social structures that separate them from ordinary society and from ourselves. Without such markings, however, cult behavior is not usually recognized, especially when this behavior is our own.

Former cult members were interviewed by the seminar research group. We talked first with a man and a woman who had escaped from the Peoples Temple camp in Guyana on the morning of the mass suicide. These witnesses were not college graduates, nor were most members of the Peoples Temple. At subsequent meetings we interviewed a married couple who had belonged to quite a different cult, one whose members were highly educated, possessing graduate degrees in psychology or related fields. (They had worked as psychotherapists and teachers, just as we in the seminar did.) After that, people spoke who had been members of a utopian rehabilitation group for ex-convicts and, still later, we heard from members and ex-members of several other new religions.

The variety of personalities involved, of differing racial, economic, religious, educational, and social backgrounds, was impressive. What was most striking was that no matter whom we interviewed, the stories of involvement in exploitive, harmful cults were similar. A distinct pattern of seduction, coercion, corruption and regression emerged, no matter what the outward trappings, no matter what dogma or purpose the group espoused. Basic human responses had been elicited by a process fundamentally the same.

The Cult Story

At the time they joined their particular cult, most of the people we interviewed had been dissatisfied, distressed, or at a transition point in their lives. Typically, they desired a more spiritual life, a community in which to live cooperatively; they wanted to become enlightened, to find meaning in serving others, or simply to belong. An encounter with an enthusiastic, attractive, friendly person served to introduce each of them to a group whose outer appearance was quite benign. At some point during that introductory phase an intense experience took place which was interpreted as validating the claim that the leader and the group were special, powerful, spiritual; that they could give the person what he or she wanted. This experience might have been an altered state of consciousness (induced by the leader of the group via meditation, chanting, or the laying on of hands), a powerful therapeutic experience, or just a wonderful feeling of being accepted and welcomed—of "coming home."

Won over, the newcomer joined the group, embracing its doctrines and practices. Soon the cult's demands increased and the new member was asked to devote increasing amounts of time, money, and energy to the group's activities. These demands were justified as necessary to fulfill the group's goals; willingness to comply was always interpreted as a measure of the recruit's commitment and sincerity. In order to continue, most did comply, sacrificing much for the sake of the stated high purposes of the group (often put in terms of saving the world).

Relationships outside the group became difficult to maintain. The former life of the new member was given up; contact with outsiders was discouraged and the demands of the new life left little opportunity for extra-group activities. However, the sacrifices were compensated for by the convert's sense of belonging and purpose. The group and the leader (at least initially) gave praise and acceptance.

Gradually, however, an iron fist was felt. Deviation from group dogma brought swift disapproval or outright rejection. The message to the convert became clear: what the group had given the group could take away. In time, he or she submitted to—and participated in—cruel, dishonest, and contradictory practices out of fear of the leader and the group, who by then had become the convert's sole source of self-esteem, comfort, and even financial support. Actions that conflicted with the convert's conscience were rationalized by various formulas provided by the leader. (For example, in one group lying to potential converts was explained as "divine deception" for the good of those deceived.) Critical evaluation of the leader and the group became almost impossible, not only because it was punished severely, but also because the view of reality presented by the cult had no challengers. Discordant information was excluded from the group's world.

Exploitation intensified and the recruit regressed into a fearful submission. Couples might be separated; members would inform on each other. Morals were corrupted and critical thinking suppressed. Often the group's leader deteriorated as well, becoming increasingly grandiose, paranoid, or bizarre. In most cases, paranoid thinking tended to mark the entire cult and reinforced the group's isolation.

Our witnesses told of how, eventually, the demands became unbearable; a mother might be told to give up her child or her husband, or a spouse directed to take a different sexual partner. Although often the person would agree to the new requirement, sometimes he or she would not. In such cases, when the member finally refused to comply with the leader or the group's demands, he or she left precipitously, often assisted by a person outside with whom some contact and trust had been maintained.

It was not uncommon for ex-converts to fear that they had been damned or had lost their souls as a consequence of leaving the group. (In some cases former members were convinced the group would hunt them down and kill them.) Many went through months of struggle to re-establish their lives, wrestling with the questions How could I have been involved in such a thing? How could I have done what I did to other members of the group? Were my spiritual longings all false? Who and what can I trust? At the same time, the closeness the group offered was often sorely missed, and until the ex-member's life was reconstituted, he or she wondered at times if leaving the group had been a mistake. This turmoil gradually diminished, but for many a sense of shame for having participated in the cult and a frustrated rage at having been betrayed lingered for a long time.

———•———

After listening to many variants of this story, I began to see that cults form and thrive not because people are crazy, but because they have two kinds of wishes. They want a meaningful life, to serve God or humanity; and they want to be taken care of, to feel protected and secure, to find a home. The first motives may be laudable and constructive, but the latter exert a corrupting effect, enabling cult leaders to elicit behavior directly opposite to the idealistic vision with which members entered the group.

Usually, in psychiatry and psychology, the wish to be taken care of (to find a home, a parent) is called *dependency* and this is a rather damning label when applied to adults. We are supposed to be autonomous, self-sustaining, with the capacity to go it alone. We do recognize that adults need each other for emotional support, for giving and receiving affection, for validation; that is acceptable and sanctioned. But underlying such mature *inter*dependency is the longing of the child, a yearning that is never completely outgrown. This covert dependency—the wish to have parents and the parallel wish to be loved, admired, and sheltered by one's group—continues throughout life in everyone. These wishes generate a hidden fantasy or dream that can transform a leader into a strong, wise, protective parent and a group into a close, accepting family. Within that dream we feel secure.

Eventually, we in the seminar were unable to maintain the belief that cults were something apart from normal society. The people telling us stories of violence, cruelty, and perversion of values were like ourselves. After listening and questioning we realized that we were not different from nor superior to the ex-cult members, that we were vulnerable to the same dependency wishes, capable of the same betrayals and cruelty in circumstances in which our sense of reality was manipulated.

When the seminar began I viewed cults as pathological entities alien to my everyday life. By the time it ended, I realized that the dynamics of cult behavior and thinking are so pervasive in normal society that almost all of us might be seen as members of invisible cults. In fact, as I will argue, society can be viewed as an association of informal cults to which everyone belongs. Yet the groups most of us belong to do not appear strange, flamboyant, esoteric, or unnatural, nor do they defy society with lurid and violent behavior. Social infrastructures and behaviors that are similar to those of the People's Temple go unnoticed.

Surely, the reader may ask, while it is true that serious consequences result from membership in extreme cults, how can you say harm comes from the groups that make up normal society? I certainly don't recognize such effects in groups to which I belong. I am indeed talking about normal society, in which the damage resulting from cult-like behavior is not as obvious as that headlined in the newspapers. Our own cult story is much less pronounced, with no noticeable beginning and no end; our perceptions, beliefs, and critical judgments are affected nonetheless.

We Americans live in a constitutional democracy, priding ourselves on the freedoms we have achieved. We live, travel and work without internal passports; we have free choice of job or profession; we may hold any belief and, within wide limits, do anything, say anything, write anything, and protest anything. We choose our governing officials from a list we have ourselves determined.

Democracy is based on an "eye-level" world in which we look directly at each other; every citizen is a peer. Political power is delegated, not inherited, not taken, not given by divine right, but bestowed by each of us. However, I believe that a danger exists even in democracies that the omnipresent authoritarian impulse will manifest itself in disguised form, will lead us toward a world in which we are always looking up at those who must be obeyed or down at those who must obey us. This is so because authoritarianism draws its strength from the same source that supports cult behavior: dependency on groups and leaders.

I believe that we need to bring into awareness the unconscious motivations and excluded information that influence our behavior and thought at the personal, national, and international levels. This requires that we first understand the dynamics of obvious cults and then address similar processes in ourselves and in ordinary society. Such understanding can provide us with tools for detecting cult behavior—our own as well as that of others—and enable us to step outside the cult circle.

Although it is important that we know about cults to avoid being caught in them, it is even more important that we study such groups to become aware of the hidden cult thinking operating unnoticed in our daily lives. Cults are mirrors of ourselves.

CHAPTER 26

*Rick Fields, Peggy Taylor, Rex Weyler,
and Rich Ingrasci*

On Cults
and Organizations

In *The Observing Self,* an eminently reasonable book about psychotherapy and mysticism, Dr. Arthur Deikman writes:

> It is important to recognize that cults and religious organizations of various kinds do perform important functions for their members. They satisfy members' needs for acceptance and protection, and often provide members with a disciplined, healthy routine of balanced living, good diet, and exercise. By also providing security, firm direction, and a controlled community life, they can have a psychotherapeutic effect, reducing anxiety and teaching more adaptive behavior. The group's dogma can provide a framework of meaning and hope absent in the lives of many of its members prior to joining. At the least, such groups provide distraction, entertainment, and social opportunities. The worst offer group and parental security at the price of destructive regression.

There are, however, certain criteria we can use as guidelines while investigating the wares in the "spiritual supermarket." Daniel Goleman, human behavior editor of the *New York Times* and the author of *Varieties of Meditative Experience,* suggests we should "be wary" of:

Taboo Topics: questions that can't be asked, doubts that can't be shared, misgivings that can't be voiced. For example, "Where does all the money go?" or "Does Yogi sleep with his secretary?"

Secrets: the suppression of information, usually tightly guarded by an inner circle. For example, the answers "Swiss bank accounts," or "Yes, he does—and that's why she had an abortion."

Spiritual Clones: in its minor form, stereotypic behavior, such as people who walk, talk, smoke, eat and dress just like their leader; in its more sinister form, psychological stereotyping, such as an entire group of people who manifest only a narrow range of feeling in any and all situations: always happy, or pious, or reduce everything to a single explanation, or sardonic, etc.

Groupthink: a party line that overrides how people actually feel. Typically the cognitive glue that binds the group; e.g., "You're fallen, and Christ is the answer" or "You're lost in *samsara*, and Buddha is the answer" or "You're impure, and Shiva is the answer."

The Elect: a shared delusion of grandeur that there is no Way but this one. The corollary: you're lost if you leave the group.

No Graduates: members are never weaned from the group. Often accompanies the corollary above.

Assembly Lines: everyone is treated identically, no matter what their differences; e.g., mantras assigned by dictates of a demographical checklist.

Loyalty Tests: members are asked to prove loyalty to the group by doing something that violates their personal ethics; for example, set up an organization that has a hidden agenda of recruiting others into the group, but publicly represents itself as a public service outfit.

Duplicity: the group's public face misrepresents its true nature, as in the example just given.

Unifocal Understanding: a single world-view is used to explain anything and everything; alternate explanations are verboten. For example, if you have diarrhea it's "Guru's

Grace." If it stops, it's also Guru's Grace. And if you get constipated, it's still Guru's Grace.

Humorlessness: no irreverence allowed. Laughing at sacred cows is good for your health. Take, for example, Gurdjieff's one-liner, "If you want to lose your faith, make friends with a priest."

CHAPTER 27

Tim Cahill

Jonestown: In the Valley of the Shadow of Death

Odell Rhodes is a soft-spoken, articulate thirty-six-year-old, an eyewitness to the first twenty minutes of the massacre at Jonestown. Odell had been a junkie for ten years. He'd been through two drug-treatment programs and both times he had gone back to drugs and some sleazy hustle on the street.

When the Peoples Temple buses came through Detroit, an alcoholic friend decided to join. The next time they came through, the friend looked up Odell. The friend was dry, sharp, well dressed. "He looked like a successful businessman," Odell said. And Odell, who had failed twice trying to kick his habit, decided to check out the temple.

Jim Jones, he said, gave him a new self-image. He was intelligent. He was useful. Odell was given a job in the San Francisco temple.

When Odell first arrived in Guyana, things seemed fine. His job was teaching crafts to children, and he was good at it. "I really loved those kids," he told me.

———•———

It was a massive job, loading up all the corpses at Jonestown, and it took eight full days. On the ninth day, the government allowed about fifty news ghouls into the jungle enclave.

We were shown a bakeshop, a machine shop, a brick-making area. We noted packets of a Kool-Aid-like drink called Fla•vor•aid lying around. The illustration showed two children sipping Fla•vor-•aid and smiling happily.

Across from the rise where the helicopter landed were forty or so cottages, painted in pleasant pastels. A guard tower stood above the cottages. Strangely, it wasn't near the roads in and out of Jonestown, but was directly over the area where most of the people lived. Someone had painted several bright seascapes on the tower, so that it appeared to be contradiction of itself, like a .357 Magnum disguised as a candy cane.

Later, back in Georgetown, I asked dissident survivor Harold Cordell about the guard tower with those painted yellow fish swimming all over it. He told me they had placed a wind-driven generator on top, but it had never worked. Finally, they had installed children's slides on the lower level. The guard tower was called the playground.

The whole process—this denial of the tower's function—reminded me of George Orwell's 1984, in which the Party re-forms language in such a way as to make "heretical thought" impossible. The language is called Newspeak and makes abundant use of euphemisms. In Newspeak, a forced labor camp is called a "joycamp." The guard tower at Jonestown was the architectural equivalent of Newspeak.

Jonestown itself had become a joycamp in its last year. There was no barbed wire around the perimeter. It wasn't needed. Escape was a dream. The jungle stretched from horizon to horizon, thick, swampy and deadly. Armed security guards patrolled the few trails, and it was their business to know where an escapee would look for food and water. Rumor had it that captured escapees had had their arms broken. Toward the end, most of them were simply placed in the euphemistically named Extra Care Unit, where they were drugged senseless for a week at a time. Patients emerged from ECU unable to carry on a conversation, and their faces were blank, as if they had been temporarily lobotomized.

They were told that even if they could survive the jungle, elude the guards and somehow make it almost 150 miles to Georgetown, they'd be stuck there. The temple held their passports as well as any money they might have had when they arrived.

Every citizen . . . could be kept . . . under the eyes of the police. . . .—1984

There were informers everywhere. They got time off, extra food, extra privileges, sometimes even a pat on the back from Father. Children informed on their parents, parents on children. Senior citizens were prized as informers. In rare moments of privacy, one resident might express "negative" opinions to another. It was unwise to reply with anything but criticism of such ideas. The person might be an informer, and any agreement would put you on the floor and result in a beating.

The aftermath of a beating used to be called "discipline," but the name was changed to the more euphemistic "public service." People in public service were transferred to a dorm patrolled by armed guards. They did double work duty, and food might be withheld if they didn't give their all.

The only way to get out of public service was to express regret for your previous attitude, to pretend to like the work, to display a "good attitude." It did something to a man's mind, public service.

[A Party member] is supposed to live in a continuous frenzy of hatred of foreign enemies and internal traitors . . . the discontents produced by his bare, unsatisfying life are deliberately turned outwards.—*1984*

The public-address system was sometimes on all night, the survivors explained, so that people could learn in their sleep. At six A.M., someone knocked on the door. Breakfast consisted of rice, watery milk and brown sugar. Promptly at seven, a typical resident reported to work in the field, which might be as much as a mile and a half away. A supervisor took his name, and the list was given to security. It seemed as if the weeds grew back to choke the crops in a single day, and workers were required to do heavy weeding in temperatures that often rose well above 100 degrees.

There was a half-hour break for lunch. Most often, the midday meal was a bowl of rice soup. The workday ended at six P.M. A resident had less than two hours to walk back from the fields, shower and eat dinner, which usually consisted of rice and gravy and wild greens. At 7:45, the public-address system began blasting out "the news."

About nine P.M., it was time for Russian class. Such phrases as "Good day, comrade," were practiced for an hour and a half. People paid attention, because supposedly they would someday visit Russia, a "paradise on earth" where the government "helped liberation movements."

At about eleven P.M., the community could knock off and fall exhausted into bed. Unless there were problems (and there were problems on average of three times a week), at which point Jones would sit on his "throne" and ask leaders to describe them. Complaints about the food were always dealt with harshly. There were maggots in the rice, and you either ate in the light and picked them out or, if too exhausted, sat in the dark and ate a lot of maggots.

Jones' answer to the problem with the inferior rice had something to do with the CIA. They couldn't allow an interracial socialist experiment to flourish. And to complain about the food was to fall into the CIA's hands, to be in league with them, to be a traitor.

Beatings were often severe enough to require a stay in the infirmary. People wept uncontrollably on the floor as they confessed their crimes and negative attitudes. Some were whipped with a leather belt. Jones encouraged senior citizens to strike others with their canes. Victims lay unconscious on the group until coming to, at which time they were expected to apologize to the community at large.

The Peoples Forum meetings might last until three A.M. Undernourished and exhausted, people took their hours of dead, dreamless sleep.

> In her opinion, the war was not happening. The rocket bombs which fell daily . . . were probably fired by the government . . . itself, just to keep people frightened—*1984*

In September 1977, shots were fired at Jones from the bush. They were real shots. Tim Carter, who was standing with Jones, swears to it. The shots were said to come from mercenaries, mercenaries hired by the Human Freedom Movement (the Berkeley group of temple defectors). The Human Freedom Movement, Jones told the community, was funded by the CIA. They were out there, in the bush. He could hear their military vehicles, could see white men in uniforms at the tree line, hear them on the shortwave radio.

It seemed absurd on the face of it. Mercenaries, hired by the shadowy hand of the CIA, make their way to Jonestown, level their sophisticated weapons, take one shot, and miss?

Nevertheless, the atmosphere of fear was such that people rose in the morning checking the tree line for mercenaries. Jones said there were sophisticated bugging devices on the trees. There weren't enough children's shoes because, as Jones explained, the customs department had broken into a shipment on the docks in Houston and taken them. The rains came early and Jones told the community that the CIA had seeded the clouds. And now there were mercenaries in the trees.

Jones despaired of defending the town. Originally, during alerts, people were to ring the perimeter with guns, crossbows, pitchforks and hoes. But what could they do against trained mercenaries? Jones began to talk of revolutionary suicide as a final statement. The early suicide drills, most people felt, had been loyalty tests. But now he was talking about reincarnation, about how death was only a step to a higher plane. Suicide was tricky. If you did it selfishly, by yourself, you'd revert 5,000 years to the Stone Age. But killing yourself for and with Father, that would be a glorious protest against repression.

Medically, paranoia refers to extreme cases of chronic and fixed delusions that develop slowly into complex, logical systems. A paranoid system may be both persecutory and grandiose. "I am great, therefore they persecute me; I am persecuted, therefore I am great." True paranoids sometimes succeed in developing a following of people who believe them to be inspired. An essential element in the paranoid personality is the ability to discover "proof" of persecution in the over-interpretation of actual facts.

In the past, Jim Jones *had* real enemies. They were, for the most part, louts, bigots and segregationists: the kind of people who referred to him as a "nigger lover" and who spat on his wife when she appeared on the street with one of their adopted black children. Sickened by racist attacks, Jones moved his ministry from the Midwest to Brazil, then to northern California, where the hostilities began anew. Vandals shot out the windows of the Redwood Valley temple, and dead animals were tossed on the lawn. In August 1973, a mysterious blaze devastated the San Francisco temple.

Legitimately harassed, Jones began making connections between events, part real, part delusion . . . Jones concluded that Mississippi Senator John Stennis, chairman of the Armed Services Committee, was spying on him.

A couple of reporters started nosing around for information for a smear campaign. One of the reporters was named George Klineman, and according to Jones, he came from a big-time German "Nazi" family. [Author's note: George is an acquaintance of mine and an honorable man. He is certainly not a Nazi.]

The Nazis hated the temple. They sent notes, on their letterhead, with ugly messages, such as: "What we did to the Jews is nothing compared with what we'll do to you niggers and nigger lovers." Now, somehow, Stennis had turned the Nazis loose on the temple.

The connections were made: Stennis, Nazi reporters, the Treasury Department. Now, an even more sinister force was against Jones. A group of temple defectors were telling "lies," speaking to the "Nazi" reporters, and for publication.

Klineman provided research for another "Nazi" reporter, Marshall Kilduff, who, along with Phil Tracy, wrote a blistering expose of the temple in the August 1st, 1977, issue of *New West* magazine. Various defectors told stories of false healings, humiliations, beatings, and financial improprieties. The article contained a sidebar arguing that the temple should be investigated. Jones used all the political clout at his disposal in a vain effort to kill the story. He fled to Guyana shortly before it was published.

The phenomenon of folie à deux *was noted in medical literature as early as 1877. It is a "psychosis of association," most often paranoid in nature, occurring frequently among people who live together intimately and in isolation.* Folie imposée *is a kind of* folie à deux *in which the delusions of a dominant individual infect one or more submissive and suggestible in-*

*dividuals who are dependent on and have a close emotional
attachment to the infector.*

In the isolation of the jungle, in the intimacy of the pavilion,
Jim Jones raged against the defectors. They were organized now,
and the traitors called themselves the Concerned Relatives. They
were plotting against him, smearing him in the media, and in
league with the shadow forces arrayed against him.

He was Father to all of them. He had taken the junkies and
prostitutes off the street. He took in lonely old folks and fed the
hungry. The young idealists had been floundering, unsure of how
to make a better world. And he showed them. Without him there
was nothing. Without him they would be back on the streets or
lying on a slab in the morgue. The community was totally dependent on him. Without him they were nothing and he told them so.
It frightened them to realize he was ill.

Jones told the community he had cancer, a kidney disorder,
diabetes, hypertension and hypoglycemia. He was God, "God
manifested a hundredfold," the only God they'd ever known. The
God of the Bible had been used to oppress people for centuries. He
was building a socialist utopia, providing economic and social
equality to the oppressed and scorned. And now traitors were
killing him with their plots . . . His hate and fear were contagious.

In May, Deborah Blakely, one of Jones' top aides, left the
Georgetown temple headquarters, obtained a temporary passport
from the American embassy and fled to the United States. The date
was May 13th, Jones' birthday. When Father heard of the betrayal,
he called a "white night," a crisis alert, and the community sat
stunned in the pavilion as he raged. They were betrayed. Wasn't
it better to die? He challenged anyone in the community to speak
for life. When they did, he battered them with arguments. He said
he was "the alpha and the omega," the beginning and the end. He
said it over and over again. The white night lasted twenty-eight
hours. No one was allowed to go to the bathroom without an armed
guard. Anyone who tried to run, he said, would be shot. Meals
were brought into the pavilion. Finally, everyone in Jonestown
voted to die.

Harold Cordell told me most of the details of this meeting. I
asked him if he too had voted to die. He nodded glumly and said,

"I figured if we just quit arguing with him, we could get some sleep."

On November 1st, [Congressman] Leo Ryan wired Jones and informed him he would be visiting Jonestown on a fact-finding mission. Ryan had been talking to traitors all summer.

The conspiracy came to a head on Saturday, November 18th, during Ryan's visit. Some temple members deserted in the morning, when security was concentrating on the Ryan party. Now others were saying they wanted to leave with Ryan. Whole families—the Parkses, the Bogues—had turned traitor.

When Ryan and his collection of traitors left for Port Kaituma, gunmen followed. The shadow forces had won.

An alert was called and the community rushed to the pavilion. Jones told them the congressman's plane would "fall from the sky." At Port Kaituma, a Jones loyalist named Larry Layton, who left with Ryan, pulled a gun. Although Layton later denied it—saying it was his idea to go after the congressman's plane—Jones may have instructed him to shoot the pilot when the plane was airborne. But the party was too large and they were going to take two planes. Layton wounded two, leveled the gun at Dale Parks's chest and fired. Dale fell back, thinking he had been shot, but the gun had jammed. He jumped Layton and, with the help of another man, wrested the gun away.

Meanwhile, gunmen arrived from Jonestown and began firing at the other plane. Ryan, Patty Parks, and newsmen Bob Brown, Don Harris and Greg Robinson were killed. Others were wounded. The gunmen retreated to Jonestown.

"Those people won't reach the States," Jones told the community. Then he said it was time for all of them to die. He asked if there was any dissent. An older woman rose and said she didn't think it was the only alternative. Couldn't the temple members escape to Russia or Cuba? The old woman continued to plead with Jones. She had the right to choose how she wanted to live, she said, and how she wanted to die. The community shouted her down. She had no such right. She was a traitor. But she held her ground, an elderly woman, all alone.

"Too late," Jones said. He instructed Larry Schact, the town doctor, to prepare the poison. Medical personnel brought the equipment into a tent that had been used as a school library. There were large syringes, without the needles, and small plastic containers full of a milky white liquid.

Jones told the community that the Guyanese Defense Force would be there in forty-five minutes. They'd shoot first and ask questions later. Those captured alive, he said, would be castrated. It was time to die with dignity. The children would be first.

A woman in her late twenties stepped out of the crowd. She was carrying her baby. The doctor estimated the child's weight and measured an amount of the milky liquid into a syringe. A nurse pumped the solution into the baby's mouth. The potassium cyanide was bitter to the tongue, and so the nurse gave the baby a sip of punch to wash it down. Then the mother drank her poison.

Death came in less than five minutes. The baby went into convulsions, and Jones—very calm, very deliberate—kept repeating, "We must take care of the babies first." Some mothers brought their own children up to the killing trough. Others took children from reluctant mothers. Some of the parents and grandparents became hysterical and they screamed and sobbed as their children died.

"We must die with dignity," Jones said. "Hurry, hurry, hurry." One thirteen-year-old girl refused her poison. She spit it out time after time and they finally held her and forced her to take it. Many people in the pavilion, especially the older ones, just watched, waiting. Others walked around, hugging old friends. Others screamed and sobbed.

Jones stepped off his throne and walked into the audience. "We must hurry," he said. He grabbed people by the arm and pulled them to the poison. Some struggled, weakly. One girl put up a fight and she had to be injected.

———•———

After an individual took the poison, two others would escort him, one on each arm, to a clearing and lay him on the ground, face down. It wouldn't do to have bodies piled up around the poison, slowing things down.

I missed the flight back to Miami and ended up spending a night in Curacao. There was a television in the hotel room and I found that, after staring into the face of horror for two weeks, all I could do was sit there and watch Popeye cartoons in Spanish while my mind spun and slipped gears.

Jones was a contradiction of everything he stood for. He denigrated sex, but he slept with any woman who pleased him. He brought homosexuals to the floor for beatings, but had sex with men. He stood for social equality, and ate platters full of meat while others ate rice. He preached racial equality, and yet the leadership of his primarily black organizations was mostly white. He railed against slavery, but he forced his followers to work twelve hours a day in the fields. He fed them maggoty rice and they called him Father instead of Massa. He feared oppression but became an oppressor. In the end, he put a bullet through his brain, killing all those things he hated with such vehemence.

Having a theory about it helped some. Mine was that Jones was paranoid, in the clinical sense, and that he infected others. The mechanism of *folie imposée* was magnified by the classic techniques of brainwashing. The mass suicides of history—Masada (the hilltop fortress where, in 73 A.D., nearly 1,000 Jews killed themselves rather than surrender to the Romans) and Saipan (under invasion from American forces, 1,000 Japanese took their lives in 1944)—had occurred when a people were under siege and surrounded by enemies. Jones and the people of Jonestown were no exception: for months they had been harassed, persecuted, surrounded and besieged by shadow forces. When the final attack was imminent and undeniable, they chose to die.

I assumed in Curacao I might finally get more than two hours of sleep. Since Tuesday, November 28th, the day after the planeload of newsmen visited Jonestown, there hadn't been much to do except sit around and touch bases for the third or fourth time with the survivors.

A few of the survivors were charging for interviews, and it seemed to me that some of them sold their exclusive story several times. I didn't pay anyone, but I didn't begrudge them the money. It was the first time many of them had had cash in their pockets in years, and some hired prostitutes from a nearby brothel to stay with them.

Some people—other survivors and newsmen—were outraged by the situation. It struck me differently. I remembered the attitude toward sex at Jonestown, and I saw that these men and women treated each other with affection. In some way it seemed to me a bittersweet affirmation of the resilience of the human spirit.

6

TOMORROW'S COMMUNITIES

Once an organic world picture is in ascendance, the working aim of an economy of plenitude will be, not to feed more human functions into the machine, but to develop further man's incalculable potentialities for self-actualization and self-transcendence, taking back into himself deliberately many of the activities he has too supinely surrendered to the mechanical system.

LEWIS MUMFORD

Let new communities arise as new springs in the desert. Around each spring tender grass will become green and the streams from the springs will eventually flow together in one current.

AGNI YOGA SOCIETY

Utopian communities are important not only as social ventures in and of themselves but also as challenges to the assumptions on which current institutions are organized . . .

ROSABETH MOSS KANTER

You see things as they are and ask "Why?" I dream things that never were and ask "Why not?"

GEORGE BERNARD SHAW

To a great extent, tomorrow's communities exist today. The Amish and Mennonites, the kibbutzim in Israel, the urban and rural communes that survived from the 1960s, the collaborative housing developments, and the more traditional small communities that dot the landscape—every one of them has something to teach us. We don't know which ones, if any, will prevail in the future. But, together, they provide us with a rich harvest of knowledge about what works and what doesn't.

The communities of the future are sure to be diverse. Hopefully, they will satisfy many of our unmet needs. Like the experimental communities of today many will exhibit a planetary consciousness that favors stewardship over exploitation. Some of today's communities are rapidly developing as international centers of education and exchange. Some are becoming more like traditional small towns, intent on meeting the common needs of their members: energy, roads, education, health care, child care, and meaningful work.

Already we can see signs of a future in which local and regional networks of small communities grow up to supplement, if not replace, dependence on big government. Community advocates Corinne McLaughlin and Gordon Davidson clearly describe this trend in their book *Builders of the Dawn: Community Lifestyles in a Changing World.* Among the local and regional networks they list are The National Federation of Egalitarian Communities, the New England Network of Light, and the Earth Community Network. Globally, they list the International Communes Network, which has members in fifteen countries; the Communities Network and the Alternative Communities Network, both in Britain; the Japanese Commune Movement; and the Green Alliance Network in Australia. McLaughlin and Davidson declare that community networks of the future will almost certainly organize within specific ecological regions. "Today's communities," they say, "remind us of both the past and the future. They tap us into our past and our tribal roots as a people. We feel the sense of security and intimacy that comes from connectedness with others and with nature—instructing us in the art of relationship and how to think in terms of the good of the whole. And communities remind us of our future by inspiring us with a vision of a better world, sounding the harmonious notes that are blended together to build a more loving society. Amidst the networks of the new communities growing all over the world, we can begin to perceive the outlines of a new culture for humanity—a new planetary culture."

And what about the cities? We're already seeing hopeful signs of community there, and we can expect to see more. As inner-city housing costs continue to climb, a lot more city dwellers will be looking at collaborative housing. More of us will band together in food co-ops to buy food in bulk. Cooperative ventures in which a group of city dwellers agrees to buy the entire season's harvest from local organic farmers will expand. Already neighborhood community gardens have expanded in numbers enough to gain the attention of the national news media. Urban communities centered around niche enterprises or public education, like the multimillion-dollar computer services company run by Kerista Village in San Francisco, or the Briarpatch business network, with its several hundred members worldwide, will become more widespread. Community trusts, in which people share common land, tools, or expensive assets like a swimming pool or recreation center, may become more widely accepted.

How will all these opportunities for community experience, whether urban or rural, fit into our desire to fulfill the great American dream? Corinne McLaughlin and Gordon Davidson would argue that the community experience gives us the greatest chance of fulfilling that dream. "The American Dream is alive and *real* in communities!" they say. "Many community members are actually well on their way to living this dream—and probably in some ways much closer to it than most Americans! The difference, of course, is that they don't live the dream *alone*. It's *shared* with fellow members.

"Intentional communities today are like small seeds that are keeping alive the spirit of community amidst the alienation and loneliness of our modern times. It is in these communities that experiences are being gained, lessons learned, and systems developed that can re-seed the community spirit when people realize their lack and look for ways to remedy it."

The crises in basic health care, jobs, and housing; the disintegration of the railroads, highways, and schools; and the seemingly endless downward spiral of the economic recession of the late 1980s and early 1990s bring home clearly the all too real possibility that fewer people than ever will achieve the American Dream—a home, a car, a good education, health care, and a decent job—without help from a community of friends and neighbors. In America politics mirrors the soul of our people. Issues are adopted by our political parties when they have become the everyday concerns of a significant portion of the population.

If government does not make the radical changes necessary to correct our many ills, what then? What can we do on our own? In chapter 28, *Achieving a Community Way of Life*, Arthur E. Morgan, a pioneering champion of community development, describes how small communities provide opportunities that are simply not available in the larger society. Young people who want to make a difference might give up when faced with the enormity of it all. But local solutions are definitely within their grasp. The power of conformity sometimes seems too great to fight. Society tends to level differences, oppressing those who would be distinct.

But it is healthy to test societal norms, especially if the testing can take place within the safety of a community of people who know and care for each other. Such testing helps create healthy individuals and introduces new ideas that actually might make life better for all of us. In this chapter Morgan helps us see not only the challenges and opportunities that take shape in a community but also the solutions.

Among the early community experiments in America, most

were guided by the principles of the Christian faith. Now, in the last half of this century, something quite unexpected has happened: Buddhism has come to America and brought community with it. Wherever it has traveled, Buddhism has absorbed the cultural trappings and some of the folk dogma of the region. But there is also buddhism with a little "b," the heart of buddhism that has remained true to its origins and to the apparent intent of its founder for more than 2,500 years. This pure form of buddhism, independent of historical fashions, roughly equates the concept of "sangha" with "community." Traditionally, sangha has referred to a community based on the ideals of cooperation, propertylessness, and spiritual authority. What will sangha become in America, when it builds on our traditions of egalitarian democracy and comes into confrontation with our strong beliefs in individualism and private property? In chapter 29, *Ecocentric Sangha,* author and environmentalist Bill Devall offers us an alternative that emphasizes planetary stewardship: our responsibility to live gently on the earth. This chapter is a futuristic look into a world in which community becomes central to life itself.

Beyond our need to belong to a group of like-minded mutual supporters, we also may have a need to belong to a place. And there is a good chance, therefore, that the communities of the future will also be more identified with geography, climate, and the plants and animals of the region, all of which make up our idea of the "place" in which we live. In chapter 30, *The Place, the Region, and the Commons,* we are introduced to the old Anglo-European concept of "the commons" by Pulitzer poet Gary Snyder. Snyder uses his well-honed poetic imagination to help us understand how a sense of place can be as important as a sense of community, and why our future survival may depend on it.

In chapter 31, *A Future Community Today: The Open Network,* information gurus and networkers extraordinaire Pat Wagner and Leif Smith describe a type of community that stretches our ordinary understanding and offers us an image of future possibilities. Many people assume that a system of many-to-many communication must be built around the information-processing capabilities of a computer, like the electronic communities described in chapter 21. But Wagner and Smith prove that it's possible to have long-distance, many-to-many connections without a massive central computer, and that it may even be preferable to rely more on people than on machines. The care, consideration, and natural intelligence that they apply to their efforts results in an unusually high incidence of synchronistic matching—the ability to hook people together using little or no rational explanation and a lot of intuition. Without human facilitation it is unlikely that the Open Network could promote diversity while focusing on members' commonalities rather than on their differences.

Chapter 32 is made up of excerpts from Ernest Callenbach's *A Future Community Tomorrow: Ecotopia*, in which the Berkeley author imagines a Pacific Northwest that has seceded from the United States to create a country whose central premises are equality of the sexes and stewardship of the land. This essay brings us full circle with a futuristic look at a community in the same northern California region we saw 200 years before the coming of the Spanish, in chapter 4 of our opening section.

CHAPTER 28

Arthur E. Morgan

Achieving a Community Way of Life

There is possible a new synthesis of small-community life. While recovering the unity which tends to emerge when all the people live and work and learn and play together and develop common interests, as in the primitive communities of ancient and medieval times, this new synthesis will include also the universality, the culture, the critical-mindedness, the sophistication, of the city and of specialized functional groups. The new synthesis will take advantage of technical developments in communication, transportation, power transmission, and other fields. It will make extensive use of specialized organizations for special purposes. But also it will strive to see the community as a unified whole, not just as an aggregation of men and of special interests and organizations. Men again may live and work with and for all the members of the community, and may have the deep emotional satisfaction which comes from common experience and association.

The wider and more numerous contacts of the present day need not destroy community traditions, but may make possible the conscious creation of greater traditions. The community can be a reservoir for the preservation and transmission of basic culture on a higher level than at any time in the past.

A clear concept of the community as a fundamental element in human affairs—as a way of life and an attitude toward life— cannot be counted on to spring up spontaneously. The idea of self-conscious, critical design for the small community, with a spirit of universality instead of provincialism, and with a conscious striving for a sense of proportion, will develop slowly, and must be transmitted by the contagion of both word and example. In the long history of numberless communities that concept seldom has emerged. When it has appeared, the results have been important in world history. Such results have been seen in the founding of Greek colonies, in the origin of the Hebrew state, and in the settlement of New England, Pennsylvania, and southern New Jersey, not to mention similarly significant undertakings in ancient East Indian civilizations.

The small community should use and recognize special or functional organizations, such as scientific and business associations, as well as its total-way-of-life or community organization. It should welcome and encourage pioneers who advance to new positions for which the community as a whole is not yet ready. There should be recognition and respect for individuality. There should be deliberate planning for active but orderly step-by-step transition from things as they are to community relations as they might be.

From the old organic community and from the modern outlook this new synthesis can borrow the elements of its purpose and program. In so doing the aim will be to seek unity, fellowship, and a sense of good proportion, so that the community shall be united in the aim of making possible for each of its members a full and varied development of his life according to the needs of the community as a whole and the needs of his own individual genius. The following are some elements of such an objective:

1. The development of neighborliness, with mutual good will, helpfulness, tolerance, and personal acquaintance.
2. A budget of community interests, consisting of matters on which the community has substantial unity, so that it can act effectively; development of the broadest possible base of unified social purpose; a policy of common efforts to common ends.
3. Suitable and effective relationships with larger units, such as region, state, and nation; common, united representation in outside relationships and issues which affect the community as a whole.

4. A policy of free, open-minded, critical inquiry, with the habit of striving for unity through sincere, patient, tolerant inquiry, rather than through compulsion or arbitrary authority.

5. The largest possible agreement on ethical principles, with conscious development of common ethical standards; no interference with pioneer standards or sincere and tolerable divergences of individuals.

6. Common community programs of education, cultural and social life, recreation, health, and other major community interests, with inclusion of the entire community population in those programs to the full extent of individual capacity and interest.

7. Recognition of community interest in land and improvements, both public and private, through programs of zoning, etc.

8. The development of co-operative community effort or group co-operative effort for supplying basic economic needs where the general welfare can be advanced thereby; community consideration of such possibilities as community-owned and operated utilities, co-operatives, credit unions, etc.

9. The habit of regularly meeting together as a community without division into social and economic classes, for the discussion of general and specific community problems, and for general community recreation and acquaintance; the attitude of working together as a community of people who have cast their lot together and who will stand or fall together in working out common problems.

10. Respect for individuality and for individual tastes and interests—the maintenance of a wholesome balance between community life in which the entire community acts together, and individual or smaller group life where diversity of individuality is recognized and respected.

The beginning point for community development is person-to-person relationships. Every person can learn the fundamentals of community life by learning to live in harmony and good will with the persons next to him. Almost every problem of the community, state, and nation is met with on a small scale in our relations with people closest to us. This is not a rhetorical expression, but a statement of specific fact. Unless we can be successful in those relationships we have not yet mastered the art of building a community. We need not wait for great programs. Each person in his day-to-day relationships can be mastering the art of community.

Regardless of the form of government and of society, most of our contacts from week to week and from year to year are these first-hand personal relations with people close to us. If these relations are fine, then the greater part of our lives is fine, and that fineness will constantly infect the community and all social units beyond the community.

CHAPTER 29

Bill Devall

Ecocentric Sangha

Buddhism wears a unique face whenever and wherever it manifests.

I suggest that in North America, as well as in Europe and Australia, Buddhists may develop an ecocentric Sangha. An ecocentric Sangha is not human-centered, but centered in the biosphere.

In an ecocentric Sangha Buddhists are members of the land community. Practice occurs in a bioregion. Bioregion refers to the life region of watersheds, deserts, or mountains which are part of the broader identification of the Sangha. Each bioregion is graced with sacred places. Each bioregion exists beyond artificial boundaries of counties, states, or nations. A Sangha may take its name from a specific mountain, forest, section of coastline, or watershed in its bioregion. The ecocentric Sangha encourages service to the place wherein all beings dwell. Members serve in order to maintain a continuous harmony within the place. Out of this wider responsibility comes great expansion of self into the greater Self of the bioregion.

I dwell in a bioregion noted for its redwood trees. Redwood trees are only one species among many in the forest, but they are very big and sometimes very old. Many people, including some ecologists, call my homeland the Redwood Forest. Instead of calling ourselves the Redwood Zendo [meditation hall] or even the Zendo in the Redwoods, it might be more appropriate to call ourselves People of the Redwoods or better still, People in Service to the Redwood Forest. When our self is very broad, deep, and tall, serving the forest is the same as serving ourselves.

The bioregion of an ecocentric Sangha might include a vast wilderness area where human beings visit, but only a few at a time, in the tradition of a pilgrimage. Sangha members practice by allowing all other creatures, especially wild creatures, all the space they need to be fruitful and happy. Buddhism teaches us that there are no real enemies in the world. Our suffering grows from delusion born of ignorance, fear, and greed.

People in an ecocentric Sangha work with the rich bounty given to them without striving for great wealth at the expense of the life forms of the bioregion. A truly rich and full life can be expected from serving "all our relatives," as Native Americans say. Great diversity characterizes the ecocentric Sanghas. Some serve the ancient forests and glaciers of southeastern Alaska, while others serve a desert.

Some will serve in nuclear waste repositories or toxic waste dumps. The level of discipline held by people in such a Sangha would make most monasteries look like models of anarchy. Their practice will be guided in part by scientific knowledge of these toxic wastes, the rates of decay, and the extent of harm that can come to beings when exposed to these toxic substances.

Knowledge of appropriate ways of handling and monitoring these toxic substances will be very highly valued. People of the Toxic Waste Dump will probably experience higher rates of cancer than most other people. Perhaps they will choose to not have children, and recruit other Sangha members to join them in nuclear practice.

The Dharma teaches us that life is impermanent. All is changing. Change, in the form of evolution, has no direction, no finality. However, evolutionary change tends to develop greater diversity. Protection of biodiversity is another precept of an ecocentric Sangha.

Dwelling in harmony means dwelling in the knowledge that life in the broadest sense, not just human life, really matters. It means liberating our minds from the shallow and anthropocentric attitudes drilled into us by a consumer culture that rewards the desire to manipulate others for selfish purposes, and a culture where violence as a way to solve problems is tolerated along with egocentric individualism and an intense fear of nature. Dwelling in place means cultivating mindfulness of the multitude of blessings that flow freely to us each day. Freed from the desire for greater worldly wealth or political power and liberated from the belief in unrestrained growth, we can settle effortlessly into the delightful flow of energy we call nature. Joyful moments and rewarding experiences multiply when socially perpetuated illusions and false needs, so artfully promoted in the dominant culture, are allowed to drop away.

Some Sanghas may be located in large cities. Nonhuman life forms can also be included in the urban Sanghas. Discussion among the members of the Sangha will concern many questions: What is the essential nature of the place where this city has been built? Where are the rivers or streams? (Under the streets, turned into sewers?) What native species are no longer found within this city? Have land owners introduced exotic plants in this city and, if so, what impact have they had on the habitat of native species? How can human beings and wildlife live harmoniously in the city? Where does the city obtain its water supply? Have dams been built that impede fish from returning to their spawning grounds? Does the city government encourage recycling?

The quality and richness of life manifests from a deep understanding of ourselves in relation to a place. In our technocratic culture there is widespread belief that we can satisfy any desire, anywhere. By participating in an ecocentric Sangha, we become more honest with ourselves and identify more profoundly with the other sentient beings in our midst. The journey home is joyful and simple. Settling down into our rightful place as human beings in harmony with our bioregions, we find rich companionship with life.

CHAPTER 30

Gary Snyder

The Place, the Region, and the Commons

> *When you find your place where you are, practice occurs.*
>
> DŌGEN

The World Is Places

We experience slums, prairies, and wetlands all equally as "places." Like a mirror, a place can hold anything, on any scale. I want to talk about place as an experience and propose a model of what it meant to "live in place" for most of human time, presenting it initially in terms of the steps that a child takes growing into a natural community. (We have the terms *enculturation* and *acculturation*, but nothing to describe the process of becoming placed or re-placed.) In doing so we might get one more angle on what a "civilization of wildness" might require.

For most Americans, to reflect on "home place" would be an unfamiliar exercise. Few today can announce themselves as someone *from* somewhere. Almost nobody spends a lifetime in the same valley, working alongside the people they knew as children. Native people everywhere (the very term means "someone born there") and Old World farmers and city people share this experience of living in place. Still—and this is very important to remember—being inhabitory, being place-based, has never meant that one didn't travel from time to time, going on trading ventures or taking livestock to summer grazing. Such working wanderers have always known they had a home-base on earth, and could prove it at any campfire or party by singing their own songs.

The heart of a place is the home, and the heart of the home

is the firepit, the hearth. All tentative explorations go outward from there, and it is back to the fireside that elders return. You grow up speaking a home language, a local vernacular. Your own household may have some specifics of phrase, of pronunciation, that are different from the *domus,* the *jia* or *ie* or *kum,* down the lane. You hear histories of the people who are your neighbors and tales involving rocks, streams, mountains, and trees that are all within your sight. The myths of world-creation tell you how *that mountain* was created and how *that peninsula* came to be there. As you grow bolder you explore your world outward from the firepit (which is the center of each universe) in little trips. The childhood landscape is learned on foot, and a map is inscribed in the mind—trails and pathways and groves—the mean dog, the cranky old man's house, the pasture with a bull in it—going out wider and farther. All of us carry within us a picture of the terrain that was learned roughly between the ages of six and nine. (It could as easily be an urban neighborhood as some rural scene.) You can almost totally recall the place you walked, played, biked, swam. Revisualizing that place with its smells and textures, walking through it again in your imagination, has a grounding and settling effect. As a contemporary thought we might also wonder how it is for those whose childhood landscape was being ripped up by bulldozers, or whose family moving about made it all a blur. I have a friend who still gets emotional when he recalls how the avocado orchards of his southern California youth landscape were transformed into hillside after hillside of suburbs.

Our place is part of what we are. Yet even a "place" has a kind of fluidity: it passes through space and time—"ceremonial time" in John Hanson Mitchell's phrase. A place will have been grasslands, then conifers, then beech and elm. It will have been half riverbed, it will have been scratched and plowed by ice. And then it will be cultivated, paved, sprayed, dammed, graded, built up. But each is only for a while, and that will be just another set of lines on the palimpsest. The whole earth is a great tablet holding the multiple overlaid new and ancient traces of the swirl of forces. Each place is its own place, forever (eventually) wild. A place on earth is a mosaic within larger mosaics—the land is all small places, all precise tiny realms replicating larger and smaller patterns. Children

218

start out learning place by learning those little realms around the house, the settlement, and outward.

———•———

One's sense of the scale of a place expands as one learns the *region*. The young hear further stories and go for explorations which are also subsistence forays—firewood gathering, fishing, to fairs or to market. The outlines of the larger region become part of their awareness. (Thoreau says in "Walking" that an area twenty miles in diameter will be enough to occupy a lifetime of close exploration on foot—you will never exhaust its details.)

The total size of the region a group calls home depends on the land type. Every group is territorial, each moves within a given zone, even nomads stay within boundaries. A people living in a desert or grassland with great visible spaces that invite you to step forward and walk as far as you can see will range across tens of thousands of square miles. A deep old-growth forest may rarely be traveled at all. Foragers in gallery forests and grasslands will regularly move broadly, whereas people in a deep-soiled valley ideal for gardens might not go far beyond the top of the nearest ridge. The regional boundaries were roughly drawn by climate, which is what sets the plant-type zones—plus soil type and landforms. Desert wastes, mountain ridges, or big rivers set a broad edge to a region. We walk across or wade through the larger and smaller boundaries. Like children first learning our homeland we can stand at the edge of a big river, or on the crest of a major ridge, and observe that the other side is a different soil, a change of plants and animals, a new shape of barn roof, maybe less or more rain. The lines between natural regions are never simple or clear, but vary according to such criteria as biota, watersheds, landforms, elevation. (See Jim Dodge, 1981.) Still, we all know—at some point—that we are no longer in the Midwest, say, but in the West. Regions seen according to natural criteria are sometimes called bioregions.

(In pre-conquest America people covered great distances. It is said that the Mojave of the lower Colorado felt that everyone at least once in their lives should make foot journeys to the Hopi mesas to the east, the Gulf of California to the south, and to the Pacific.)

———•———

Every region has its wilderness. There is the fire in the kitchen, and there is the place less traveled. In most settled regions there used to be some combination of prime agricultural land, orchard and vine land, rough pasturage, woodlot, forest, and desert or mountain "waste." The de facto wilderness was the extreme backcountry part of all that. The parts less visited are "where the bears are." The wilderness is within walking distance—it may be three days or it may be ten. It is at the far high rough end, or the deep forest and swamp end, of the territory where most of you all live and work. People will go there for mountain herbs, for the trapline, or for solitude. They live between the poles of home and their own wild places.

Recollecting that we once lived in places is part of our contemporary self-rediscovery. It grounds what it means to be "human" (etymologically something like "earthling"). I have a friend who feels sometimes that the world is hostile to human life—he says it chills us and kills us. But how could we *be* were it not for this planet that provided our very shape? Two conditions—gravity and a livable temperature range between freezing and boiling—have given us fluids and flesh. The trees we climb and the ground we walk on have given us five fingers and toes. The "place" (from the root *plat*, broad, spreading, flat) gave us far-seeing eyes, the streams and breezes gave us versatile tongues and whorly ears. The land gave us a stride, and the lake a dive. The amazement gave us our kind of mind. We should be thankful for that, and take nature's stricter lessons with some grace.

Understanding the Commons

I stood with my climbing partner on the summit of Glacier Peak looking all ways round, ridge after ridge and peak after peak, as far as we could see. To the west across Puget Sound were the farther peaks of the Olympic Mountains. He said: "You mean there's a senator for all this?" As in the Great Basin, crossing desert after desert, range after range, it is easy to think there are vast spaces on earth yet unadministered, perhaps forgotten, or unknown (the endless sweep of spruce forest in Alaska and Canada)—but it is all mapped and placed in some domain. In North America there is a lot that is in public domain, which has its problems, but at least they are problems we are all enfranchised to work on. David Foreman, founder of the Earth First! movement, recently stated his radical provenance. Not out of Social Justice, Left Politics, or Feminism did I come—says David—but from the Public Lands Conservation movement—the solid stodgy movement that goes back to the thirties and before. Yet these land and wildlife issues were what politicized John Muir, John Wesley Powell, and Aldo Leopold—the abuses of public land.

American public lands are the twentieth-century incarnation of a much older institution known across Eurasia—in English called the "commons"—which was the ancient mode of both protecting and managing the wilds of the self-governing regions. It worked well enough until the age of market economies, colonialism, and imperialism. Let me give you a kind of model of how the commons worked.

Between the extremes of deep wilderness and the private plots of the farmstead lies a territory which is not suitable for crops. In earlier times it was used jointly by the members of a given tribe or village. This area, embracing both the wild and the semi-wild, is of critical importance. It is necessary for the health of the wilderness because it adds big habitat, overflow territory, and room for wildlife to fly and run. It is essential even to an agricultural village economy because its natural diversity provides the many necessities and amenities that the privately held plots cannot. It enriches the agrarian diet with game and fish. The shared land supplies firewood, poles and stone for building, clay for the kiln, herbs, dye plants, and much else, just as in a foraging economy. It is especially important as seasonal or full-time open range for cattle, horses, goats, pigs, and sheep.

In the abstract the sharing of a natural area might be thought of as a matter of access to "common pool resources" with no limits or controls on individual exploitation. The fact is that such sharing developed over millennia and always within territorial and social contexts. In the peasant societies of both Asia and Europe there were customary forms that gave direction to the joint use of land. They did not grant free access to outsiders, and there were controls over entry and use by member households. The commons has been defined as "the undivided land belonging to the members of a local community as a whole." This definition fails to make the point that the commons is both specific land *and* the traditional community institution that determines the carrying capacity for its various subunits and defines the rights and obligations of those who use it, with penalties for lapses. Because it is traditional and *local*, it is not identical with today's "public domain," which is land held and managed by a central government. Under a national state such management may be destructive (as it is becoming in Canada and the United States) or benign (I have no good examples)—but in no case is it locally managed. One of the ideas in the current debate on how to reform our public lands is that of returning them to regional control.

An example of traditional management: what would keep one household from bringing in more and more stock and tempting everyone toward overgrazing? In earlier England and in some contemporary Swiss villages (Netting, 1976), the commoner could only turn out to common range as many head of cattle as he could feed over the winter in his own corrals. This meant that no one was allowed to increase his herd from outside with a cattle drive just for summer grazing. (This was known in Norman legal language as the rule of *levancy and couchancy*: you could only run the stock that you actually had "standing and sleeping" within winter quarters.)

The commons is the contract a people make with their local natural system. The word has an instructive history: it is formed of *ko*, "together," with (Greek) *moin*, "held in common." But the Indo-European root *mei* means basically to "move, to go, to change." This had an archaic special meaning of "exchange of goods and services within a society as regulated by custom or law." I think it might well refer back to the principle of gift economies: "the gift must always move." The root comes into Latin as *munus*, "service performed for the community" and hence "municipality."

There is a well-documented history of the commons in relation to the village economies of Europe and England. In England from the time of the Norman Conquest the enfeoffed knights and over-lords began to gain control over the many local commons. Legislation (the Statute of Merton, 1235) came to their support. From the fifteenth century on the landlord class, working with urban mercantile guilds and government offices, increasingly fenced off village-held land and turned it over to private interests. The enclosure movement was backed by the big wool corporations who found profit from sheep to be much greater than that from farming. The wool business, with its exports to the Continent, was an early agribusiness that had a destructive effect on the soils and dislodged peasants. The arguments for enclosure in England—efficiency, higher production—ignored social and ecological effects and served to cripple the sustainable agriculture of some districts. The enclosure movement was stepped up again in the eighteenth century: between 1709 and 1869 almost five million acres were transferred to private ownership, one acre in every seven. After 1869 there was a sudden reversal of sentiment called the "open space movement" which ultimately halted enclosures and managed to preserve, via a spectacular lawsuit against the lords of fourteen manors, the Epping Forest.

Karl Polanyi (1975) says that the enclosures of the eighteenth century created a population of rural homeless who were forced in their desperation to become the world's first industrial working class. The enclosures were tragic both for the human community and for natural ecosystems. The fact that England now has the least forest and wildlife of all the nations of Europe has much to do with the enclosures. The takeover of commons land on the European plain also began about five hundred years ago, but one-third of Europe is still not privatized. A survival of commons practices in Swedish law allows anyone to enter private farmland to pick berries or mushrooms, to cross on foot, and to camp out of sight of the house. Most of the former commons land is now under the administration of government land agencies.

A commons model can still be seen in Japan, where there are farm villages tucked in shoestring valleys, rice growing in the *tanbo* on the bottoms, and the vegetable plots and horticulture located on the slightly higher ground. The forested hills rising high above the valleys are the commons—in Japanese called *iriai*, "joint entry." The boundary between one village and the next is often the very crests of the ridges. On the slopes of Mt. Hiei in Kyoto prefecture, north of the remote Tendai Buddhist training temples of Yokkawa, I came on men and women of Ohara village bundling up slender brush-cuttings for firewood. They were within the village land. In the innermost mountains of Japan there are forests that are beyond the reach of the use of any village. In early feudal times they were still occupied by remnant hunting peoples, perhaps Japanese-Ainu mixed-blood survivors. Later some of these wildlands were appropriated by the government and declared "Imperial Forests." Bears became extinct in England by the thirteenth century, but they are still found throughout the more remote Japanese mountains, even occasionally just north of Kyoto.

In China the management of mountain lands was left largely to the village councils—all the central government wanted was taxes. Taxes were collected in kind, and local specialties were highly prized. The demands of the capital drew down Kingfisher feathers, Musk Deer glands, Rhinoceros hides, and other exotic products of the mountains and streams, as well as rice, timber, and silk. The village councils may have resisted overexploitation of their resources, but when the edge of spreading deforestation reached their zone (the fourteenth century seems to be a turning point for the forests of heartland China), village land management crumbled. Historically, the seizure of the commons—east or west—by either the central government or entrepreneurs from the central economy has resulted in degradation of wild lands and agricultural soils. There is sometimes good reason to kill the Golden Goose: the quick profits can be reinvested elsewhere at a higher return.

———•———

In the United States, as fast as the Euro-American invaders forcefully displaced the native inhabitants from their own sorts of traditional commons, the land was opened to the new settlers. In the arid West, however, much land was never even homesteaded, let alone patented. The native people who had known and loved the white deserts and blue mountains were now scattered or enclosed on reservations, and the new inhabitants (miners and a few ranchers) had neither the values nor the knowledge to take care of the land. An enormous area was de facto public domain, and the Forest Service, the Park Service, and the Bureau of Land Management were formed to manage it. (The same sorts of land in Canada and Australia are called "Crown Lands," a reflection of the history of English rulers trying to wrest the commons from the people.)

In the contemporary American West the people who talk about a "sagebrush rebellion" might sound as though they were working for a return of commons land to local control. The truth is the sagebrush rebels have a lot yet to learn about the place—they are still relative newcomers, and their motives are not stewardship but development. Some westerners are beginning to think in long-range terms, and these don't argue for privatization but for better range management and more wilderness preservation.

The environmental history of Europe and Asia seems to indicate that the best management of commons land was that which was locally based. The ancient severe and often irreversible deforestation of the Mediterranean Basin was an extreme case of the misuse of the commons by the forces that had taken its management away from regional villages (Thirgood, 1981). The situation in America in the nineteenth and early twentieth centuries was the reverse. The truly local people, the Native Americans, were decimated and demoralized, and the new population was composed of adventurers and entrepreneurs. Without some federal presence the poachers, cattle grazers, and timber barons would have had a field day. Since about 1960 the situation has turned again: the agencies that were once charged with conservation are increasingly perceived as accomplices of the extractive industries, and local people—who are beginning to be actually local—seek help from environmental organizations and join in defense of the public lands.

Destruction extends worldwide and "encloses" local commons, local peoples. The village and tribal people who live in the tropical forests are literally bulldozed out of their homes by international logging interests in league with national governments. A well-worn fiction used in dispossessing inhabitory people is the declaration that the commonly owned tribal forests are either (1) private property or (2) public domain. When the commons are closed and the villagers must buy energy, lumber, and medicine at the company store, they are pauperized. This is one effect of what Ivan Illich calls "the 500-year war against subsistence."

———•———

So what about the so-called tragedy of the commons? This theory, as now popularly understood, seems to state that when there are open access rights to a resource, say pasturage, everyone will seek to maximize his take, and overgrazing will inevitably ensue. What Garrett Hardin and his associates are talking about should be called "the dilemma of common-pool resources." This is the problem of overexploitation of "unowned" resources by individuals or corporations that are caught in the bind of "If I don't do it the other guy will" (Hardin and Baden, 1977). Oceanic fisheries, global water cycles, the air, soil fertility—all fall into this class. When Hardin et al. try to apply their model to the historic commons it doesn't work, because they fail to note that the commons was a social institution which, historically, was never without rules and did not allow unlimited access (Cox, 1985).

In Asia and parts of Europe, villages that in some cases date back to neolithic times still oversee the commons with some sort of council. Each commons is an entity with limits, and the effects of overuse will be clear to those who depend on it. There are three possible contemporary fates for common pool resources. One is privatization, one is administration by government authority, and the third is that—when possible—they become part of a true commons, of reasonable size, managed by local inhabitory people. The third choice may no longer be possible as stated here. Locally based community or tribal (as in Alaska) landholding corporations or cooperatives seem to be surviving here and there. But operating as it seems they must in the world marketplace, they are wrestling with how to balance tradition and sustainability against financial success. The Sealaska Corporation of the Tlingit people of southeast Alaska has been severely criticized (even from within) for some of the old-growth logging it let happen.

———•———

We need to make a world-scale "Natural Contract" with the oceans, the air, the birds in the sky. The challenge is to bring the whole victimized world of "common pool resources" into the Mind of the Commons. As it stands now, any resource on earth that is not nailed down will be seen as fair game to the timber buyers or petroleum geologists from Osaka, Rotterdam, or Boston. The pressures of growing populations and the powers of entrenched (but fragile, confused, and essentially leaderless) economic systems warp the likelihood of any of us seeing clearly. Our perception of how entrenched they are may also be something of a delusion.

Sometimes it seems unlikely that a society as a whole can make wise choices. Yet there is no choice but to call for the "recovery of the commons"—and this in a modern world which doesn't quite realize what it has lost. Take back, like the night, that which is shared by all of us, that which is our larger being. There will be no "tragedy of the commons" greater than this: if we do not recover the commons—regain personal, local, community, and peoples' direct involvement in sharing (in *being*) the web of the wild world—that world will keep slipping away. Eventually our complicated industrial capitalist/socialist mixes will bring down much of the living system that supports us. And, it is clear, the loss of a local commons heralds the end of self-sufficiency and signals the doom of the vernacular culture of the region. This is still happening in the far corners of the world.

The commons is a curious and elegant social institution within which human beings once lived free political lives while weaving through natural systems. The commons is a level of organization of human society that includes the nonhuman. The level above the local commons is the bioregion. Understanding the commons and its role within the larger regional culture is one more step toward integrating ecology with economy.

Bioregional Perspectives

The Region is the elsewhere of civilization.

MAX CAFARD

The little nations of the past lived within territories that conformed to some set of natural criteria. The culture areas of the major native groups of North America overlapped, as one would expect, almost exactly with broadly defined major bioregions (Kroeber, 1947). That older human experience of a fluid, indistinct, but genuine home region was gradually replaced—across Eurasia—by the arbitrary and often violently imposed boundaries of emerging national states. These imposed borders sometimes cut across biotic areas and ethnic zones alike. Inhabitants lost ecological knowledge and community solidarity. In the old ways, the flora and fauna and landforms are *part of the culture*. The world of culture and nature, which is actual, is almost a shadow world now, and the insubstantial world of political jurisdictions and rarefied economies is what passes for reality. We live in a backwards time. We can regain some small sense of that old membership by discovering the original lineaments of our land and steering—at least in the home territory and in the mind—by those rather than the borders of arbitrary nations, states, and counties.

Regions are "interpenetrating bodies in semi-simultaneous spaces" (Cafard, 1989). Biota, watersheds, landforms, and elevations are just a few of the facets that define a region. Culture areas, in the same way, have subsets such as dialects, religions, sorts of arrow-release, types of tools, myth motifs, musical scales, art styles. One sort of regional outline would be floristic. The coastal Douglas Fir, as the definitive tree of the Pacific Northwest, is an example. (I knew it intimately as a boy growing up on a farm between Lake Washington and Puget Sound. The local people, the Snohomish, called it *lukta tciyats*, "wide needles.") Its northern limit is around the Skeena River in British Columbia. It is found west of the crest through Washington, Oregon, and northern California. The southern coastal limit of Douglas Fir is about the same as that of salmon, which do not run south of the Big Sur River. Inland it grows down the west slope of the Sierra as far south as the north fork of the San Joaquin River. That outline describes the boundary of a larger natural region that runs across three states and one international border.

The presence of this tree signifies a rainfall and a temperature range and will indicate what your agriculture might be, how steep the pitch of your roof, what raincoats you'd need. You don't have to know such details to get by in the modern cities of Portland or Bellingham. But if you do know what is taught by plants and weather, you are in on the gossip and can truly feel more at home. The sum of a field's forces becomes what we call very loosely the "spirit of the place." To know the spirit of a place is to realize that you are a part of a part and that the whole is made of parts, each of which is whole. You start with the part you are whole in.

As quixotic as these ideas may seem, they have a reservoir of strength and possibility behind them. The spring of 1984, a month after equinox, Gary Holthaus and I drove down from Anchorage to Haines, Alaska. We went around the upper edge of the basin of the Copper River, skirted some tributaries of the Yukon, and went over Haines Summit. It was White and Black Spruce taiga all the way, still frozen up. Dropping down from the pass to saltwater at Chilkat inlet we were immediately in forests of large Sitka Spruce, Skunk Cabbage poking out in the swamps, it was spring. That's a bioregional border leap. I was honored the next day by an invitation to Raven House to have coffee with Austin Hammond and a circle of other Tlingit elders and to hear some long and deeply entwined discourses on the responsibilities of people to their places. As we looked out his front window to hanging glaciers on the peaks beyond the saltwater, Hammond spoke of empires and civilizations in metaphors of glaciers. He described how great alien forces—industrial civilization in this case—advance and retreat, and how settled people can wait it out.

Sometime in the mid-seventies at a conference of Native American leaders and activists in Bozeman, Montana, I heard a Crow elder say something similar: "You know, I think if people stay somewhere long enough—even white people—the spirits will begin to speak to them. It's the power of the spirits coming up from the land. The spirits and the old powers aren't lost, they just need people to be around long enough and the spirits will begin to influence them."

Bioregional awareness teaches us in *specific* ways. It is not enough just to "love nature" or to want to "be in harmony with Gaia." Our relation to the natural world takes place in a *place*, and it must be grounded in information and experience. For example: "real people" have an easy familiarity with the local plants. This is so unexceptional a kind of knowledge that everyone in Europe, Asia, and Africa used to take it for granted. Many contemporary Americans don't even *know* that they don't "know the plants," which is indeed a measure of alienation. Knowing a bit about the flora we could enjoy questions like: where do Alaska and Mexico meet? It would be somewhere on the north coast of California, where Canada Jay and Sitka Spruce lace together with manzanita and Blue Oak.

But instead of "northern California" let's call it Shasta Bioregion. The present state of California (the old Alta California territory) falls into at least three natural divisions, and the northern third looks, as the Douglas Fir example shows, well to the north. The boundaries of this northern third would roughly run from the Klamath/Rogue River divide south to San Francisco Bay and up the delta where the Sacramento and San Joaquin rivers join. The line would then go east to the Sierra Crest and, taking that as a distinct border, follow it north to Susanville. The watershed divide then angles broadly northeastward along the edge of the Modoc Plateau to the Warner Range and Goose Lake.

East of the divide is the Great Basin, north of Shasta is the Cascadia/Columbia region, and then farther north is what we call Ish River country, the drainages of Puget Sound and the Straits of Georgia. Why should we do this kind of visualization? Again I will say: it prepares us to begin to be at home in this landscape. There are tens of millions of people in North America who were physically born here but who are not actually living here intellectually, imaginatively, or morally. Native Americans to be sure have a prior claim to the term native. But as they love this land they will welcome the conversion of the millions of immigrant psyches into fellow "Native Americans." For the non-Native American to become at home on this continent, he or she must be *born again* in this hemisphere, on this continent, properly called Turtle Island.

That is to say, we must consciously fully accept and recognize that this is where we live and grasp the fact that our descendants will be here for millennia to come. Then we must honor this land's great antiquity—its wildness—learn it—defend it—and work to hand it on to the children (of all beings) of the future with its biodiversity and health intact. Europe or Africa or Asia will then be seen as the place our ancestors came from, places we might want to know about and to visit, but not "home." Home—deeply, spiritually—must be here. Calling this place "America" is to name it after a stranger. "Turtle Island" is the name given this continent by Native Americans based on creation mythology (Snyder, 1974). The United States, Canada, Mexico, are passing political entities; they have their legitimacies, to be sure, but they will lose their mandate if they continue to abuse the land. "The State is destroyed, but the mountains and rivers remain."

But this work is not just for the newcomers of the Western Hemisphere, Australia, Africa, or Siberia. A worldwide purification of mind is called for: the exercise of seeing the surface of the planet for what it is—by nature. With this kind of consciousness people turn up at hearings and in front of trucks and bulldozers to defend the land or trees. Showing solidarity with a region! What an odd idea at first. Bioregionalism is the entry of place into the dialectic of history. Also we might say that there are "classes" which have so far been overlooked—the animals, rivers, rocks, and grasses—now entering history.

These ideas provoke predictable and usually uninformed reactions. People fear the small society and the critique of the State. It is difficult to see, when one has been raised under it, that it is the State itself which is inherently greedy, destabilizing, entropic, disorderly, and illegitimate. They cite parochialism, regional strife, "unacceptable" expressions of cultural diversity, and so forth. Our philosophies, world religions, and histories are biased toward uniformity, universality, and centralization—in a word, the ideology of monotheism. Certainly under specific conditions neighboring groups have wrangled for centuries—interminable memories and hostilities cooking away like radioactive waste. It's still at work in the Middle East. The ongoing ethnic and political miseries of parts of Europe and the Middle East sometimes go back as far as the Roman Empire. This is not something that can be attributed to the combativeness of "human nature" per se. Before the expansion of early empires the occasional strife of tribes and natural nations was almost familial. With the rise of the State, the scale of the destructiveness and malevolence of warfare makes a huge leap.

In the times when people did not have much accumulated surplus, there was no big temptation to move in on other regions. I'll give an example from my own part of the world. (I describe my location as: on the western slope of the northern Sierra Nevada, in the Yuba River watershed, north of the south fork at the three-thousand-foot elevation, in a community of Black Oak, Incense Cedar, Madrone, Douglas Fir, and Ponderosa Pine.) The western slope of the Sierra Nevada has winter rain and snowfall and a different set of plants from the dry eastern slope. In pre-white times, the native people living across the range had little temptation to venture over, because their skills were specific to their own area, and they could go hungry in an unfamiliar biome. It takes a long education to know the edible plants, where to find them, and how to prepare them. So the Washo of the Sierra east side traded their pine nuts and obsidian for the acorns, yew bows, and abalone shells of the Miwok and Maidu to the west. The two sides met and camped together for weeks in the summer Sierra meadows, their joint commons. (Dedicated raiding cultures, "barbarians," evolve as a response to nearby civilizations and their riches. Genghis Khan, at an audience in his yurt near Lake Baikal, was reported to have said: "Heaven is exasperated with the decadence and luxury of China.")

There are numerous examples of relatively peaceful small-culture coexistence all over the world. There have always been multilingual persons peacefully trading and traveling across large areas. Differences were often eased by shared spiritual perspectives or ceremonial institutions and by the multitude of myths and tales that cross language barriers. What about the deep divisions caused by religion? It must be said that most religious exclusiveness is the odd specialty of the Judeo/Christian/Islamic faith, which is a recent and (overall) minority development in the world. Asian religion, and the whole world of folk religion, animism, and shamanism, appreciates or at least tolerates diversity. (It seems that the really serious cultural disputes are caused by different tastes in food. When I was chokersetting in eastern Oregon, one of my crew was a Wasco man whose wife was a Chehalis woman from the west side. He told me that when they got in fights she would call him a "goddamn grasshopper eater" and he'd shout back "fish eater"!)

Cultural pluralism and multilingualism are the planetary norm. We seek the balance between cosmopolitan pluralism and deep local consciousness. We are asking how the whole human race can regain self-determination in place after centuries of having been disenfranchised by hierarchy and/or centralized power. Do not confuse this exercise with "nationalism," which is exactly the opposite, the impostor, the puppet of the State, the grinning ghost of the lost community.

So this is one sort of start. The bioregional movement is not just a rural program: it is as much for the restoration of urban neighborhood life and the greening of the cities. All of us are fluently moving in multiple realms that include irrigation districts, solid-waste management jurisdictions, long-distance area code zones, and such. Planet Drum Foundation, based in the San Francisco Bay Area, works with many other local groups for the regeneration of the city as a living place, with projects like the identification and restoration of urban creeks (Berg and others, 1989). There are groups worldwide working with Third and Fourth World people revisualizing territories and playfully finding appropriate names for their newly realized old regions (*Raise the Stakes*, 1987). Four bioregional congresses have been held on Turtle Island.

As sure as impermanence, the nations of the world will eventually be more sensitively defined and the lineaments of the blue earth will begin to reshape the politics. The requirements of sustainable economies, ecologically sensitive agriculture, strong and vivid community life, wild habitat—and the second law of thermodynamics—all lead this way. I also realize that right now this is a kind of theater as much as it is ecological politics. Not just street theater, but visionary mountain, field, and stream theater. As Jim Dodge says: "The chances of bioregionalism succeeding . . . are beside the point. If one person, or a few, or a community of people, live more fulfilling lives from bioregional practice, then it's successful." May it all speed the further deconstruction of the superpowers. As "The Surre(gion)alist Manifesto" says:

> Regional politics do not take place in Washington, Moscow, and other "seats of power." Regional power does not "sit"; it flows everywhere. Through watersheds and bloodstreams. Through nervous systems and food chains. The regions are everywhere & nowhere. We are all illegals. We are natives and we are restless. We have no country; we live in the country. We are off the Inter-State. The Region is against the Regime—any Regime. Regions are anarchic. (Cafard, 1989)

Finding "Nisenan County"

This year Burt Hybart retired from driving dump truck, backhoe, grader, and Cat after many years. Roads, ponds, and pads are his sculpture, shapes that will be left on the land long after the houses have vanished. (How long for a pond to silt up?) Burt still witches wells, though. Last time I saw him he was complaining about his lungs: "Dust boiling up behind the Cat you couldn't see from here to there, those days. When I worked on the Coast. And the diesel fumes."

———•———

Some of us went for a walk in the Warner Range. It's in the far northeast corner of California, the real watershed boundary between the headwaters of the Pit River and the *nors* of the Great Basin. From the nine-thousand-foot scarp's high points you can see into Oregon, Goose Lake, and up the west side of the Warners to the north end of Surprise Valley. Dry desert hills to the east.

Desert mountain range. A touch of Rocky Mountain flora here that leapfrogs over desert basins via the Steens Mountains of southeastern Oregon, the Blue Mountains, and maybe the Wallowas. Cattle are brought up from Eagleville on the east side, a town out of the 1880s. The proprietor of the Eagleville Bar told how the sheepherders move their flocks from Lovelock, Nevada, in early March, heading toward the Warners, the ewes lambing as they go. In late June they arrive at the foot of the range and move the sheep up to the eight-thousand-foot meadows on the west side. In September the flocks go down to Madeline—the lambs right onto the meat trucks. Then the ewes' long truck ride back to Lovelock for the winter. We find the flock in the miles-long meadow heavens of Mule-ear flowers. The sheep business is Basque-run on all levels. Old aspen grove along the trail with sheepherder inscriptions and designs in the bark, some dated from the 1890s.

Patterson Lake is the gem of the Warners, filling an old cirque below the cliffs of the highest peak. The many little ledges of the cliffs are home to hawks. Young raptors sit solemnly by their nests. Mt. Shasta dominates the western view, a hub to these vast miles of Lodgepole and Jeffrey Pine, lava rock, hayfield ribbons, rivers that sink underground. Ha! This is the highest end of what we call "upriver"—and close to where it drains both ways, one side of the plateau tipping toward the Klamath River, the other to the Pit and the Sacramento. Mt. Shasta visible for so far—from the Coast

Range, from Sierra Buttes down by Downieville—it gleams across the headwaters of all of northern California.

———•———

Old John Hold walks up a streambed talking to it: "So that's what you've been up to!" Reading the geology, the wash and lay of the heavy metal that sinks below the sand, never tarnishing or rusting—gold. The new-style miners are here, too, St. Joseph Minerals, exploring the "diggings," the tertiary gravels. The county supervisors finally approved the EIR and the exploratory drilling begins. This isn't full-scale mining yet, and they'll come back in eighteen months with their big proposal (if they do). The drilling's not noticeable: a little tower and a trailer lost in the gravel canyons and ridges that were left from the days of hydraulicking.

———•———

There were early strong rains this fall, so the springs started up. Then the rain quit and the springs stopped. A warm December. Real rains started in January, with heavy snows above six thousand feet and not much below that. This year more kids go skiing. Resistance to it (as a decadent urban entertainment) crumbles family by family. Most adults here never were mountain people, didn't climb, ski, or backpack. They moved up from the city and like to think they're in a wilderness. A few are mountain types who moved down to be here, and are glad to be living where there are some neighbors. The kids go to Donner Pass to be sliding on the white crystals of future Yuba River waters. I get back to downhill skiing myself; it feels wonderful again. Downhill must have provided one of the fastest speeds human beings ever experienced before modern times. Cross-country ski trips in Sierra Buttes too. On the full moon night of April (the last night of the month) Bill Schell and I did a tour till 2 A.M. around Yuba Pass, snow shining bright in the moonlight, skis clattering on the icy slabs. Old mountain people turned settlers manage to finally start going back into the mountains after the house is built, the garden fenced, the drip-systems in. February brought ten inches of rain in six days. The ponds and springs stream over, the ground's all silvery with surface glitter of a skin of water. Fifteen feet of snow at Sugarbowl near Donner Pass.

———•———

Two old gents in the Sacramento Greyhound station. I'm next to an elder who swings his cane back and forth, lightly, the tip pivoting on the ground—and he looks about the room, back and forth, without much focus. He has egg on his chin. A smell of old urine comes from him, blows my way, time to time. Another elder walks past and out. He's very neat: a plastic-wrapped waterproof blanket-roll slung on his shoulder, a felt hat, a white chin beard like an Amish. Red bandanna tied round his neck, bib overalls. Under the overall bottoms peep out more trousers, maybe suit pants. So that's how he keeps warm, and keeps some clothes clean! Back in my traveling days men said, "Yeah, spend the winter in Sac."

I caught the bus on down to Oakland. In Berkeley, on the wall of the Lucas Books building, is a mural that shows a cross section of Alta California from the Northwest Coast to the Mojave Desert. I walked backward through the parking lot to get a look at it whole, sea lions, coyote, redtail hawk, creosote bush. Then noticed a man at one corner of it, touching it up. Talked to him, he is Lou Silva, who did the painting. He was redoing a mouse, and he said he comes back from time to time to put in more tiny fauna.

———•———

Spring is good to the apples, much fruit sets. Five male deer with antler velvet nubs walk about the meadow in the morning. High-country skiing barely ends and it's time to go fishing. Planting and building. This area is still growing, though not as rapidly as several years ago. The strong spirit of community of the early seventies has abated somewhat, but I like to think that when the going gets rough this population will stick together.

———•———

San Juan Ridge lies between the middle and south forks of the Yuba River in a political entity called Nevada County. New settlers have been coming in here since the late sixties. The Sierra counties are a mess: a string of them lap over the mountain crest, and the roads between the two sides are often closed in winter. A sensible

236

redrawing of lines here would put eastern Sierra, eastern Nevada, and eastern Placer counties together in a new "Truckee River County" and the seat could be in Truckee. Western Placer and western Nevada counties south of the south fork of the Yuba would make a good new county. Western Sierra County plus a bit of Yuba County and northern Nevada County put together would fit into the watershed of the three forks of the Yuba. I would call it "Nisenan County" after the native people who lived here. Most of them were killed or driven away by the gold rush miners.

People live on the ridges because the valleys are rocky or brushy and have no level bottoms. In the Sierra Nevada a good human habitat is not a valley bottom, but a wide gentle *ridge* between canyons.

CHAPTER 31

Leif Smith and Pat Wagner

A Future
Community Today:
The Open Network

When David first visited our office in Denver, after months of working in Singapore, he expressed concern that he would be in our way. After all, his engineering skills were not needed amidst the piles of letters and brochures. He wanted to be more than an idle tourist, but what kind of contribution could he make?

"What could I possibly do to be of service?" he asked. A few minutes later, the phone rang. Did we know about Connie, the caller asked? Her husband was just transferred to Singapore, and she was frantically trying to find out about living conditions there. Had Connie contacted us yet for assistance? David's jaw sagged in astonishment when we told him he had his first assignment.

We phoned Connie and explained that we had an expatriate American in the office who was currently living in Singapore. Would she like to talk to him? Would she?!! For the next hour or so, David proceeded to tell Connie everything she needed to know to smooth her family's move to Singapore. When David returned to Singapore, he maintained his friendship with Connie and her family during their stay there and has continued to do so since then.

The Office for Open Network, a project Leif started more than seventeen years ago, puts people in touch with each other for mutual benefit. It is fueled, not by some monster computer system, but rather by the hearts and minds of hundreds of people. These people, our clients and friends, tend to be adventurers, poised on the edge of a great wilderness, of which they know little. They come to us for maps, tools, and introductions to fellow travelers.

The Office for Open Network is not [just] a network; it is a network generator. It is not [just] a community; it is a contribution to many communities, some existing and others yet to be conceived. Our clients tend to be people who cherish their own ideas about the world, but still like the concept of being in touch with other explorers, no matter what the destination.

People initially sign up with us for many reasons. (The service is based on a yearly fee of $60; a lifetime account is currently $250.) They might be starting a new business, a new non-profit, or a new book project. They might be liberal, conservative, socialist, libertarian, green, or red.

Abe teaches businesses how to decrease bad debt. Rebecca sews bridal gowns. Jeff is bringing together some experienced, international coal brokers to examine a deal involving mines in Siberia. Liz, an official in a government agency, needs information to help her evaluate hardware and software for a multi-agency online clearinghouse. Fran wants to know the feasibility of setting up a home business doing writing projects for medical journals.

Jan needs to sell some antique furniture and find someone to dig up her prize iris garden. Ginny is fundraising for a social venture foundation. Jim is looking for participants for his men's group. Elizabeth needs a clinical psychologist to keynote a health conference. Marilyn is looking for ways to make her diabetic cat more comfortable. Carl is moving to Seattle and reviving his music career. Kathy is looking for a new boyfriend, and Kendra is trying to understand her economics homework.

It is not necessary, in most cases, for us to have detailed histories of each person. It is enough if we know something of the person's past experience in the region of current interest and something of the trajectory of the quest. For example, we need to know if Marilyn already has consulted a number of veterinarians on behalf of her cat, if she prefers hi-tech to holistic solutions, and how much money and time she has budgeted. We also need to have a sense of what Marilyn "really" needs. Is she looking for a supportive friend or a clinically-objective expert?

One part of what we pay attention to is the content of the information exchange, parameters often defined by when, how much, how far, and what for. Here is where the links of common interests join people in communities based on connections as tenuous as a shared love of fast cars or a mutual interest in participating in oil lease partnerships. For the task-oriented person, it is enough to find an electrician or locate a source of bat dung.

Some of our clients still cling to the notion that the monster computer really does exist and that their requests are fed into a giant database. Some of them seem to be wary of the ambiguity of our processes and are still not prepared to believe that, when they contact our office, human beings will begin to think about what they need and make educated guesses about whom they should talk with, and why. The part of our work that encompasses the process of building working relationships among our clients is the part that puzzles the task-oriented folks who want us to be a mechanized clearinghouse, and pleases those relationship-oriented people who prefer fellowship to immediate, measurable results.

However, the people who focus too much on the relationships also may misunderstand what we are doing. They think that the warm feelings that exist among many of our clients, those feelings of trust and friendship that were not really part of the original purpose, but are a reality for many people, are a product of . . . what? They are not sure how the warm feelings came to be, and this failure to understand is reflected in requests for access to people and their resources without consideration for their boundaries. From the sincere businesswoman who asked for a list of rich people to call in order to bail her boyfriend out of financial trouble to the spiritual workshop leader who couldn't understand why we wouldn't give him the phone numbers of everybody we know, they are usually extremely friendly, but without a sense for the substance needed to make a successful connection.

We sometimes bluntly ask these folks to explain to us what benefit it would be to the other party to be put in touch with them. They don't like having to put a cost to the time and resources someone else is going to invest in them, or to consider that cost when they contact another person. They want instant rapport and trust, and, oftentimes, an instant entry into the other person's territory and personal communities. When it is not forthcoming, they sometimes accuse us of elitist practices.

What these people don't understand is the necessity of boundaries in creating good community. Each person must be able to decide for themselves what those boundaries are. Over the years we have discovered that the easier we make it for people to say "no," the more likely they are to say "yes." Our clients' ability to request boundaries and our ability (which is far from perfect) to respond to those requests help keep the networks of relationships vigorous and stable.

Attracting adventurers works. Keeping a balance between results and relationships works. Respecting boundaries works. What else promotes the health of the Office for Open Network?

Much of the vitality springs from its diversity; we are an "open network" office. Our clients range from wealthy industrialists to communitarian rural Greens, from suburban housewives who play tennis and stay at home to raise their families to itinerant fitness junkies who peddle mountain bikes in Germany. We have clients who think nuclear energy is wonderful and others who think it is the Devil's own handmaiden. We have clients who hate Republicans and others who serve on the state Republican committee. Pick an issue, and, within the hour, we could probably supply you with the phone numbers of at least three sets of articulate, interesting people with conflicting points of view.

Journalists and librarians understand us best, and they know the great delight we get from the wonderful combinations of ideas and purposes visible from the walls of our outpost. Each client is like a multifaceted jewel, whose light splinters into a unique pattern of color and energy. Each individual pattern, which is constantly changing, contributes to the overall pattern, which also is constantly changing. The patterns represent shifting alliances, based on the most unlikely connections.

For example, the holistic therapist who hates food irradiation and the engineer who loves the idea are united in their appreciation of the mountain parks of the Front Range of Colorado. Often, the "enemy" has the information and perspective we need to solve a problem, and if the "enemy" is accessible to us, and we are motivated to do something for them in return, our world is better. Our office, and what it stands for, creates a neutral ground for the exploration of ideas without the fear of punishment or humiliation.

Some of our clients do not like the idea that their worst enemy also might be a client of the Office for Open Network. We once received a phone call from a woman active in local environmental issues who wanted us to know that as long as "that man" was a client, she would never sign up with us. If we followed her logic, we would have to clear the acceptance of any client into our service with all the other clients, like the old private club "blackball." The makeup of our clientele would be bland indeed.

Where do the walls of the Office for Open Network end? Our clients are mostly white, mostly middle-class, mostly thirty-five to fifty, mostly educated. It pleases us, however, that our contacts run deep into every part of the city, so that when someone is doing a project that involves speaking to and working with minorities and non-mainstream types, we usually come through.

We have connections with gun-toting survivalists, lesbian feminists, Native Americans, conservative Christians, Afro-American Marxists, Wiccan priestesses, people who use DOS computers (or Amigas or Nexts), and even a rare politician or two.

We take it as a good sign that less than 15% of our clients appear to share our philosophical biases. If we believed that we had special access to truth we might declare that connections made by us constitute "the one true network," and we might ask people to commit themselves to it, forsaking all others. Instead, we see the Office for Open Network as a tool that people may employ to extend and enrich their own networks and to create new networks for themselves, their friends, and their allies.

Our hope is that through our work, and through the work of others, the sense of open network, the feeling that each individual is more likely to be ally than enemy, will become the possession of every human being. More listening posts resembling ours, established on the same frontier, whether formal or informal, will do much to achieve this end. Respect for boundaries, together with the willingness to serve all explorers, is crucial for success.

The shared expectation that a civilization fit for explorers may arise among us is not sufficient to constitute community, but it is an essential part of the ground on which many differently constituted communities may thrive, in peace, affording one another mutual aid, adventure, and joy.

CHAPTER 32

Ernest Callenbach

A Future Community
Tomorrow: Ecotopia

San Francisco, May 7. Under the new regime, the established cities of Ecotopia have to some extent been broken up into neighborhoods or communities, but they are still considered to be somewhat outside the ideal long-term line of development of Ecotopian living patterns. I have just had the opportunity to visit one of the strange new minicities that are arising to carry out the more extreme urban vision of this decentralized society. Once a sleepy village, it is called Alviso, and is located on the southern shores of San Francisco Bay. You get there on the interurban train, which drops you off in the basement of a large complex of buildings. The main structure, it turns out, is not the city hall or courthouse, but a factory. It produces the electric traction units—they hardly qualify as cars or trucks in our terms—that are used for transporting people and goods in Ecotopian cities and for general transportation in the countryside. (Individually owned vehicles were prohibited in "car-free" zones soon after Independence. These zones at first covered only downtown areas where pollution and congestion were most severe. As minibus service was extended, these zones expanded, and now cover all densely settled city areas.)

Around the factory, where we would have a huge parking lot, Alviso has a cluttered collection of buildings, with trees everywhere. There are restaurants, a library, bakeries, a "core store" selling groceries and clothes, small shops, even factories and workshops—all jumbled amid apartment buildings. These are generally of three or four stories, arranged around a central courtyard of the type that used to be common in Paris. They are built almost entirely of wood, which has become the predominant building material in Ecotopia, due to the reforestation program. Though these structures are old-fashioned looking, they have pleasant small balconies, roof gardens, and verandas—often covered with plants, or even small trees. The apartments themselves are very large by our standards—with 10 or 15 rooms, to accommodate their communal living groups.

Alviso streets are named, not numbered, and they are almost as narrow and winding as those of medieval cities—not easy for a stranger to get around in. They are hardly wide enough for two cars to pass; but then of course there *are* no cars, so that is no problem. Pedestrians and bicyclists meander along. Once in a while you see a delivery truck hauling a piece of furniture or some other large object, but the Ecotopians bring their groceries home in string bags or large bicycle baskets. Supplies for the shops, like most goods in Ecotopia, are moved in containers. These are much smaller than our cargo containers, and proportioned to fit into Ecotopian freight cars and onto their electric trucks. Farm produce, for instance, is loaded into such containers either at the farms or at the container terminal located on the edge of each minicity. From the terminal an underground conveyor belt system connects to all the shops and factories in the minicity, each of which has a kind of siding where the containers are shunted off. This idea was probably lifted from our automated warehouses, but turned backwards. It seems to work very well, though there must be a terrible mess if there is some kind of jam-up underground.

My guides on this expedition were two young students who have just finished an apprenticeship year in the factory. They're full of information and observations. It seems that the entire population of Alviso, about 9,000 people, lives within a radius of a half mile from the transit station. But even this density allows for many small park-like places: sometimes merely widenings of the streets, sometimes planted gardens. Trees are everywhere—there are no large paved areas exposed to the sun. Around the edges of town are the schools and various recreation grounds. At the northeast corner of town you meet the marshes and sloughs and saltflats of the Bay.

A harbor has been dredged for small craft; this opens onto the ship channel through which a freighter can move right up to the factory dock. My informants admitted rather uncomfortably that there is a modest export trade in electric vehicles—the Ecotopians allow themselves to import just enough metal to replace what is used in the exported electric motors and other metal parts.

Kids fish off the factory dock; the water is clear. Ecotopians love the water, and the boats in the harbor are a beautiful collection of both traditional and highly unorthodox designs. From this harbor, my enthusiastic guides tell me, they often sail up the Bay and into the Delta, and even out to sea through the Golden Gate, then down the coast to Monterey. Their boat is a lovely though heavy-looking craft, and they proudly offered to take me out on it if I have time.

We toured the factory, which is a confusing place. Like other Ecotopian workplaces, I am told, it is not organized on the assembly-line principles generally thought essential to really efficient mass production. Certain aspects are automated: the production of the electric motors, suspension frames, and other major elements. However, the assembly of these items is done by groups of workers who actually fasten the parts together one by one, taking them from supply bins kept full by the automated machines. The plant is quiet and pleasant compared to the crashing racket of a Detroit plant, and the workers do not seem to be under Detroit's high output pressures. Of course the extreme simplification of Ecotopian vehicles must make the manufacturing process much easier to plan and manage—indeed there seems little reason why it could not be automated entirely.

Also, I discovered, much of the factory's output does not consist of finished vehicles at all. Following the mania for "doing it yourself" which is such a basic part of Ecotopian life, this plant chiefly turns out "front ends," "rear ends," and battery units. Individuals and organizations then connect these to bodies of their own design.

The battery units, which seem to be smaller and lighter than even our best Japanese imports, are designed for use in vehicles of various configurations. Each comes with a long reel-in extension cord to plug into recharging outlets.

The factory does produce several types of standard bodies, to which the propulsion units can be attached with only four bolts at each end. (They are always removed for repair.) The smallest and commonest body is a shrunken version of our pick-up truck. It has a tiny cab that seats only two people, and a low, square, open box in back. The rear of the cab can be swung upward to make a roof, and sometimes canvas sides are rigged to close in the box entirely.

A taxi-type body is still manufactured in small numbers. Many of these were used in the cities after Independence as a stop-gap measure while minibus and transit systems were developing. These bodies are molded from heavy plastic in one huge mold.

These primitive and underpowered vehicles obviously cannot satisfy the urge for speed and freedom which has been so well met by the American auto industry and our aggressive highway program. My guides and I got into a hot debate on this question, in which I must admit they proved uncomfortably knowledgeable about the conditions that sometimes prevail on our urban throughways—where movement at *any* speed can become impossible. When I asked, however, why Ecotopia did not build speedy cars for its thousands of miles of rural highways—which are now totally uncongested even if their rights of way have partly been taken over for trains—they were left speechless. I attempted to sow a few seeds of doubt in their minds: no one can be utterly insensitive to the pleasures of the open road, I told them, and I related how it feels to roll along in one of our powerful, comfortable cars, a girl's hair blowing in the wind. . . .

We had lunch in one of the restaurants near the factory, amid a cheery, noisy crowd of citizens and workers. I noticed that they drank a fair amount of the excellent local wine with their soups and sandwiches. Afterward we visited the town hall, a modest wood structure indistinguishable from the apartment buildings. There I was shown a map on which adjacent new towns are drawn, each centered on its own rapid-transit stop. It appears that a ring of such new towns is being built to surround the Bay, each one a self-contained community, but linked to its neighbors by train so that the entire necklace of towns will constitute one city. It is promised that you can, for instance, walk five minutes to your transit station, take a train within five minutes to a town ten stops away, and then walk another five minutes to your destination. My informants are convinced that this represents a halving of the time we would spend on a similar trip, not to mention problems of parking, traffic, and of course the pollution.

What will be the fate of the existing cities as these new mini-cities come into existence? They will gradually be razed, although a few districts will be preserved as living museum displays (of "our barbarian past," as the boys jokingly phrased it). The land will be returned to grassland, forest, orchards, or gardens—often, it appears, groups from the city own plots of land outside in the country, where they probably have a small shack and perhaps grow vegetables, or just go for a change of scene.

After leaving Alviso we took the train to Redwood City, where the reversion process can be seen in action. Three new towns have sprung up there along the Bay, separated by a half mile or so of open country, and two more are under construction as part of another string several miles back from the Bay, in the foothills. In between, part of the former suburban residential area has already been turned into alternating woods and grassland. The scene reminded me a little of my boyhood country summers in Pennsylvania. Wooded strips follow the winding lines of creeks. Hawks circle lazily. Boys out hunting with bows and arrows wave to the train as it zips by. The signs of a once busy civilization—streets, cars, service stations, supermarkets—have been entirely obliterated, as if they never existed. The scene was sobering, and made one wonder what a Carthaginian might have felt after ancient Carthage was destroyed and plowed under by the conquering Romans.

———•———

Gilroy Hot Springs, June 22. The more I have discovered about Ecotopian work habits, the more amazed I am that their system functions at all. It is not only that they have adopted a 20-hour week; you can't even tell when an Ecotopian is working, and when he is at leisure. During an important discussion in a government office, suddenly everybody will decide to go to the sauna bath. It is true they have worked out informal arrangements whereby, as their phrase has it, they "cover" for each other—somebody stays behind to answer phones and handle visitors. And it is also true that even in the sauna our discussion continued, on a more personal level, which turned out to be quite delightful. But Ecotopian society offers so many opportunities for pleasures and distractions that it is hard to see how people maintain even their present levels of efficiency.

Things happen in their factories, warehouses, and stores which would be quite incredible to our managers and supervisors. I have seen a whole section close down without notice; somebody will bring out beer or marijuana, and a party will ensue, right there amid the crates and machines. Workers in Ecotopian enterprises do not have a normal worker's attitude at all. Perhaps because of their part ownership of them, they seem to regard the plants as home, or at least as their own terrain. They must be intolerable to supervise: the slightest change in work plans is the occasion for a group discussion in which the supervisors (who are elected and thus in a weak position anyway) are given a good deal of sarcastic questioning, and in which their original plans are seldom accepted without change. The supervisors try to take this with good grace, of course, even claiming that the workers often come up with better ideas than they do; and they believe that Ecotopian output per person hour is remarkably high. It may be.

Incidentally, many rather intellectual people seem to be members of the ordinary factory and farm work force. Partly this seems to be due to the relative lack of opportunity for class differentiation in Ecotopia; partly it is due to a deliberate policy which requires students to alternate a year of work with each year of study. This is perhaps one of the most startling arrangements in the whole Ecotopian economy—for not only is the students' education prolonged, but their ideological influence is responsible for many of the new policies that prevail in Ecotopian enterprises. (I was told, for example, that it was students who were originally behind the whole movement toward workers' control.)

Ecotopians are adept at turning practically any situation toward pleasure, amusement, and often intimacy. At first I was surprised by the ease with which they strike up very personal conversations with casual strangers. I have now gotten used to this, indeed I usually enjoy it, especially where the lovely Ecotopian women are concerned. But I am still disconcerted when, after speaking with someone on the street in a loose and utterly unpressured way for perhaps ten minutes, he mentions that he is working and trots off. The distinction between work and non-work seems to be eroding away in Ecotopia, along with our whole concept of jobs as something separate from "real life." Ecotopians, incredibly enough, *enjoy* their work.

Unemployment does not seem to worry Ecotopians in the slightest. There were many unemployed just before Independence, but the switch to a 20-hour week almost doubled the number of jobs—although some were eliminated because of ecological shutdowns and simplifications, and of course the average real income of most families dropped somewhat. Apparently in the transition period when an entirely new concept of living standards was evolving, the country's money policy had to be managed with great flexibility to balance sudden inflationary or deflationary tendencies. But the result now seems to be that, while enterprises are not seriously short of member-workers, there is also no significant number of people involuntarily unemployed. In any case, because of the minimal-guaranteed income system and the core stores, periods of unemployment are not considered disasters or threats by individuals; they are usually put to use, and sometimes deliberately extended, for some kind of creative, educational or recreational purposes. Thus in Ecotopia friends who are unemployed (usually through the collapse of their previous enterprise) often band together and undertake studies that lead them into another enterprise of their own.

If it is sometimes hard to tell whether Ecotopians are working or playing, they are surprisingly generous with their time. I was told, for instance, that many workers in factories put in extra hours to fix machines that have broken down. They evidently regard the 20-hour week quota as applying to productive time only, and take the repair of machinery almost as a sideline responsibility. Or perhaps it is just that they enjoy tinkering: despite the de-emphasis of goods in Ecotopia, people seem to love fixing things. If a bicycle loses a chain or has a flat tire, its rider is soon surrounded by five people volunteering to help fix it. . . .

Epilogue

> *We are all part of a huge family. Within the family our acts of caring, insignificant as they may seem, are nevertheless an integral part of a vast network of compassionate acts that are occurring throughout the universe at each moment. Just as billions of tiny acts of ignorance, greed, violence, and exploitation have created most of the suffering and breakdown that now exist, so the billions of tiny actions of compassion—which include wisdom and skillful means and joy—preserve and heal the situation.*
>
> RAM DASS

There is far more information available about community than would ever fit in a single book. The major influence on my knowledge of community is, however, my personal experience living and working in community. The work on community in the fields of ecology, sociology, and psychology has been of immense help in deepening my knowledge. As a way of closing this collection I would like to summarize what these fields have to say.

Community: Lost, Saved, and Liberated

Sociology is the study of groups. No wonder then that experts in the field have always taken a big interest in the ways that groups come together in community. Until the 1960s, sociologists were hotly engaged in the "community has been lost" argument that several authors in this collection refer to. Thirty years ago sociologists had a long list of the ills which they believed were caused by the centralization of manufacturing and distribution that occurred during the industrial revolution: masses of workers migrated to the centralized cities which became empty, hostile streets ruled by unfeeling bureaucracies; community ties became weaker and fewer in number; and individuals became isolated from "mass society" developing a dependence on the impersonal bureaucracies for care and protection.

The small decentralized communities of town and village had provided a nurturing and control that kept crime rates down, said these observers. Then, in cities where there was no sense of community, crime rates rose.

In the 1960s, another group of sociologists decided to go out into the cities for first-hand observation. What they found was a surprising contrast to the opinions of the previous observers. Strong neighborhood and kinship groups were in abundance, they told us. Rather than disappearing, community had blossomed. Neighborhood and family alliances had grown up to provide emotional and financial support and a haven from the outside world.

But, like all black and white arguments, this one presents only a partial picture. Both groups of observers limited their definition of community to groups that had common interests and values; occurred in a neighborhood settings; and grew out of family kinship bonds. This is not an adequate picture of the possibilities of community, which, as we have seen in this collection, occur in an almost infinite variety of situations.

In the 1970s, a third group of scholars focused on the impact of high-speed transportation and communication and turned up at least one alternative viewpoint: the so-called "liberated" community. Cheap, safe, timely, long-distance transportation and communication made it possible for people to create another kind of community that was held together across great distances, by friendship and mutual interest in commerce, as well by the kinship ties of scattered families. The Briarpatch, electronic computer systems like the WELL, and loose affiliations like the Office for Open Network are examples of this new kind of informal community.

From yet another school of social thought, the environmental movement, comes an additional point of view. Environmentalists point to a series of changes that have taken place in small communities as a direct result of the centralization of the economy that accompanied the industrial revolution. Small communities, they say, have given up local self-reliance and have become dependent on big government or large corporations for natural gas and electricity, heating oil and gasoline, schools and hospitals, and in many cases even food. People buy too much outside of their towns. As a result they have lost their focus, their sense of place. By becoming dependent they have had to submit to regulation of many local community issues by these larger institutions. Because the regulators often are not involved in the local community, a weakening of control by local people over their own standards, goals, and self-regulation has occurred. This loss of control has led to an increase in alienation and a marked decline in efforts to take care of local problems at a local level.

Today, observers of groups, both sociologists and environmentalists, are telling us that in an increasing number of cases centralization is not working. They point to the disrepair of our highways and roads; the reduction in school budgets for communities that rely on state or national funding; the skyrocketing costs of purchasing energy from big corporations; the lack of support for conservation and local energy systems based on solar or hydroelectric sources. If that were not enough, today's observers add, while most people believe that high-quality health care is widely available, more than 35 million Americans have limited or no access to it.

The good news, as we have tried to point out in this collection, is that there are solutions to these problems. And these solutions, based on creating a renewed sense of community, bring with them not only the rewards of increased physical security but psychological and spiritual growth as well.

The Needs of the One Versus the Needs of the Many

Psychology is the study of behavior. Psychologists have had a long-standing interest in the behavior of individuals, whether alone or within groups. Their emphasis, however, is less on the social aspects and more on mental and emotional qualities. After more than 100 years of research, psychology has formulated an understanding of human behavior that very closely echoes many of the ancient spiritual models.

This new view of what it means to be human comes from three different branches of psychology: humanistic psychology, depth psychology, and transpersonal psychology. Beginning with William James and Sigmund Freud, and building on the contributions of Harry Stack Sullivan, Alfred Adler, Erik Erikson, Carl Jung, Abraham Maslow, Carl Rogers, Jean Piaget, Lawrence Kohlberg, and others, this new view provides powerful insights into the relationship between the needs of the one and the needs of the many. It teaches us that who we are and what makes us happy comes directly from the balance we create between our individual needs and the needs of our group.

We start in life with the basic needs of food, shelter, and clothing. If we meet these basic survival needs, then comfort and pleasure can come into focus. Once we've mastered personal well-being, say these scientists, we become attracted to activities that bring others into our lives. We begin to embrace the values of family, clan, race, and community. We learn to conform to the expectations of the group to which we belong and, for many people today, this is as far as we get. We become "belongers."

Those of us who finally belong, then, have the opportunity to move into a new level of *self*-interest characterized by introspection that leads to insights about how life really works. For a time, self-exploration tends to set us apart. We move away from identifying with our group and become almost completely immersed in our newly discovered inner-self. No longer willing to accept the group's expectations with blind faith, we start to question everything, in order to learn how the world actually works. Our own inner growth and fulfillment of our personal potential become our most important goals.

Those of us who make it through this phase, psychologists

observe, turn back to the community. This is not a turning away from personal growth but rather a transformation of their introspective interest into a renewed interest in others. Metaphorically speaking, we become open to the energy of the heart. We develop a desire to serve, to return gifts to the whole. We explore the universal values of peace and human fellowship, and launch ourselves with vigor into activities that serve the common good. Ultimately, this new exploration helps lay the best foundation for a real sense of community. It is at this stage that we finally come to realize: *Living without others is more than undesirable, it is impossible.*

In the Company of Others

In the company of others I can find comfort or pain. In the company of others I can belong or be shunned. In the company of others I can become who I truly am or be bent and twisted beyond recognition.

Torn between a need to be a unique individual and a need to belong to family, tribe, and clan, each of us struggles to find a balance we can live with. For most of us it is equally wrong to turn away from society or to give up our identity to a group.

We are *human* beings. The word itself is a mixture of the Latin *homo,* which means "like kind," and the Sanskrit *manas,* which means "mind or mental." To be human means that we are simultaneously *with* members of our own kind and *alone* in the self-consciousness of our own minds. To be a whole and healthy human being, we must know both of our own innermost self and the love of our fellow human beings.

Whether we find comfort or pain, belonging or shunning, self-actualization or deformity depends on the values and standards of the communities we choose. It behooves us then to choose carefully. Freedom of choice, diversity of membership, shared responsibility, and the kind of patience that nurtures growth are the chief traits we will want to look for in a community experience. Their absence or their opposites—authority without appeal, uniformity in membership, blame and shame, and an effort to make people change—are sure signs of a community gone awry.

It is my hope that the essays and the profiles included in this collection have helped you to see what works and what can go wrong, what choices you have and what skills you need to build and maintain a community, and how you might make community an active part of your future. As psychologist and spiritual teacher Ram Dass so aptly puts it, "We are all part of a huge family."

And the future is ours to create.

Contributors

MARGO ADAIR is a teacher, mediator, and consultant who has created numerous self-help tapes, written for many anthologies and magazines, and is the author of *Working Inside Out: Tools for Change* and coauthor with Sharon Howell of the forthcoming *Patterns of Power*. She lives and works in San Francisco.

KRISTIN ANUNDSEN is a San Francisco freelance writer who covers subjects ranging from management and technology to travel and community living. She is coauthor of the forthcoming book *Creating Community Anywhere* (Tarcher).

JUANITA BROWN is an international strategic management consultant, a fellow of the World Business Academy, and has served as program faculty at the John F. Kennedy University School of Management and the California Institute of Integral Studies. She lives in Mill Valley, California.

TIM CAHILL, who lives in Livingston, Montana, is the author of *Buried Dreams, Jaguars Ripped My Flesh*, and *A Wolverine Is Eating My Leg*. He is also a columnist and founding editor of *Outside* magazine and a contributing editor to *Rolling Stone*.

Author ERNEST CALLENBACH's books include *Ecotopia, Ecotopia Emerging*, and *A Citizen Legislature* (with Michael Phillips). He founded the critical journal *Film Quarterly* in 1958 at the University of California Press and served as its editor until 1991. He lives with his wife, Christine, in Berkeley, California.

MIHALY CSIKSZENTMIHALYI is former chairman of the Department of Psychology at the University of Chicago and author of *Flow: The Psychol-*

ogy of Optimal Experience, Beyond Boredom and Anxiety and coauthor of *The Creative Vision, Optimal Experience: Studies in Flow Consciousness,* and *Television and the Quality of Life.*

Psychologist and spiritual teacher RAM DASS (a.k.a. Richard Alpert, Ph.D.) is author of many inspirational books including *Be Here Now, The Only Dance There Is, Grist for the Mill* (with Stephen Levine), *Journey of Awakening, Miracle of Love, How Can I Help?* (with Paul Gorman), and most recently *Compassion in Action* (with Mirabai Bush). He lives in the San Francisco Bay Area.

ARTHUR J. DEIKMAN is clinical professor of psychiatry at the University of California at San Francisco. He is the author of *The Observing Self: Mysticism and Psychotherapy* and *The Wrong Way Home: Uncovering Patterns of Cult Behavior.*

BILL DEVALL lives in Arcata, California, where he writes extensively on the environmental movement. He is the author of *Simple in Means, Rich in Ends* and *Deep Ecology: Living as if Nature Mattered.*

DUANE FICKEISEN, who lives on Bainbridge Island, near Seattle, Washington, is Administrator of the Context Institute; associate editor of *In Context* magazine; and works as an organizational development consultant to non-profits.

RICK FIELDS is the coauthor of *Chop Wood, Carry Water: A Guide to Finding Spiritual Fulfillment in Everyday Life; How the Swans Came to the Lake: A Narrative History of Buddhism in America;* and *The Code of the Warrior: In History, Myth, and Everyday Life.* He lives in Boulder, Colorado. His coauthors on *Chop Wood, Carry Water* included Peggy Taylor, founder of *New Age Journal;* Rex Weyler, founder of Greenpeace; and Rick Ingrasci, M.D., a holistic health physician.

FRANCES FITZGERALD lives in New York City and is author of *Cities on the Hill, America Revised,* and the bestselling *Fire in the Lake,* which was awarded a Pulitzer Prize, the National Book Award, and the Bancroft Prize for history. Her articles on Vietnam, Cuba, Northern Ireland, and the Middle East have appeared in *The New Yorker, Atlantic Monthly, The New York Review of Books,* and *Harper's.*

ROBERT K. GREENLEAF was Director of Management Research at AT&T and visiting lecturer at M.I.T.'s Sloan School of Management and Harvard Business School. He wrote extensively on the topic of "servant leadership" in the decade before his death in 1991.

MARK HOLLOWAY is a historian with a special interest in utopian communities. He lives in Sussex, England.

SHARON HOWELL is a community organizer, speaker, and writer living in Detroit. She is the author of *Reflections of Ourselves: Mass Media and the Women's Movement*, and coauthor with Margo Adair of the forth-coming *Patterns of Power*.

STEPHANIE KAZA is a Zen student of Kobun Chino Roshi. She lives in Burlington, Vermont, is assistant professor in the Environmental Program at the University of Vermont, and serves on the board of the Buddhist Peace Fellowship.

GEOPH KOZENY has visited intentional communities across North America for the past several years. He is a guest editor of *Communities: Journal of Cooperation*, coauthor of *The Directory of Intentional Communities*, and founder of The Community Catalyst Project in San Francisco, which provides technical assistance for established and emerging communities.

AMIA LIEBLICH lived with her husband and children in Jerusalem and taught psychology at the Hebrew University. She is a Gestalt therapist and author of *Kibbutz Makom* and *Soldiers on Jerusalem Beach*.

WAYNE LIEBMAN is a physician in private practice in Los Angeles, California. He has been active in the men's movement and is the author of *Tending the Fire: The Ritual Men's Group*.

MICHAEL LINTON, who works on the development of local currency systems, lives in British Columbia. He is founder of Landsman Community Services, developers of the "Local Employment and Trading System" which has been successfully implemented worldwide.

MALCOLM MARGOLIN has written numerous articles for national and local magazines and several books, including *The Earth Manual* and *The Ohlone Way: Indian Life in the San Francisco-Monterey Bay Area*. He lives in Berkeley, California.

KATHRYN MCCAMANT, CHARLES DURRETT, and ELLEN HERTZMAN are coauthors of a book on Danish and American "living communities" entitled *CoHousing: A Contemporary Approach to Housing Ourselves*. They live and work in the San Francisco Bay Area, where they offer workshops, consulting, and architectural services to people interested in CoHousing communities.

CORINNE MCLAUGHLIN and GORDON DAVIDSON are the co-founders of the Sirius Community, a non-profit educational center in Massachusetts, and coauthors of *Builders of the Dawn: Community Lifestyles in a Changing World*. Former members of the Findhorn Community in Scotland, they lecture on alternative communities and social change.

STEPHANIE MILLS is a bioregionalist wordsmith who lives in the northeast of Lake Michigan's watershed. Her books include *Whatever Happened to Ecology?* and *In Praise of Nature*.

ARTHUR E. MORGAN (1878 to 1975) was president of Antioch College, where he and his wife developed the Antioch College Plan of wholeness and balance in education. He helped bring about the League of Nations, protected the Florida Everglades, and championed the small community. He was a prolific author of books, including *Industries for Small Communities, The Community of the Future and the Future of Community*, and *Nowhere was Somewhere: How History Makes Utopias How Utopias Make History*. Morgan's work continues under the auspices of Community Service, Inc., of Yellow Springs, Ohio, an educational organization he founded in 1940.

Zen monk THICH NHAT HANH founded Van Hanh Buddhist University in Saigon and the School of Youth for Social Service. In 1966, he visited the United States to describe the enormous suffering of the Vietnamese people. He was nominated by Martin Luther King, Jr., for the Nobel Peace Prize. Today he is head of Plum Village in France, headquarters for a worldwide community of meditators and activists. He is author of *Being Peace, The Miracle of Mindfulness, The Sun My Heart*, and many other books.

Psychologist M. SCOTT PECK is author of the bestselling *The Road Less Traveled*, as well as *People of the Lie* and *The Different Drum: Community Making and Peace*. He is also founder of the Foundation for Community Encouragement, a non-profit organization promoting community and world understanding. He lives in New Preston, Connecticut.

CAROLYN R. SHAFFER is a hypnotherapist in private practice in Berkeley, California. She is the coauthor of *City Safaris: A Sierra Club Explorers Guide to Urban Adventures for Grownups and Kids* and a contributor to *The Womanspirit Sourcebooks* and *The Politics of Women's Spirituality*. She is the coauthor of the forthcoming *Creating Community Anywhere* (Tarcher).

LEIF SMITH and PAT WAGNER are information consultants, network facilitators, authors of *The Networking Game*, and founders of The Office for Open Network in Denver, Colorado.

GARY SNYDER is a Pulitzer Prize–winning poet and teacher of literature and wilderness thought at the University of California at Davis. His poetry collections include *Turtle Island, Axe Handles*, and *Earth Household* and his best-known essay collections include *The Real Work* and *The Practice of the Wild*. He is founder of the Ring of Bone Zendo community and lives with his family on San Juan Ridge in the Sierra foothills.

CHARLENE SPRETNAK is the author of *The Spiritual Dimension of Green Politics, Green Politics* (with Fritjof Capra), *The Lost Goddesses of Early Greece*, and most recently *States of Grace: The Recovery of Meaning in the Postmodern Age*. She is the founder of the Committees of Correspondence, a major Green political organization in the United

States. Her work also has contributed to the framing of the women's spirituality and ecofeminist movements. She lives in Berkeley, California.

STARHAWK is a peace activist and leader in the feminist spirituality and ecofeminist movements in the United States and Europe. She is the author of the bestsellers *The Spiral Dance*, *Dreaming the Dark*, and *Truth and Dare*. She lives in San Francisco.

Resources

Center for Communal Studies
University of Southern Indiana
8600 University Boulevard
Evansville, IN 47712
812-464-1727

An international clearing house for community information; research facility with a communal database and an archival collection of manuscripts, photographs, recordings, publications, and artifacts from 100 historic and nearly 400 contemporary intentional communities; sponsor of conferences, classes, seminars, speakers, publications, small research grants, and related educational projects. Inquiries welcome.

Center for Good Work
P.O. Box 77086
San Francisco, CA 94107–7086
415-648-2667

A mail-order catalog of books on mindfulness, community, right livelihood, and simple living. Write for free catalog.

The CoHousing Company
48 Shattuck Square, #15
Berkeley, CA 94704
510-549-9980

A design and development company formed specifically to build collaborative housing communities. Service areas include group formation and facilitation, site search and acquisition, real estate brokerage, land development, architectural design, project management, and finance. Emphasis in northern California, but consulting services offered nationwide.

Community Bookshelf
Route 1, Box 155
Rutledge, MO 63563
816-883-5543

A mail-order catalog of books on community, co-ops, and other aspects of joyous alternative lifestyles and politics. Write for free catalog.

Community Service, Inc.
Box 243
Yellow Springs, OH 45387
513-767-2161

A non-profit educational organization offering a bi-monthly newsletter of articles and book reviews on community, a mail-order book service, and host of an annual conference which explores various aspects of community. Write or call for more information, a sample newsletter, or a booklist.

Cult Awareness Network
2421 West Pratt Blvd., #1173
Chicago, IL 60645
312-267-7777

A national non-profit organization founded to educate the public about the harmful effects of mind control used by destructive cults. CAN confines its concerns to unethical or illegal practices including coercive persuasion or mind control, and does not judge doctrine or beliefs. Provides a newsletter, information, and support for families as well as assistance to former followers during their reentry to society.

EcoHome
4344 Russell
Los Angeles, CA 90027

An urban community organized around a belief in environmental preservation. Practices recycling, composting, etc. Provides a community resource center and an ecology library.

EcoNet
Institute for Global Communications
18 De Boom Street
San Francisco, CA 94107
415-442-0220

A computer-based communication system ("electronic bulletin board") dedicated to helping the world environmentalist community communicate more effectively. Accessible in the U.S. and in 70 foreign countries. Offers more than 80 public conferences in which users keep abreast of worldwide environmental issues. Access requires a computer with modem.

Federation of Egalitarian Communities
c/o East Wind Community
Box DC-9
Tecumseh, MO 65760

An organization of democratically run and communally owned communities promoting equality, cooperation, participatory government, ecology, and non-violence.

Fellowship of Intentional Communities
c/o Center for Communal Studies
University of Southern Indiana
8600 University Boulevard
Evansville, IN 47712
812-464-1727

Provides alliance building, support services, and referrals for intentional communities, community networks, individuals seeking community, and other interested organizations.

Foundation for Community Encouragement
7616 Gleason Road
Knoxville, TN 37919
615-690-4334

Offers community building workshops based on the stages of community described by M. Scott Peck in *A Different Drum*. Also involved in community networking, aspiring to encourage and help strengthen all other communities and community building organizations.

Landsman Community Services Ltd.
1600 Embleton Crescent
Courtenay, BC, Canada V9N 6NB
604-338-0213

A consulting service helping communities create local currency systems. Developers of the "Local Employment and Trading System," which has been successfully implemented in several dozen communities in North America, 140 in Australia, 60 in New Zealand, and 40 in the United Kingdom.

Pattern Research
Box 9845
Denver, CO 80209
303-778-0880

Offers consulting on designing and maintaining "network generators." Workshops on communication, information management, networking, and other kinds of information projects. Specializes in non-technological solutions to communication issues. Call or write for free information.

Shared Living Resource Center
2375 Shattuck Avenue
Berkeley, CA 94704
510-548-6608

Creates supportive shared living communities that integrate housing with cooperative living, affordability, and ecological design. Workshops, consultation sessions, slide-talk presentations, building and site surveys, architectural design, and construction drawings for shared living communities.

Tools for Change
349 Church Street
San Francisco, CA 94114
415-861-6838

An adult education institute dedicated to transforming domination of one another and nature to living in harmony, where diversity is a source of strength, and the sanctity of all life is honored. Offers facilitation, mediation, training, and consulting services along with a variety of publications.

The WELL
27 Gate Five Road
Sausalito, CA 94965
415-332-4335

An online computer network affiliated with the *Whole Earth Review*. Offers many public conferences on topics of interest to the readers of its affiliated magazine *Whole Earth Review*. Access requires a computer with modem.

Bibliography

Auerbach, Nina. *Communities of Women: An Idea in Fiction* (Cambridge, MA: Harvard University Press, 1978).

Bellah, Robert N., Richard Madsen, William M. Sullivan, Ann Swidler, and Steven M. Tipton, eds. *Habits of the Heart: Individualism and Commitment in American Life* (New York: Harper & Row, 1985).

Best, James. *Another Way to Live: Experiencing Intentional Community* (Wallingford, PA: Pendle Hill Publ., 1978).

Boyte, H. C. *Community is Possible* (New York: Harper & Row, 1984).

Carlin, Vivian F. and Ruth Mansber. *If I Live to Be a Hundred: Congregate Housing for Later Life* (West Nyack, NY: Parker Publishing, 1984).

Fellowship for Intentional Community and Communities Publications Cooperative. *Directory of Intentional Communities: A Guide to Cooperative Living* (Evansville, Indiana: Fellowship for Intentional Community, updated annually).

Fromm, Dorit. *Collaborative Communities: Co-housing, Central Living, and Other New Forms of Housing With Shared Facilities* (New York: Van Nostrand Reinhold, 1991).

Hawxhurst, Donna. *Living Our Visions: Building Feminist Community* (Fourth World, May, 1984).

Kolbenschlag, Madonna. *Lost in the Land of Oz: The Search for Identity and Community in American Life* (New York: Harper & Row, 1988).

Komar, Ingrid. *Living the Dream: A Documentary Study of the Twin Oaks Community* (Norwood, PA: Twin Oaks Community, 1983).

Kriyananda, Swami. *Cooperative Communities: How to Start Them and Why* (Nevada City, CA: Ananda Publications, 1968).

Miller, Ronald S. and the editors of *New Age Journal. As Above, So Below: Paths to Spiritual Renewal in Daily Life* (Los Angeles: Jeremy P. Tarcher, 1992).

269

Morehouse, Ward, ed. *Building Sustainable Communities: Tools and Concepts for Self-Reliant Economic Change* (New York: Bootstrap Press, 1989).

Morgan, Griscom. *Guidebook for Intentional Communities* (Yellow Springs, OH: Community Services, Inc., 1988).

Morrison, Roy. *We Build the Road as We Travel: Mondragon, a Cooperative Social System* (Philadelphia, PA: New Society Publishers, 1991).

Partners for Livable Places Staff. *The Better Communities Catalog: A Sourcebook of Ideas, People, & Strategies for Improving the Place Where You Live* (Reston, VA: Acropolis, 1989).

Patty, Catherine. *Community Spirit* (Jonesboro, AR: ESP, 1976).

Pilisuk, Marc and Susan Parks-Hillier. *The Healing Web: Social Networks and Human Survival* (University Press of New England, 1986).

Powers, Elvin M. *Building a Caring-Sharing Community of Believers* (Beacon-Hill, 1983).

Raimy, Eric. *Shared Houses, Shared Lives* (Los Angeles: Jeremy P. Tarcher, 1979).

Riddell, Carol. *The Findhorn Community: Creating a Human Identity for the 21st Century* (Moray, Scotland: Findhorn Press, 1990).

Rohrlich, Ruby and Elaine Hoffman Baruch. *Women in Search of Utopia: Mavericks and Myth Makers* (New York: Schocken Books, 1984).

Sher, Barbara and Annie Gottlieb. *Teamworks! Building Support Groups that Guarantee Success* (New York: Warner Books, 1989).

Soleri, Paolo. *Arcosanti: An Urban Laboratory?* (San Diego, CA: Avant Books, 1984).

The Training Action Affinity Group. *Building Social Change Communities* (Santa Cruz: New Society Publishers, 1979 [out of print]).

Turnbull, Colin M. *The Forest People: A Study of the Pygmies of the Congo* (New York: Simon & Schuster, 1962).

Turner, Victor, ed. *Celebration: Studies in Festivity and Ritual* (Washington, DC: Smithsonian Institution Press, 1982).

Walters, Donald. *Cities of Light: What Communities can Accomplish, and the Need for Them in Our Times* (Nevada City, CA: Crystal Clarity Publ., 1987).

Weiss, Michael *Living Together: A Year in the Life of a City Commune.* (New York: McGraw-Hill, 1984).

Wolff-Salin, M. K. *The Shadow Side of Community and the Growth of Self* (New York: Crossroads Publ., 1988).

Notes

CHAPTER 18

1. Adams, John D. "A Health Cut in Costs," *Personnel Administrator*, August 1988.
2. Srivastva, Suresh, David Cooperriter and Associates. *Appreciative Management and Leadership: The Power of Positive Thought and Action in Organization* (San Francisco: Jossey-Bass, 1990).
3. Trachtenberg, Alan. *The Incorporation of America: Culture and Society in the Gilded Age* (New York: Hill and Wang, 1982).

CHAPTER 23

1. Frantz, Douglas. *Levine & Co.: Wall Street's Insider Trading Scandal* (New York: Henry Holt, 1987).
2. "Lincoln Memo Listed Likely Bond 'Targets,'" Associated Press, *San Francisco Chronicle*, 31 March 1990.
3. Helmore, Kristin. "Growing Food With Pride," *Christian Science Monitor*, 1 March 1989.
4. Wallis, Jim. "Idols Closer to Home: Christian Substitutes for Grace," in *The Rise of Christian Conscience* (San Francisco: Harper & Row, 1987), 191.
5. Wallis. "Idols Closer to Home," 196.

CHAPTER 30

1. Berg, Peter, and others. *A Green City Program for San Francisco Bay Area Cities and Towns* (San Francisco: Planet Drum, 1989).
2. Cafard, Max. "The Surre(gion)alist Manifesto." *Mesechabe*, Autumn 1989.
3. Cox, Susan Jane Buck. "No Tragedy in the Commons." *Environmental Ethics*, Spring 1985.
4. Dodge, Jim. "Living by Life." *CoEvolution Quarterly*, Winter 1981.

271

5. Hardin, Garret and John Baden. *Managing the Commons* (San Francisco: W. H. Freeman, 1977).

6. Kroeber, A. L. *Cultural and Natural Areas of Native North America.* (Berkeley: University of California Press, 1947).

7. Netting, R. "What Alpine Peasants Have in Common: Observations on Communal Tenure in a Swiss Village." *Human Ecology*, 1976.

8. Polanyi, Karl. *The Great Transformation* (New York: Octagon Books, 1975).

9. *Raise the Stakes.* Journal of the Planet Drum Foundation, P.O. Box 31251, San Francisco, California, 94131.

10. Snyder, Gary. *Turtle Island* (New York: New Directions, 1974).

11. Thirgood, J. V. *Man and the Mediterranean Forest: A History of Resource Depletion* (New York: Academic Press, 1981).

Permissions and Copyrights

321, Indianapolis, Indiana, 46200. Reprinted by permission of the Robert K. Greenleaf Center.

Chapter 9 is an article from *Creation Spirituality* magazine, July/August 1988. ($17/year [6 issues]; single issues $1.50); P.O. Box 19216, Oakland, California, 94619.

Chapter 10 is excerpted from *Kibbutz Makom: Report from an Israeli Kibbutz* by Amia Lieblich. Copyright © 1981 by Amia Lieblich. Reprinted by permission of Pantheon Books.

Chapter 11 is excerpted from *Flow: The Psychology of Optimal Experience.* Copyright © 1990 by Mihaly Csikszentmihayli. Reprinted by permission of HarperCollins Publishers.

Chapter 12 is excerpted from *How Can I Help?* Copyright © 1985 by Ram Dass and Paul Gorman. Reprinted by permission of Alfred A. Knopf.

Chapter 13 is excerpted from *Truth or Dare* by Starhawk. Copyright © 1987 by Miriam Simos. Reprinted by permission of HarperCollins Publishers.

Chapter 14 is from "Community As a Resource" by Thich Nhat Hanh, reprinted by permission from *The Mindfulness Bell*, Vol. 1, No. 1, January 1990 ($12/year; single issues $3), Parallax Press, P.O. Box 7355, Berkeley, California, 94707. Copyright © 1990 by Parallax Press.

Chapter 15 is excerpted from issue No. 29 of *In Context: A Quarterly of Humane Sustainable Culture* ($24/year; single issues $6), P.O. Box 11470, Bainbridge Island, Washington, 98110.

Chapter 16 is an original essay created for this collection by Geoph Kozeny. Copyright © 1992 Geoph Kozeny. All rights reserved. Printed by permission of Community Catalyst Project, c/o The Purple Rose, 1531 Fulton, San Francisco, California, 94117.

Chapter 17 is excerpted from *Tending the Fire: The Ritual Men's Group* by Wayne Liebman, copyright © 1991 Wayne Liebman. Reprinted by permission of Ally Press, St. Paul, Minnesota.

Chapter 18 is excerpted from "Corporation as Community: A New Image for a New Era," *New Traditions in Business: Spirit & Leadership in the 21st Century*, John Renesch, editor (1992), San Francisco, CA, Berrett-Koehler Publishers, Inc.

Chapter 19 is excerpted from the second edition of *CoHousing: A Contemporary Approach to Housing Ourselves,* copyright © 1988, 1993 Ten Speed/Habitat Press. For more information about The CoHousing Company or the book, write to 1250 Addison Street #113, Berkeley, California, 94702. "CoHousing" is a service mark of McCamant and Durrett. All rights reserved.

Chapter 20 is excerpted from *Utne Reader,* March/April 1991 ($18/year [bi-monthly]; single issues $4), Box 1974, Marion, Ohio, 43305. Copyright © 1992 by Stephanie Mills. Reprinted by permission of Stephanie Mills.

Chapter 21 is from "Electronic Communities" by Kristen Anundsen and Carolyn R. Shaffer. Published in *Creating Community Anywhere: Finding Support and Connectedness in a Fragmented World* by Carolyn R. Shaffer and Kristin Anundsen, Jeremy P. Tarcher (Putnam) 1993.

Chapter 22 is excerpted from *Cities on the Hill* by Frances Fitzgerald. Copyright © 1988 by Frances Fitzgerald. Reprinted by permission of Simon and Schuster.

Chapter 23 is excerpted from *States of Grace: The Recovery of Meaning in the Postmodern Age.* Copyright © 1991 by Charlene Spretnak. Reprinted by permission of HarperCollins.

Chapter 24 is excerpted from "The Subjective Side of Power" by Margo Adair and Sharon Howell, which first appeared in *Healing the Wounds: The Promise of Ecofeminism* (Philadelphia: New Society, 1989). The article is copyright © 1989 by Margo Adair and Sharon Howell. Reprinted by permission of Margo Adair and Sharon Howell.

Chapter 25 is excerpted from *The Wrong Way Home: Uncovering Patterns of Cult Behavior* by Arthur Deikman. Copyright © 1990 by Arthur Deikman. Reprinted by permission of Beacon Press, Boston.

Chapter 26 is excerpted from *Chop Wood, Carry Water: A Guide to Finding Spiritual Fulfillment in Everyday Life.* Copyright © 1984 by Rick Fields and the editors of *New Age Journal.* Reprinted by permission of Jeremy P. Tarcher, Inc., Los Angeles, California.

Chapter 27 is from "In the Valley of the Shadow of Death" by Tim Cahill, *Rolling Stone*, January 25, 1979. Copyright © 1979 by Tim Cahill. Reprinted by permission of the author.

Chapter 28 is an edited chapter from Arthur E. Morgan's *The Small Community: Foundation of Democratic Life.* It is used with permission of the publisher, Community Service, Inc., P.O. Box 243, Yellow Springs, Ohio, 45387.

Chapter 29 is reprinted by permission from "Ecocentric Sangha" by Bill Devall, in *Dharma Gaia: A Harvest of Essays in Buddhism and Ecology*, edited by Alan Hunt Badiner, Parallax Press, Berkeley, California, copyright © 1990.

Chapter 30 is reprinted from *The Practice of the Wild* by Gary Snyder. Copyright © 1990 by Gary Snyder. Reprinted by permission of North Point Press, Berkeley, California, a division of Farrar, Straus, & Giroux, Inc. New York.

Chapter 31 is an original essay created for this collection by Pat Wagner and Leif Smith. Copyright © 1992 Pat Wagner and Leif Smith. All rights reserved. Reprinted by permission of Pattern Research, Denver, Colorado.

Chapter 32 is excerpted from *Ecotopia* by Ernest Callenbach. Copyright © 1975 by Ernest Callenbach. Reprinted by permission of Bantam Books, a division of Bantam Doubleday Dell Publishing Group, Inc.

About the Editor

CLAUDE WHITMYER is the coordinator of the Briarpatch community, a worldwide network of several hundred businesses and community organizations that practice right livelihood and simple living. He has more than twenty years of experience as a community organizer, environmental activist, entrepreneur, and international consultant. He is the coauthor of *Running A One-Person Business* (Berkeley: Ten Speed Press, 1989, with Salli Rasberry) and editor of the anthology *Mindfulness and Meaningful Work: Explorations in Right Livelihood* (Berkeley: Parallax Press, 1993).

Mr. Whitmyer has developed a unique consulting process, Good Work Guidance℠, that helps individuals use mindfulness practice and their own community to find and maintain meaningful work. Readers may write to Mr. Whitmyer at The Center for Good Work, P.O. Box 77086, San Francisco, California, 94107–7086.